What My Heart Would Tell You

Amanda Page

Catmandu
PRESS

Catch up on all the excitement of the Flyboys series:

INTO THE FIRE
OUT OF THE BLUE

And Flyboys Historical Romance:

WHAT MY HEART WOULD TELL YOU

To the brave World War II RAF pilots, especially those who gave their lives; and to the men and women who toiled in secret at Bletchley Park, knowing that their contributions might forever remain unacknowledged.

"My life may not be long, but it will be wide."

- Art Donahue, DFC, American pilot in the RAF, from a letter to his parents

"Never in the field of human conflict was so much owed by so many to so few."

- Winston Churchill

Published by Catmandu Press

amandapagebooks.com

ISBN: 978-0-9989884-8-1

Cover art by Andrea Orlic

Prologue

June, 1940
Kansas, USA

Jenny was going to kill him. Literally.

And just like a woman. After everything Hank had done to keep her airworthy, all the attention he'd lavished on her woefully outdated clunker of an engine, here he was, dropping out of the sky like a stone. Not exactly like a stone, he'd begun a tail spin which made the situation all the more dire. His ailerons and elevators were useless in this situation so he pounded down the port side of the rudder bar with both feet, fighting the spin. Sparing a brief glance away from the controls, the field below him became individual stalks of wheat.

This is not good.

Hank Clarkson was not a vulgar man by any stretch but every obscene word he'd ever heard flew out of his mouth as the ground rose up to meet him. His efforts with the rudder were blessedly lessening the spin and

1

he cranked the engine for all it was worth, begging, praying for it to start. At twenty-three he had a lot more life yet to live, if only he could make it back down in one piece.

He was only eighty feet up and plunging toward the ground like an arrow. He could hear his heartbeat in his ears.

Okay, obscenities hadn't helped.

"Come on, Jenny. You're my best girl, don't let me down now."

Hank had genuinely expected those words to be his last but, like any other woman, Jenny responded predictably to sweet talk and the JN-4's antiquated engine sprang back to life. He hauled back hard on the stick and the nose of the plane obligingly pulled out of the dive just in time. Hank winced as the wheels smacked against the tops of the wheat. He'd been hired to dust the crops, not harvest them. The plane slowly climbed back up into the sky but Hank kept the stick taut between his thighs until he'd gained enough altitude to breathe easily again.

Jenny's engine stayed reliable and Hank let out a sigh of relief when Art's barn appeared in the distance. Angling the plane to head into the wind, he cut the engine and nosed the machine over to the appropriate glide path, just like he'd done a hundred times before. When he reached six feet off the ground he leveled the wings and the plane skimmed along, slowing and lowering until the wheels and tail skid hit the earth.

The minute the plane was motionless Hank hauled his big frame out of the cockpit and vaulted to the ground, sinking down to his knees in the dirt, just enjoying the feeling of terra firma beneath him. It wasn't the first time that plane had almost killed him, and if he stuck around it probably wouldn't be the last. Not that anyone would particularly mourn for the loss.

Hank's father argued that if God had intended for man to fly he'd have given him wings. But like most things with his father, Hank took it with a grain of salt and went his own way.

He'd been dusting crops for Art Rasmussen since right out of high school, when Art had discovered his aptitude with machines. Art had bought Jenny for $50 after the Great War, when the military was trying to unload the planes as quickly as possible. Art had seen the possibilities for a variety of uses for the little plane and was now the sole proprietor of the only crop dusting business in northern Kansas. Of course, Hank would be a lot happier if Art would invest in something a little more modern than Jenny, but a job was a job. And considering the number of jobs for which he wasn't qualified, he was lucky to have this one.

Hank looked up at the barn and noticed that Art's beat up old truck was parked outside. He jumped to his feet and trotted through the huge sliding door.

"Art?" he called.

"Back here," a gravelly voice came through the open space.

Sunlight shone through large hay doors above, illuminating dust motes floating in the air. Hank breathed in the comfortingly familiar smell of hay bales and manure. He'd grown up on a farm and this smell, unpleasant as it was to some, would always make him think of home.

Hank found the older man sitting at his weather-beaten writing desk, paging through an accounts book.

"My eyes are getting too old for this." It was a familiar complaint. Hank never offered to help, Art already knew why he couldn't.

"Jenny stalled again."

The understatement of the year.

"You went up too fast, didn't you?" Art turned to him with a stern expression.

It said a lot about their relationship that the news an airplane had stopped in midair with Hank in it didn't faze the older man. Of course, Hank was standing right in front of him, clearly in one piece.

"I know the proper angle of climb as well as you, she's just getting unreliable."

"You always say that, but you always manage to get her back in shape." Art squinted. "What're you dancing around for? You look twitchy."

"It came," Hank said without preamble. "The letter from the Army."

He reached into his pocket and pulled out a battered envelope, handing it to Art.

"You didn't even open it?" Art asked, taking it from Hank's outstretched hand.

"I wanted to be sure of what it said," Hank answered.

Art gave him a look over his half glasses that conveyed exactly what he thought of Hank's response, but he pulled out a letter opener and cut through the seal. He seemed to be moving in slow motion and Hank began to pace, knowing that the contents of this letter would determine his future. Art pulled the single sheet from the envelope and snapped it open, pushing his glasses back up on his nose and clearing his throat.

"Dear sir," he began. "We regret to inform you that at this time we have no position to offer you in the United States Army Air Corps—"

Art stopped abruptly as Hank made an anguished sound and balled his fists at his sides.

"Do you want me to read the rest?" he asked gently.

"No, I can guess what it says," Hank replied. "How could they turn me down? Don't they know there's a war in Europe? The Germans just took France."

"I don't know, son." Art scanned the rest of the letter, looking for any hopeful information he could pass on to Hank and finding none.

"But what about the letter of recommendation you wrote? You told them I can fly anything? Fix anything?"

Art sighed. "I told them everything you asked me to. It's your grades, Hank. They can't put just anyone up in those new military planes. They need to know you'll be able to learn everything you need to know. Look, you're the most natural pilot I've ever met. I'd trust you to fly any plane I owned. But the Army can't take that chance, even with my say so."

Hank sat down heavily on a hay bale and pondered his future. He'd been sure that with Art being an experienced aviator and successful businessman the Army might take him at his word and give Hank a chance.

He shook his head. "I've got to get out of here."

"I know," Art said sadly.

Hank knew that Art had been counting on him to take over the business when Art retired. Hank regretted that he'd be letting down the one person who had never let him down, but there was no way Hank could just keep dusting crops when there was a war going on. A war that the United States would enter sooner or later.

And right now Hank had every reason to leave this place. Leave the failure and the humiliation behind him.

Art sighed heavily. "There is another way."

Hank's head came up.

"Don't get too excited. There's a big catch."

"Tell me. I'll do anything."

"That's what I'm afraid of."

Hank looked like he was about to come out of his skin, so Art figured he'd better finish what he'd started. "The RAF, Britain's Royal Air Force, is hiring Canadian pilots. If you go up to Canada you'll probably get sent over to England to fly for the Brits."

Hank's eyes lit up with the possibility of not just leaving home, but actually joining the war effort. "When can I leave?"

"Now hold on a minute there, son. You'll be flying in a real fighter plane. Not just an antique crop duster. I have no doubt that you can pilot any plane man's hands have built, but you'll be up against Nazis. Getting shot at. That's not something you want to rush into."

"That's what's got you worried? That I'll get shot down?"

"Not just that. I said there was a catch."

"And?"

Art sighed again, knowing that to a twenty-three year old man, especially the one sitting in front of him, what he was about to say probably wouldn't make much difference. But he couldn't in good conscience let him go without knowing everything.

"The United States is a neutral country. There are laws that say we can't fight against Germany. If you do this, if you go up to Canada and get recruited by the RAF, you could lose your citizenship. If they catch you, you might even be prosecuted. Thrown in jail."

At least that news made Hank pause.

"The world is at war, Art," he said finally, resting his elbows on his knees. "Even if the United States won't admit it yet. Hitler's out to conquer the world and we're a part of it. If he's not stopped over there, he'll come over here."

Art didn't disagree with Hank's words but he'd lived through a war himself, flown planes in that war. He knew how many young men like Hank wouldn't come home. The idea of this young man getting shot down over foreign soil somewhere didn't sit right with him.

"Have you really thought this through? You're willing to risk your home, your life, to go and fight in a war halfway around the world? What will your parents say?"

"You think my father would lose any sleep if I didn't come home?" Hank's angry words made Art ache for him. "He doesn't care what I do."

"I know it must seem like that sometimes, but he just wants what's best for you. Better 'n he had."

"You sound like mom."

Hank paused for a minute to think about his mother. While his dad might not worry after him, his mom would. But he wanted her to be proud of the son she'd raised, and that wasn't going to happen if he stayed here.

"Do I even qualify for this? What are the requirements?" Hank's stomach lurched at the thought that he'd have to endure the torture of another written test.

"You need to be over nineteen and under thirty-two, have good eyesight, three hundred hours of certified flying time, and a high school diploma."

Hank's fists clenched at the words "high school diploma." To his eternal humiliation, he'd finally graduated from high school at age nineteen. Thinking he might never graduate, his father tried to pull him out at seventeen to work on the farm but his mother, a school teacher, wouldn't hear of it. She was determined that Hank would get that diploma no matter how long it took or how hard it was. In truth he'd never worked so hard for anything in his life, and as the eldest child of a farmer that was saying something. But he'd done it. He'd graduated.

"So that's it? Shoot, I had the flying hours done my first six months here. Wait." Hank looked over at the older man. "You knew all that off the top of your head? You figured I'd ask about it? That I'd need it?"

"I thought the Army might not work out, and you'd be lookin' for another way."

Hank knew better than to be offended Art had guessed the Army would turn him down. He supposed it was foolish for him to have thought that his abysmal school performance wouldn't disqualify him from the military. At least Art believed in him enough to want to give him another chance.

"Then you understand why I have to leave. It's not just Irene." Hank stumbled a little on her name. "I need a chance to be a good man. A better man. That's not going to happen if I stay here."

"So what's your pop going to do about the farm? You work for me, but I know you still help out back home."

"Danny's old enough to pitch in. Dad wouldn't lose a step if I left."

"You're really convinced this is what you want?"

"I'm convinced I'm not going to find what I want if I stay here," Hank replied honestly. "At least over there I'll be doing some good."

Art took a minute to consider his words, but didn't put up any more of a fight.

"Can you help me? I'll need you to certify the flight hours."

Art gave him a long look, knowing it was unlikely there was anything he could say to prevent Hank from going.

"I'll give you the certification and connect you with someone who can get you where you want to go." Art shook his head. "And I'll pray that you live long enough to work out whether you made the right decision."

Hank's handsome face broke out in a broad grin and his heart lightened, as though he were already flying overhead in one of those British fighter planes. He was finally going to escape this place that had brought him little but frustration. He knew he was more than just a bad student, more than a jilted lover, more than a disappointment as a son.

And now he'd get his chance to prove it.

Chapter One

June, 1940
Bletchley Park, UK

"It's going to France!"

Charity Spence called out in what her mother referred to rather disparagingly as her "barker voice." A girl of Cherry's breeding evidently should not shout under any circumstances, but Cherry had never been one for rule following.

Gilda and Walter rushed over to her chair and peered over her shoulder. The printouts on the strips of tape in front of her would have looked like gibberish to most Brits, but Cherry was enough of a German scholar to be able to decipher even the fragmented and cryptic commands that passed through the small cottage behind the Bletchley Park mansion.

"Look at this," Cherry excitedly laid the strips out in front of her. The text was hard to read in the dim light of the bare bulb hanging from the ceiling, but by now all three codebreakers were used to working under such conditions.

"These are the orders for the *Prince Heinrich*. They're not being sent from Wilhelmshaven. It's being controlled from France, I'm sure of it." She looked up at Gilda and Walter, hoping to see signs of agreement.

News of a skirmish had hit Bletchley Park that morning. The British battleship *Duke of Cambridge* and battlecruiser *Howe* had taken on the German battleship, *Prince Heinrich* in the Strait of Denmark. The *Duke of Cambridge* had been damaged and forced to withdraw, and the *Howe* had been sunk. The *Prince Heinrich* had managed to limp away, the full extent of its damage undetermined. The battleship would be a grand prize for the British Royal Navy, and its whereabouts were a top priority for the codebreakers at the secretive Bletchley Park, known generally as Station X.

Cherry had spent the long hours of her night shift searching for any clue that might give away the ship's location or ultimate destination. Finally she'd hit upon something.

Excitement cut through the fatigue on Gilda's beautiful face. Cherry was perpetually envious of the other woman's ability to look lovely under the most trying of circumstances. While Cherry was on the short side with mouse brown hair and eyes, Gilda was tall, blonde, and willowy in a marvelously elegant way. Cherry's modiste would have been in raptures had she Gilda to dress rather than Cherry. As it was, the poor dressmaker had done her best to draw attention away from what she considered Cherry's "rather vulgar excess" in the bust area and make her look taller.

In a prime example of the odd humor of the eccentric codebreakers at Station X, they had come to refer to Cherry and Gilda as "Duck" and "Swan" respectively, in honor of the Duck and Swan pub located in the nearby town of Bletchley.

Cherry had always found her body to be perfectly satisfactory. It's true she wasn't the type to inspire odes and sonnets. (Percy Wainwright at university didn't count, he'd cribbed Lord Byron. Cloudless climes indeed.) But it had never bothered Cherry that she was sturdy. The age of wispy flappers had come and gone. Cherry's body was strong and capable, and the extra padding here and there didn't hinder her contributions to the war effort one bit.

Despite Gilda's obvious enthusiasm for Cherry's discovery, Walter was more reserved.

"Common sense says it would be less risky for them to route it to Norway for repairs," he argued.

"But we've seen this before," Cherry argued. "Every ship that has received orders from France has put in to port there. My guess would be Brest."

His face wavered, then looked resolute. It generally didn't take Cherry long to persuade Walter when she was convinced she was right, even though she was a woman. He was quite reasonable that way, if a bit of a worrywart. He was extremely bright but came from a meager background. His father drove a horse and cart for the ironworks, and Walter's keen intelligence had likely confounded his elder. Cherry had helped to pitch in for Walter's birthday gift a few months back, a much needed second pair of grey flannel trousers. He was slight of stature and wore glasses that seemed too big for his face. But he was a brilliant analyst and read German as though he'd been born there.

The problem now became that Walter wasn't the one she really had to convince.

"I'm going to take this to Hugh," she said, jumping up. "Unless…" She trailed off, turning to Walter.

"You're the one who found it," he said. "You should show it to him."

She turned to Gilda. "I'm with Walter," she shrugged.

Cherry took a deep breath and grabbed up the translation tapes. "Wish me luck!" she called, as she headed out into the pitch black night.

The only thing lighting her path was the dim glow of a waning moon. For most people the blackouts were unnerving. Especially those who had been raised in the city, where even on the darkest night the outdoors was lit up like a circus tent. Cherry had been raised on her grandfather's estate in the country, and there had often been nights with no light but the moon. The blackouts didn't rattle her, she knew their purpose.

She expected the conversation she was about to have would leave her frustrated, for one reason or another. But the work she and her colleagues did was important and every little bit helped. Every piece of information

17

she could glean from the puzzling snippets she was given helped to bring about an end to this war.

Hugh Fitzpatrick was technically her immediate supervisor on this night shift, and would be the one to pass along her information to the Admiralty. At least, she hoped he would. It could occasionally be difficult to convince some of the other codebreakers that you were correct, especially considering how convoluted the path of information was.

Somewhere out in the dark, all along the coast of Britain, wireless stations were intercepting signals from the Germans. The signals floated through the air like insects, being picked up by this or that antenna. The signals were then deciphered from Morse code and taken down. Some were scrambled, some weren't. They all ended up here at Bletchley Park.

The scrambled information was given to the Decoding Room, the rest was given to translators. Then the resulting messages were analyzed by yet another group. Sometimes it seemed the whole thing was just a game of Chinese whispers. Hopefully, enough real information got through to help the British military anticipate Hitler's movements and form an appropriate strategy. Cherry believed that the information she possessed could make a significant difference to the war effort.

She knocked on the door of Hut 3 and entered swiftly as the door was opened.

"Hugh?" she asked the woman who'd admitted her. The young woman nodded toward the far end of the room where a small group of men were huddled over a card table. Cherry's heels clacked on the wooden floor as she strode as quickly as her short legs would allow.

"Hugh, I've got something." A tall, slender man with wavy brown hair turned to her and gave her something just short of a smirk.

"What've you got, Duck?" he asked.

"We've determined where the *Prince Heinrich* is going."

He glanced down at the printouts clutched in her hand.

"All by yourselves? Quite an accomplishment. The intelligence analysts seem to think it's headed to Norway."

"It's going to France. Probably Brest. We need to alert the Admiralty." She was all but tapping her toes, knowing that every second wasted on this insufferable fop was one less second the British Navy would have to respond to the information.

"If you'd sweeten your tone, I'd be much more inclined to give your words the consideration you'd like." The smirk became a leer.

Cherry could never understand why Hugh had singled her out for inappropriate comments over the lithe beauty who shared the Cottage. Perhaps it was because, unlike a number of other young ladies at the Park, she completely rebuffed his advances. Not that he'd ever propositioned her directly, it was all sly innuendo. But it made situations where she needed his assistance unpleasant. If she'd thought Walter would have been equally emphatic about the certainty of her findings she would have asked him to go.

She took a deep breath, got hold of her temper, and laid out the message tapes on the table, explaining in detail why she believed the battleship was headed to France.

As obnoxious as Hugh could be, he was not stupid. Nobody at Station X was stupid, although a number of them would have been considered certifiable anywhere but where they were. After several long moments she managed to convince him that she was probably right. He got on the direct line from Hut 3 to the Admiralty and attempted to pass along Cherry's information.

While a number of individuals in the highest positions, including the Prime Minister himself, respected Bletchley Park and understood what was happening there, most of the lower ranking commanders and even the intelligence analysts failed to take information seriously when it came from Station X. The biggest problem being that most of them weren't allowed to know how the codebreakers got their information. To protect the secret that the Brits had broken the German Engima machines, only those at the top of the military leadership knew where the information really came from. The rest assumed, or were told, that it had come from spies, who were notoriously unreliable. In addition, information from Station X occasionally directly contradicted what the Admiralty analysts themselves had concluded. Like in this situation.

Cherry listened as Hugh patiently explained, just as she had to him, what her conclusion was and how she had arrived at it. It didn't help that the Admiralty was apparently very busy. Trying to locate the *Prince Heinrich*.

Hugh finally hung up the phone and turned to Cherry with a shrug.

"I did my best, Duck. And it should help to know that I believe you."

Cherry gave him a look that conveyed exactly what she thought about her need for his endorsement and headed back to the Cottage. She spent the rest of her shift sorting through the incoming messages, looking for any confirmation that her theory was correct. She stayed a few hours past her normal quitting time the next morning until she was almost cross-eyed with fatigue, just to be sure she hadn't missed anything.

After a fitful day of attempts at sleep, she reported back to work that evening for another night shift. Walter and Gilda were already there, looking excited.

"You did it, Cherry. You were right." Even Gilda's well-modulated voice couldn't hide her excitement.

Cherry looked quizzically at Walter.

"Yesterday after you went off shift one of the decoders in Hut 4 saw the word 'Brest.' Your information that Hugh had passed along had already been tentatively incorporated into the battle plan, but the Hut 4 decode confirmed the information. Rated it A1."

A1 was the highest grade intelligence could be given, meaning there was absolutely no doubt about its veracity.

"Apparently some high ranking German general had a son on the *Prince Heinrich* and High Command wired him the ship was headed to Brest. The Royal Navy sank her an hour ago."

Cherry gave a very undignified whoop and did a little dance, right there in the middle of the Cottage. Her heart bubbled over with the knowledge that she had helped, in a very small way of course, with the sinking of a German battleship.

Walter produced a notable bottle of sherry from somewhere and three small glasses.

"To the end of the war," he said, raising his glass.

"And our hastening of it," Cherry added. Gilda just smiled as they all clinked glasses.

Chapter Two

It was only his first day in England and already Hank felt his luck was changing. The trip across the Atlantic had been a grand adventure. It had marked the first time he'd even seen the ocean, much less crossed it. Come to think of it, since leaving Kansas his life had been one long series of exciting firsts. His trip to Canada had been his first time out of the country. Heck, he'd never really been outside of Kansas except for a few trips up to Nebraska for farm exhibitions.

He hadn't had much difficulty crossing the border. He'd had to answer a few questions, but Art had told him what answers to give about his business in Canada. He'd said he was going up "for some shooting," which was technically the truth. He just didn't admit he'd be shooting at Nazis. Hank felt the falsehood was a small sin compared to what the Germans were doing to the citizens of Europe. To his great relief, he hadn't been required to put anything in writing.

The ocean crossing had been uneventful, although the captain had done some fancy maneuvering as the boat neared the British Isles to avoid possible targeting by U-boats. Hank recalled one evening he'd spent on the deck of the large ship, gazing over the railing at the black water below. He'd looked up and seen what he'd taken to be a deck crane but had actually turned out to be a large cannon. The sight of the armament on an otherwise peaceful night brought home the truth that he was joining a war where weapons were shot and people were killed. Rather than instilling fear, it had filled him with determination. He would finally be of some use.

The crossing had been so smooth that the ship had arrived in port a full twelve hours ahead of schedule. The arrival party that was supposed to meet Hank had sent word to the porter's office that he could either find his own way up to RAF Chicksands in Bedfordshire where he'd be training, or he could entertain himself in town and wait for his contact that evening. Hank had never been much for waiting around so he'd decided to do what he could to get up to his billet.

Hitchhiking had been common in Kansas, especially since the Depression. He'd hitched countless times and had met a lot of interesting folks. He figured people were probably the same everywhere, and considering his meager funds, felt it was worth a try. He'd had good luck at first, making it all the way up to Luton before he'd been stranded. All that sitting, both on the ship and then in kindly strangers' automobiles, had him itching for some exercise so he hauled his duffel bag over one shoulder and started out along the road towards Bedford.

Even under the June sun, the English heat wasn't near as bad as Kansas. And Hank felt a sense of purpose as he strode continually closer to his post, closer to sitting in the cockpit of a plane, closer to putting a dent in Hitler's armor. He whistled as he walked, enjoying the pleasantly familiar vista of farms dotting the countryside. Although there were no red barns, like in Kansas, all the buildings here appeared to be made of stone.

A few hours on foot had only slightly shortened his stride, but he was glad to catch sight of the first vehicle he'd seen in a long while. It was a small bus, pulled off to the side of the road. Hank couldn't tell why it was stopped, but if it was engine trouble then he'd offer to lend a hand. Hank's father had never been one for compliments but had grudgingly admitted that he'd never met a machine his son couldn't fix.

Hank hitched the bag up higher on his shoulder and trotted over to the bus.

Cherry wrenched the bonnet of the bus open and peered inside, not sure entirely what she was looking for or how she would know if she found it. She stared at the mass of metal parts, experimentally poking at things without the first clue as to what she should do.

She'd given up one of her precious free afternoons to cover the bus run so her friend Evelyn in the Motor Transport Corps could go to London to see her boyfriend on shore leave. Cherry didn't have a sweetheart, but she could support the morale of the troops by making their sweethearts available to them.

Everything had been going so well. Cherry was a perfectly competent driver, and she'd had little difficulty handling the large green bus used to ferry codebreakers and other workers to and from Bletchley. Her lone difficulty being that the brake pedal was so far forward it exceeded the length of her leg and she'd found she had to point her toe to depress it completely.

Despite this shortcoming, she'd managed to drop off all of the morning shift workers at their billets and was heading back to BP herself when steam began pouring out from under the bonnet of the bus. The engine shuddered and ground to a halt, just as Cherry managed to maneuver it to the side of the road. Even this far inland, it was important to keep the roads cleared for military and other vehicles.

Now here she stood, staring glumly at the still steaming engine without a clue as to what might be wrong. She leaned over to get a better view and scraped her leg on the bumper, putting a ladder in her stocking.

Blast.

Not that Cherry was one to complain about minor inconveniences, but since the war had started, stockings were precious so she did her best to maintain them. Silk was the best material for parachutes and powder bags for naval guns. Some girls actually went without, but Cherry was fortunate enough to have an influential family and a superficial mother who kept her supplied.

Because of the scarcity of silk, Cherry knew she could turn the stockings in to be reused for the war effort. It would be wise to remove them now, rather than risk further damage. She glanced self-consciously around her and, upon seeing no one, lifted her skirt and unclipped her stockings from her garter belt. She slid them down her legs, enjoying the feeling of freedom as the air hit her bare skin.

Better put these in my purse so I don't lose them. She stepped inside the front of the bus and stuffed them down into her already overflowing bag. A delicate clutch would have been more ladylike, but Cherry was practical and knew that it was good to be prepared for any eventuality. One never knew when they might be called upon to produce a handkerchief, or mirror, or safety pins, or a pen, or a notebook, or possibly even a sandwich.

Now what to do?

Having deposited the remains of her stockings in her bag, Cherry was at a loss as to how to proceed. She was fairly certain that the last house, or rather farm she'd passed was a good way down the road. She didn't feel comfortable leaving the bus unattended, and it was possible someone would come along and be able to offer assistance. Then again, she hadn't seen another vehicle for quite a while. Unsure of what would be the best course of action, she sat on the bus step and looked down at her dusty shoes. She'd only been sitting for a minute or two when she heard a voice.

"Excuse me ma'am, anything I can do to help?"

Cherry blinked up into the blinding sun and there before her stood the most beautiful man she had ever seen. Not in an overly coiffed way, like the boys at the horrid debutante balls, but in an utterly masculine way. He had a strong jaw and straight, patrician nose, and a surprisingly full bottom lip for a man. He was decidedly rough around the edges, but that just made him all the more real and appealing.

It took her brain a moment to register that he was actually standing there and not just a mirage conjured up by the heat coming off the ground. When it sank in she jumped to her feet and had the idiotic urge to cover her shockingly stocking-free legs. Realizing there was really nothing to be done about it, she gathered her wits enough to respond.

"I'm afraid it's knackered," she stated, motioning toward the engine.

He smiled broadly, just short of a laugh. "I'm pretty good with vehicles, would you mind if I had a look?"

The most she could manage was to shake her head no, so he set down the large duffel bag he'd been carrying and rolled up his sleeves, revealing muscular forearms covered in fair hair. He stepped to the front of the bus and smoothly lifted the bonnet, propping it open.

He moved in an easy way, his body fluid grace. His clothes were rather shabby. His checkered shirt looked soft to the touch but had seen better days, and his brown pants were dusty at the ankles. His shoes were dirty and worn as well. He must have been walking for a while. The sunlight gleamed on his dark blonde hair, lighter streaks hinting at time spent in the sun.

The stranger studied the engine and began checking this part and that. Cherry watched him for a minute, and then delicately sat back down on the bus step, attempting to hide her sinfully naked legs beneath her skirt.

"So what're you doing out here?" he asked.

Cherry was an accomplished liar when it came to discussing her job, but in this case she was able to stick pretty close to the truth.

"Taking people home after work."

"You're a bus driver?" he asked, cranking something in the engine.

"Just today. I'm covering for a friend of mine."

"Women bus drivers, huh?"

"We all do our part for the war," she said, a little more sharply than she'd intended. He stopped what he was doing and looked at her with eyes so blue she fell in a little.

"I'm sorry," he said softly. "I didn't mean to offend you. I admire you for pitching in this way."

His voice was very pleasant, deep and mellow, although distinctively not British. Cherry guessed he was Canadian. There were a number of Canadian men who had come to the UK to join the war effort. He must be one of them.

"It's all right," she said, attempting to temper her earlier remark. "It must seem a bit odd. We get to break all sorts of rules with the war on. I certainly wouldn't be in this position, alone with a strange man, if it weren't for the war. I can't imagine what my mother would say."

The words came tumbling out, as though there were no filter between her brain and her mouth. Cherry clamped her lips shut, afraid of what might come out next. The man just turned to her and smiled. She loved his smile. She was used to smiles that were polite or cynical, but his was magnificently genuine.

He stepped forward and held out his hand to her.

"Hank Clarkson."

Cherry stood up to take it but he pulled it away as he noticed it was streaked with grease. She held out her own hand, showing that it was likewise soiled, and they both laughed as she took his big hand in her much smaller one.

"Charity Spence. Cherry. How do you do?"

His hand was warm and rough, probably from fixing buses and doing other useful things. She liked the way it felt holding hers. Much better than the limp handshakes she'd gotten from all the "good matches." She took hers back reluctantly.

"I guess we're not strangers anymore," he said, stepping back to the engine. "Hopefully that would make your mom rest easier."

Not if she knew I'd introduced myself by a pet name, thought Cherry.

The truth was, she'd been living in a shockingly modern way since starting at Bletchley. The women were treated quite evenly with the men. Their clothing was different of course, but even that was very lax. Women wore all sorts of fanciful colored stockings that wouldn't have been allowed in most office environments. Women ran shifts, gave instructions to men who worked with them, and pretty much fetched and carried for themselves. Initially there had been rules about men and women not working alone together during night shifts but, as with most things, silly rules like that had gone by the wayside in the face of necessity.

"Where are you from?" she asked. Since she was breaking all rules of etiquette in this exchange she might as well satisfy her curiosity.

"What gave it away?" *Answering my question with a question. He'd do well at Bletchley*, she thought.

"Your accent, mostly."

"Ottawa. Canada." He reached back down into the bowels of the engine and said, "Here's your problem."

Unsure of what she could offer by way of a solution, Cherry nevertheless jumped up and went over to stand next to him.

Being in such close proximity to Hank flooded her senses. Every sinew about him was overtly male. His shirt stuck to him with sweat, detailing the muscles in his broad shoulders and back. Something about the way he moved and manipulated the engine made Cherry believe those muscles had been forged through real work, hard work, not the vanity that shaped men in her circle.

It was queer, she was almost breathless just looking at him. She had never had a reaction like this to any other man, even the notoriously dashing Marquess of Huntingdon. Her whole body responded, coming alive. Her pupils dilated, pulse kicked up. Her skin tingled and a warmth spread through her, from her face down to her very core.

Her poise, which had been drilled so expertly into her by Emily Farnsworth of the eponymous finishing school, completely disappeared. She could do nothing but stand mutely next to him, hoping he wouldn't notice her inexplicable physical reaction to his presence. Fortunately, he seemed oblivious to her lapse.

"Looks like your engine overheated." He pointed down toward one of the parts which all looked the same to Cherry.

"Is there any hope?" she managed to squeak out, finally finding her voice.

"There's always hope," he replied and winked at her, the scoundrel! His smile was so inviting the corners of her own mouth turned up involuntarily. "Do you have any water?" he asked.

She took in the sweat drenched shirt and watched a bead of moisture as it slowly rolled down the side of his tanned face.

"Yes, of course," she said, springing into action and fetching the canteen from the front of the bus. Her face burned with guilt at not offering the poor man a drink before now.

He took the canteen and, rather than take it in his mouth as she'd expected, he poured it into something under the bonnet.

"You've got a slow leak in your radiator. I don't have a welding torch out here, but the water should get you back into town or wherever you need to go before it breaks down again."

"Thank you so much," she said. "I thought I was going to be stranded out here all day."

"My pleasure," he said, slamming the bonnet down. He wiped his hands on a bandana he'd pulled out of his pocket. "Let's give it a try."

He gave her another smile and her knees melted. She tried to cover by scrambling up into the drivers' seat. She turned the key in the ignition and the engine made an encouraging sound and roared to life.

Cherry let out one of her unladylike whoops and beamed at Hank in the doorway.

"May I?" he asked, motioning towards the bus interior.

"Of course," she replied. He grabbed up his bag and stepped into the bus, taking a seat immediately behind her.

"I'd volunteer to drive, but your whole country seems to travel on the wrong side of the road," he said. "I'm not sure how you manage to avoid accidents."

"Don't worry," she said. "Despite appearances I'm actually quite an adequate driver." She turned to him, conspiratorially. "And truthfully, we think the same about your country."

Hank laughed at her spunk. He'd had no idea how lucky he'd been when he'd spied the stranded bus. No way of knowing it would be piloted by this pert little pixie with a body like one of the pinups in the magazines Art stashed in the bottom drawer of his desk. With her red lips and rosy cheeks she reminded him of a juicy cherry. He couldn't stop smiling at her.

Her curvy shape left him wanting to put his hands around her waist, but her prim little blouse and skirt made her seem untouchable. Made him worry he'd soil her with his dirty hands. Fortunately for him, there was a little smudge of grease on her nose that ruined the overall perfection of her appearance. That smudge of grease was the only reason he allowed himself to believe she might really be looking at him with a spark of interest.

Her voice was like something from the movies. Like Vivien Leigh in *Dark Journey*. Hank had met British passengers on the ship during his Atlantic voyage and he'd enjoyed listening to them talk, although a lot of it sounded like nonsense to him. They seemed to have slang words for everything and spoke so quickly it was all he could do to keep up.

But Cherry's voice was something different. It was crisp but with a breathiness that provided an intriguing contrast to her buttoned up exterior. He wanted to soak in that voice, watch those red lips move. Try to make her smile again.

"So where can I take you?" she asked.

He pulled out a packet of papers from his bag. He'd prepared for this exact situation and thus far had done a good job of maintaining appearances.

"It says here," he started, pointing at the top of the first page. "I'm supposed to report to RAF Chicksands in Shefford."

Hank had developed a trick in school of preparing to read aloud. He simply memorized the text the night before and pretended to read as he went. It had generally worked, unless the teacher had produced new material and required him to read it on the spot. Knowing that he'd be expected to communicate his intended destination to strangers, Hank had spent several days on the ship painstakingly memorizing everything in the RAF information packet he'd been given in Canada.

Cherry put the bus in gear and pulled slowly away from the side of the road.

"I know where that is generally, although I've never been to the station itself. I've got a map here somewhere. Perhaps you could help direct me when we get close."

Hank's stomach clenched. He'd looked at a few maps of the area and had a pretty good idea of where the base was, but Cherry would probably be expecting him to point out roads and villages.

He'd already noticed that the British had a habit of adding extra letters to place names for absolutely no reason. On the ship he'd been schooled on the pronunciation of "Worcester," which apparently was pronounced "Wust-er" rather than "Wor-chest-er" like it was spelled. And for some reason, Gloucester rhymed with "Foster." It helped that Hank was a foreigner and was excused from knowing the proper way to pronounce certain words, but it made it more difficult to sound things out with all those extra letters.

"Am I keeping you from something?" he asked, concerned that a long detour to his base might further inconvenience Cherry after her engine troubles.

"Oh, no," she assured him. "I was just on my way back to drop the bus."

"Drop it where?" he asked. It hit him that his time with this appealing girl was drawing to an end, and it would be helpful to find out more about her if he wanted to see her again.

"I work at Bletchley Park," she said blandly. *Bletchley Park.* He made a mental note of the name.

"And you're the mechanic?" he joked, hoping to elicit more information without looking like he was prying.

She laughed, which he considered a bonus. "No, I'm a secretary." He liked the way she said it. *Sec-re-tree.*

"What is Bletchley Park?"

The smile left her face but she did answer his question. "It's used as a Headquarters for Government Communications. I'm sure it's all quite important, I just deal with the correspondence."

Hank looked at her carefully. He'd only just met her, but there was something odd about her response. As though she were reciting it. And Hank got the impression she was far too genteel to just be a sec-re-tree. Then again, today she was a bus driver.

"So what do people do for fun around here?" he asked, wanting to see her again, but not wanting to be too forward.

"Oh, lots of things. Grab a bite, see a picture. The air station actually holds dances."

"They hold dances on the base?" he asked, intrigued.

"Oh yes. I suppose they can't leave that many men alone for too long," she joked, and then seemed to blush at her own words.

Gosh, she was adorable. Hank really liked her but he'd only just arrived in this country and didn't know what the rules were for asking out a girl he'd just met.

"Do you ever go to the dances?" he asked.

"I haven't been able to, thus far. My work schedule is a little erratic," she replied. "But I'd like to go," she added, casting a quick glance in his direction.

He took this as a very favorable sign and was about to ask if she'd like to accompany him to the next dance when she handed him a folded up map.

"We've reached the extent of my directional capability," she said. "Would you mind taking a look? We're on Warren Lane, just south of Clophill."

Hank spread the map open on his lap and took a deep breath. Despite his difficulty with words, Hank was excellent with pictures and had a good memory for where things were in relation to other things. He knew London was a huge dot in the Southeast, so he got his bearings and quickly located his destination. But there were a lot of tiny little roads and villages between the two, and he knew it would take him way too long to find their current location on the map.

"I believe I've found the next turn, but I'm not quite sure how to pronounce it." He took a wild stab, hoping the road would have some exotic name that would make sense of his comment.

She pulled to a stop right in the middle of the deserted road.

"No trouble, let's take a look." She turned around and bent her head over the map, rotating it a quarter turn so they could both read the names.

Hank was not intending to do anything unseemly, but as Cherry leaned forward to look at the map he couldn't help but catch a quick glimpse of creamy skin covered in peach satin and lace down the neck of her blouse. He immediately averted his gaze, feeling as though he'd betrayed her somehow. Still, the pictures from Art's magazine popped back into his head, making it even more difficult to concentrate on the map.

"Here we are, Ampthill Road," she said, oblivious to his ogling. "That is a bit of a mouthful. It should be just up on the right." She turned back to the front of the bus and set it in motion.

Hank exhaled long and slow. Crisis averted. Although that meant he was about to have to leave this bus and Cherry. He was looking forward to a new adventure as a real military pilot, but he was suddenly struck by the idea that he might not see her again. He'd developed a fondness for her that was all out of proportion to the amount of time he'd spent in her company.

She turned onto the oddly named Ampthill Road, and before he knew it they were at the gate to the aerodrome. There was a little wooden guardhouse with a man in uniform. Hank grabbed his bag and slung it back over his shoulder, reluctantly turning to say goodbye.

"Thanks for the ride," he said.

"Thanks for the rescue," she replied with a grin, holding out her hand. He took it in his and just held it for a minute.

He wanted to say something else, anything to let her know how much he wanted to see her again, but his mind was a blank. After holding her hand for what must have been an inappropriately long time, he grudgingly relinquished it and stepped off the bus. Just before she closed the door, he turned back to her with a smile.

"Cherry, if you do make it to the next dance, would you save me one?"

She smiled brightly and called "Of course!" as she pulled the door shut and drove off. Hank whistled a tune as he turned to show his papers to the guard.

Chapter Three

"I heard a rumor that you were rescued by a handsome stranger," Gilda remarked slyly, stirring the tea in her cup.

Cherry's hand stalled briefly with the cream in midair before continuing to her own cup. Once the shift started there wasn't much time for small talk, but Cherry enjoyed sharing a cup of tea with her colleagues when she arrived early.

"That's the trouble with working for an intelligence gathering organization," she muttered.

"Care to confirm or deny?" Gilda's cheek dimpled prettily and Cherry sighed.

"I can confirm the intelligence as A1," she replied. Gilda raised an eyebrow, intrigued. "The bus broke down and he got it running again. I dropped him at Chicksands before returning to BP."

"So what did the mystery man look like?"

By now Cherry had a mouthful of tea and the best she could do by way of a response was mutely turn bright red. Her pulse quickened just thinking about Hank's smile. She'd dreamt about it. About him. Doing things to her she'd only read about in books. Well, one book really.

Cherry had spent a year in Germany to perfect her study of the language, and one of her well-connected classmates had managed to get hold of a copy of the notorious D. H. Lawrence novel *Lady Chatterley's Lover*. It had been passed around from girl to girl until it was quite well worn. Certain pages, anyway. Cherry did not believe Hank had anything in common with the story's embittered gamekeeper, Oliver Mellors, but some of the more racy scenes had provided her fertile brain with ample inspiration from which to draw.

Her cheeks burned as her traitorous mind conjured up images of Hank's strong hands on her, pulling her to him, kissing her senseless, laying her down on the soft grass...

"That handsome?" Gilda teased, noting Cherry's reaction. "My goodness,"

"I've never seen anyone like him," Cherry admitted, having managed to swallow her tea.

"So who is he?"

"I have no idea. His name is Hank Clarkson from Ottawa, Canada. I think he's some sort of mechanic."

"Not a suitable match, I'm afraid," Gilda remarked.

"While my parents may be silly and superficial about some things, I'm quite sure they intend to give me the bulk of the decision making there. Especially since I'm now a twenty-one year-old spinster with no 'Deb's Delights' in sight."

Gilda raised a skeptical eyebrow at Cherry's use of the word "spinster," but didn't disagree. She'd been through the London Season as well, although she was only nineteen and not quite the has-been that Cherry considered herself to be.

Cherry had looked forward to the Season, but found the reality to be thoroughly disappointing. The gents considered to be good matches had been rather tedious in conversation, and seemed more interested in catching her behind a darkened staircase than learning what made her tick. Many of the girls were just as shallow, coming to town from their country estates in an attempt to snag a husband and move out to his country estate. It was like children collecting dolls. They all seemed to be playing house. Cherry wanted someone she could count on for stimulating discussions, someone who felt things and had experienced things and wanted to share adventures together. Not just buy more horses.

And so she had rejected the easy life of a country aristocrat to join the war effort. She'd initially thought to get trained up as a nurse, but once the government had discovered her proficiency in German she was told to report to the Bletchley train station one gloomy afternoon and fetched by a man who had asked his companion "Do we blindfold her, or use the covered van?" Thankfully, they'd decided on the covered van.

Starting that day, her life had been a long slog of translating and decoding German transmissions, punctuated by the ever so rare success story.

Until yesterday.

"You're really not going to tell me anything else about him?" Gilda asked.

"As I may never see the man again, I probably shouldn't dwell too much on his virtues. It'll just make me sad. And we have more important things to do," Cherry replied, carrying her tea to her desk. Or rather her section of table. The Cottage handled so many transmissions it was always crowded with stacks of papers and rolls of translation tapes, leaving little open workspace for the codebreakers who toiled there.

They'd gotten about half an hour into the shift when Gilda summoned Cherry to her area. "What do you make of this? I don't believe I've ever seen this word."

Cherry's German was better than Gilda's, especially in regards to slang. Cherry's schooling had taught her proper language and forms, but the year she'd spent in Munich had been the real education. In contrast, Gilda spoke and read passable German but she was mostly hired because of her training as an actress.

Legendary codebreaker Bertie Cross was in charge of the work done in the Cottage. His codebreaking went all the way back to the Great War, where he'd worked in the famous Room 40 and had helped decrypt the Zimmerman Telegram that had brought the United States into the war.

Bertie had been responsible for the hiring of all the codebreakers in the Cottage and he'd chosen people with a variety of different backgrounds, knowing that they would bring different strengths. Because of her training as an actress, Gilda had a nuanced understanding of the rhythms of the messages. Bertie had also selected a mathematician, a speech therapist, a historian, and others from various fields who all contributed talents to the pool.

Nobody really knew what made a good codebreaker. Individuals selected for placement at Bletchley had arrived there through a number of avenues. There were chess champions, crossword experts, linguists, bridge enthusiasts, professors. Even actresses.

Cherry glanced over Gilda's shoulder. "Futzä-Schläcker. Literally it translates as 'cunt licker,' but it's usually used to refer to a small dog." Gilda looked up at Cherry with a mix of horror and wonder. "Because it sits on a woman's lap all day," Cherry explained. "It's actually Swiss-German, but you know how slang gets around."

Cherry didn't enjoy vulgarity, but as a translator part of her job was to be precise. It would do no good to dance around a word, simply because it was uncomfortable to say. They weren't teaching etiquette here, they were trying to win the war.

"I do apologize if I offended you, Gilda, but if the Germans choose to use foul language it's not our place to clean it up. We are only useful as long as we are accurate."

Gilda shook her head and smiled. "You didn't offend me, darling. I am forever envious of your title as expert in German dirty words. And you're absolutely right."

"On the other hand, it is a rude little expression. I wonder if the transmitter kisses his German mother with that mouth."

Gilda laughed, and Cherry suddenly gasped and brought a hand to her mouth.

"Mother!" she cried. "I wonder if…"

Cherry trailed off and went back to her workspace, searching through a pile of translated messages. Gilda did not remark on it. It happened nearly weekly that some bolt of lightning hit Cherry and she came to some terribly clever conclusion. Dirty words weren't the only thing that made Gilda a little jealous of Cherry, but that didn't lessen her affection for the other woman. On the contrary, it increased it.

Cherry's search was quickly rewarded as she pulled out a translation tape with a triumphant shout.

"Here! Listen to this. 'Tomorrow we celebrate the birthday of my mother. I hope for her continued good health.'" Cherry looked up at Gilda and Walter, who had just returned from fetching a new batch of transmissions.

The message was a little odd, but it was not unheard of to receive something of a personal nature rather than just orders and coordinates. There was an entire army of men sending notes back and forth. Some of them were bound to be personal.

Cherry had translated one dispatch where the transmitter had been trying to get a message to his mother through German headquarters and was told repeatedly "In code! In code!" He had been transmitting in the open because the Eighth Army tanks were on his doorstep and he just wanted to get the message out before they came through the door.

But Gilda and Walter were clearly at a loss as to why news of a German wireless operator's mother's birthday garnered such enthusiasm.

"I don't think this is actually someone's birthday, I think they're signaling some type of military action," Cherry explained. "We had another message like this a while back, something about it being 'mother's birthday' and I seem to remember the message preceded a large scale attack."

"You could be right," Walter replied. "But we've translated thousands of messages. It would probably take you the full two weeks just to locate the other message, and even if you did there's no way of knowing what type of attack it would be or how to counteract it."

"Or if the higher ups would believe you," Gilda added.

"I suppose you're right," Cherry admitted. "But I may send this up to Bertie anyway."

"He'll accuse you of being on a wild Duck chase," Walter joked.

"Possibly. Or maybe it'll just be the tip that shortens the war," Cherry replied cheerily, turning back to her translations. In this line of work it was important to remain optimistic.

Chapter Four

"Ready to go up?" Dickie asked casually, his lean frame propped against a wing.

Hank walked the perimeter of the plane, a British-made craft called a Miles Master. It was a two seater, a training plane, to help prepare him for the more advanced Hurricane and Spitfire fighter aircraft. He ran his hand along the wing, marveling at the sophistication of the ship. It had a top speed of over 240 miles per hour, which was more than twice as fast as he'd ever flown in his life.

He couldn't wait.

"I was born ready!"

Hank turned to his companion with a grin, and Dickie's mustache twitched with amusement at the enthusiasm of his new acquaintance. Hank clambered up onto the wing and jumped into the student's seat, while Dickie followed with a much more sedate embarkment.

"Now let's see if I still remember how to fly," Hank joked, setting his oxygen mask and microphone and pulling on his helmet and gloves.

"I do hope so, or this may be the shortest flight in history."

Hank smiled at Dickie's pronunciation of "hiss-tray." He'd met quite a few Brits by now but never tired of their accent. His British batman had awakened him this morning at seven a.m. with a cheery "Tea for you, sir?" A "batman" was like a butler and every pilot had one. He straightened Hank's quarters, made his bed, woke him in the morning, and took care of his uniforms.

Hank had never been waited on in his life, certainly not by another man. It was true that on the farm his mother had done the cooking and cleaning, but that was no more being waited on than his father harvesting the wheat. On the farm each person did their own chores, whatever they were best at, and everything got done.

Hank was glad he'd have someone to help keep all of his new clothes in order. He'd been issued a Class A uniform with close-fitting short coat and two pairs of pants, a raincoat, a great-coat, an overseas cap, a billed cap, two shirts, two neckties, gloves, black socks and shoes. His coat, called a "tunic," had the wings of an RAF pilot already embroidered above the left breast pocket. Hank thought the pants were a little strange. They didn't have any belt loops and had to be held up with suspenders. But the uniform really made him start to feel like a military pilot, and it was better than most any of the clothes he had from home. He felt proud, wearing those wings, although he also felt he had yet to earn the right to wear them.

Hank had met Dickie Fox in the Officer's Mess the day before. Dickie was a new RAF pilot himself, although he had six weeks jump on Hank. He'd just been through pilot training and his first assignment was to help get Hank trained up. Dickie reminded Hank of the dashing young RAF pilots from the newsreels; tall, dark, and slender with a quick smile beneath a neatly trimmed mustache.

Hank was relieved to see that the Miles Master cockpit looked relatively familiar, albeit with considerably more controls than old Jenny had. But he recognized the important things, and after the practice Dickie had given him in the Link trainer he felt more than ready to get that beauty off the ground.

He didn't have to taxi much, the whole aerodrome was a runway. Just one big grassy open field so planes could take off in any direction depending on the wind. Hank started the engine, throttled forward, and before he knew it his wheels were off the ground.

He always felt as though a weight had been lifted the moment he was airborne. When he looked down at the patchwork of fields below him, his problems all seemed smaller and more manageable. Flying helped him put things in perspective. In the airplane there was only the sky, the ground, and his craft. As long as he kept his wits about him he could master all three. It had only been a few weeks since he'd been up, but the familiar rush of adrenaline surged through him, brightening the grey, cloudy skies over Shefford.

The English weather presented some new and unique challenges to Hank who, like most American pilots, was used to flying in excellent conditions. British pilots, on the other hand, had learned to fly with the clouds and fog common in the English countryside. It required a lot more reliance on instruments than visual cues.

Dickie had Hank put the plane through its paces, providing Hank with an opportunity to show his skills as well as beginning to acquire the expertise necessary to be a successful RAF pilot. This sortie was not for dogfighting or formation flying, but rather to let Hank get a feel for the aircraft and let Dickie get a feel for Hank's ability level.

"God, it feels good to be up here," Hank said, as he rose above the cloud bank.

"That was one of the smoothest takeoffs I've seen from a novice," Dickie remarked.

"Well, I may not have flown this model before, but I've taken off from just about the craziest places you can imagine." Hank didn't want to get into too much detail. He tried to keep things general when referencing his background.

"Does it look much like home from up here?" Dickie asked.

Hank reflected briefly on the fact that his entire frame of reference about Canada was the day and a half he'd spent there, and decided to just answer the question honestly.

"Pretty much," he replied. "More stone fences and buildings. Ours are mostly wood."

Hank didn't like lying to his new friend. He was proud to be from America, proud that he'd stepped up to fight in this war. But he knew how much he'd be risking if anyone found out where he was really from. He figured that someday, after this was all over, he'd be able to talk openly with his comrades about his background. If any of them made it through this.

"Things must be dreadfully dull in Canada, if you're desperate enough for excitement to risk your life flying for us," Dickie said.

"I think even back home people are starting to realize that this war isn't going to end any time soon. I'd rather be here fighting than waiting for it to land on our doorstep." Hank meant every word. "What about you? What made you join up?"

"Well, we've all been conscripted of course, but I got out of it for a while with an engineering apprenticeship at Metrovicks. It's considered a reserved occupation so I was exempt." Dickie paused. "We lost one hundred and forty-five planes at the Battle of Dunkirk. One of them was a school chum. It didn't feel right, continuing my studies while my mates were out risking their lives over the Channel."

Dickie's voice hadn't changed much, just softened a little at the end. The Brits Hank had met were very matter of fact about the losses they'd suffered. Even the personal ones.

"I'm sorry," Hank said.

He wasn't here fighting because he'd lost anyone, but he knew that the longer he stayed and the more pilots and soldiers he met the more likely it was that someone he knew would be killed. That was part of war.

Dickie didn't seem inclined to discuss it any further, so Hank changed the subject.

"How long do you think before I get to fly a Spitfire?" he asked.

"With the way you're handing this ship, I'd say you should be ready to try one in a few days."

And he was. On the fourth day after his first flight in the Miles Master, Hank found himself sitting at the edge of the field in a Supermarine Spitfire, arguably the most sophisticated fighter aircraft in the world. He had his helmet on with oxygen mask flowing, his parachute clipped on and seat harness hooked up. The summer heat beat down on him, but there was a slight breeze blowing through the open cockpit.

He flipped the ignition switch, hit the starter, and immediately felt the Merlin V-12 engine spring to life. He opened the throttle and sat back in the Bakelite seat as the plane accelerated to ninety miles per hour, easing back on the power as the craft took flight. Hank raised the flaps instinctively but had to remind himself to also raise his wheels. He was still adjusting to piloting a plane with retractable landing gear.

Hank pulled the cockpit windscreen shut on its rails and locked it into place. Open cockpits didn't bother him, they were all he'd ever flown. But at the altitudes he'd be occupying it was safer to have a closed cockpit. He quickly decided as prestigious as it was to fly, the Spitfire hadn't been designed with someone of his proportions in mind. Once the cockpit was closed he felt as though his head was about to bump the windscreen, and his shoulders almost touched on either side. Still, it was like driving a sports car after operating tractors.

And suddenly he was in the clouds. Hank took a cleansing breath and calmed his racing heart, giddy as a schoolkid to be manning this ship but aware that he needed to familiarize himself with the sensitive controls before trying anything fancy. There was no trainer for a Spitfire. It was a single seat craft, so your first time piloting it was a solo flight.

The plane was incredibly responsive. It was as though he simply had to think his intention and the plane complied. Hank tried an aileron roll, where the nose and tail of the plane stay stationary and the plane rotated in place. The plane spun so quickly that by the time he'd brought the spade grip back to center he'd gone around twice.

There was a lot to think about in any airplane, but once Hank got comfortable with the instruments and controls his mind wandered to other subjects. Namely, Cherry. He hadn't been able to stop thinking about her, even with all of the flying and training he'd been doing. He'd told Dickie about his encounter with the bus, and his new friend had given a knowing smile and guessed that Cherry was a member of the Motor Transport Corps. Apparently the MTC was made up of daughters from wealthy families who wanted to help the war effort and were known for being well-dressed lookers.

Hank had mentioned that Cherry had been covering for a friend and was herself a secretary at some place called Bletchley Park.

Dickie had just shrugged and said maybe Cherry would bring her pretty driver friend to the next dance. Apparently secretaries didn't have the same reputation as the MTC. That was fine with Hank. He knew exactly how pretty Cherry was and didn't want to have to compete with Dickie for her affections.

Hank was snapped out of his reverie by controls that suddenly felt a bit sluggish. He looked down at his instrument panel and was astonished to see that he was traveling at 280 miles per hour. He pulled back on the stick to begin a loop, and as the centrifugal force pushed him back into the seat a tunnel of grey began to close off his vision. He eased the stick forward and was relieved that his vision returned immediately.

Whew, that's going to take some getting used to.

He'd flown Jenny in circles in the skies over Kansas without suffering any ill effects, but her top speed was only seventy-five miles per hour. Even pulling tight loops, his heart had been able to keep the blood pumping to his brain. But in this ship, if he turned too tightly he apparently blacked out. Hank spent some time experimenting with how fast he could go and how tightly he could turn. He knew this information would be vital once he was up here dogfighting with German planes. Blacking out during a skirmish could mean death for a pilot.

Hank discovered that at about 220 miles per hour he could execute a fairly tight turn, and if he leaned forward and held his breath he could get that up to about 250. He'd have to ask Dickie if there were any other techniques he could try to increase his speed without risking a blackout.

By this time the fog was starting to close in and he wanted to return to the aerodrome before it disappeared. Back in America every precaution was taken to make air fields as easy as possible to see from the sky. In England the opposite was true. Aerodromes were designed to blend in with their surroundings. Everything was painted in a mixture of drab colors, hopefully making it more difficult for German bombers to target. Unfortunately, it also made them harder for RAF pilots to locate.

Hank got on his R.T., radio transmitter, and requested a heading from Control. A cheery female voice directed him back to Chicksands. He headed in that direction and prepared for his first Spitfire landing. It was general knowledge that these birds were a menace to bring down. Four out of ten landings ended in some sort of accident. The landing gear was narrow and the long nose meant you had to swing the plane from side to side to see what was ahead of you. But Hank was up for the challenge.

He came in low on initial approach, circling the landing field at about twenty feet. Then he looped around, reminding himself to drop his landing gear, and lowered the flaps as he straightened out on final approach. As he settled down to the field, he closed the throttle and worked the rudder to keep her straight. The wheels touched down with the delicacy of a first kiss. The plane taxied a short distance and the ground crew immediately ran up to service her and get her ready to head back out.

Hank cracked the canopy and climbed out onto the wing before lowering himself to the ground. He couldn't scrape the smile off his face.

"Good flight?" the mechanic asked.

"Hopefully the first of many," Hank tossed back with a smile as he jogged towards his quarters.

Chapter Five

Cherry headed for the building known mainly as "the Index" because that's what was kept there. A lovely no-nonsense woman named Sarah managed the process by which every intercepted message was filed and cross-filed according to names, places, and military units. It was painstaking work, but necessary to organize and make sense of the massive amount of intelligence that had been gathered and translated.

It wasn't as though the Germans were sending messages that laid out entire battle plans. The big picture had to be assembled by studying hundreds of small bits of information about troop movements and shipments of supplies. Putting all this intelligence together was far beyond Cherry's humble station, and for that matter beyond Sarah's as well. But each person at Bletchley Park, from Mr. Turing all the way down to the women who cooked the food, did their part and brought Britain closer to winning the war.

Cherry had decided not to bring her theory to Bertie until she had at least confirmed that there had been a previous message involving a mother's birthday. With the long hours, changing shifts, and repetitive work it was easy for one's mind to go a bit haywire.

It would be thoroughly embarrassing to bother Mr. Cross with some hair-brained theory that turned out to have been created out of whole cloth by Cherry's overworked brain.

The downside to this was that Cherry was not authorized to go off on her own missions when she already had work that was assigned to her, so she would have to locate the other message during her free time. She'd just finished a shift and although her brain felt a bit raw, she still wanted to start the process of tracking down her birthday message.

The Index was dark and quiet with a stillness that reminded Cherry of the libraries back at Oxford. There were wooden tables laden with boxes and boxes of index cards upon which messages were stored. It all looked impossibly complicated, but Sarah was a wonder and could generally put her finger on anything you needed within minutes. At least Cherry hoped she could today.

"Sarah, I've got a challenge for you." Cherry managed to locate her target quickly, huddled over a stack of intercepts. She kept her voice low, so as not to disturb the other women who were engaged in card sorting.

Sarah looked up and smiled warily, familiar with Cherry's "challenges." This was not the first time she had come in with a peculiar request.

"What can I help you find?" Sarah asked.

"Well, I'm looking for a mother's birthday."

"I beg your pardon?" Sarah was always pleasant to her, but Cherry knew the other woman was busy and endeavored to get immediately to the point of her visit.

"I'm quite sure I translated a message recently about it being someone's mother's birthday and I'd like to locate it."

"Do you know whose mother's birthday it was? Hitler's? Goering's?" Sarah asked hopefully.

"Nobody that important, I'm afraid. Just the wireless operator's mum."

"Oh." Sarah's face fell.

"We've received another similar transmission and I believe it's some kind of code foreshadowing an attack."

Cherry provided an explanation knowing Sarah would never have asked why she wanted the message. It was one of the strange things about working at BP. Everyone kept so many secrets that nobody would ever think of probing a colleague about their work. When anyone met outside of work they talked about books or films or where to get the best beans on toast, but never about what they did back at Bletchley.

Despite this, Cherry believed that in certain circumstances providing more information would help her find what she was looking for. Nobody knew how the cataloguing system worked better than Sarah. There may be a method she could suggest that Cherry wouldn't have found on her own if she understood Cherry's goal.

Sarah's face got grim and she slowly shook her head.

"Was there anything else in the message? Anything about specific places or names?" she asked.

"No," Cherry replied sadly. "I think it was left deliberately vague so nobody would pay it any mind."

Sarah pursed her lips and led Cherry to a table holding several large boxes of cards.

"What are these?" Cherry asked.

"Personal messages," Sarah replied. "We initially had them all together with 'miscellaneous,' meaning those messages that did not include any information that would be catalogued elsewhere. But you're lucky, last week we went through miscellaneous and sorted out those that included personal information. If there is another message about a mother's birthday it will be in these piles."

Cherry looked down at the boxes containing hundreds of cards and sighed.

"Well," she said. "If I'm to get through these before my next shift I'd best get started."

"I'll have one of the girls get you some tea," Sarah offered. "Looks like it's going to be a long night for all of us."

"So what did you think of your first group sortie?" Dickie asked Hank as the two men removed their flight gear.

"Man alive!" Hank replied, shaking his head. "That formation flying is going to take some getting used to. With all the work involved in not hitting the guy next to you, how does anyone have time to spot the Germans?"

"I know it seems strange, but once you become accustomed to it there's a sense of safety in numbers, knowing you've got comrades just off your wing."

"I suppose," Hank admitted, shedding his harness. "I wanted to ask you about something. When I went into a dive I noticed the engine stalled for a minute and then caught again. Has that ever happened to you?"

Hank had been trying to shake another Spitfire in a mock dogfight and sent his craft plunging downward toward the earth when the smooth hum of his engine had sputtered before restarting. He'd turned to see he'd left a cloud of black smoke in the sky behind him. He'd been used to Jenny's temperamental behavior and it hadn't fazed him when she unexpectedly cut out. But to have the same thing happen in what was supposed to be the world's foremost fighter was a surprise.

"I'm afraid that's one of the charming eccentricities of the Spit," Dickie replied. "I believe it's got something to do with the carburetor. It only cuts out for a second, and when you pull up it resolves."

"But if you lose engine power, doesn't that give the other guy an advantage? The plane you're chasing?"

"Maybe for a second, but Spits have got their own advantages. A tighter, faster turn, and more maneuverability. And if we keep up our training, superior piloting skills should count in our favor," Dickie said with a smile. "But now's not the time to fixate on the flaws of our fine British aircraft. There's a dance tonight, my boy!" He clapped Hank on the back.

"A dance?" Hank asked, following his friend out of the changing room.

"I'm sure you must have heard of the ritual, even in Canada," Dickie joked. "Every Saturday all the local girls are brought round to keep us civilized. It's not a bad way to spend an off evening."

Suddenly the problems of a prickly Spitfire carburetor were the last thing on Hank's mind. He thought back to Cherry's promise to save him a dance, and his heart raced with the thought that he might not only see her again, but get to hold her in his arms.

Hank surged ahead of Dickie, heading for his quarters. Spending an afternoon wedged in a cramped cockpit under the July sun left him smelling more like a barn than a date. If he was going to have a shot at courting Cherry, a shower and shave were sorely needed.

"Save a few girls for me!" Dickie called gaily after him.

Cherry pushed a strand of hair out of her face and picked up another stack of cards. This was the second evening she'd spent poring over transmissions, searching for her elusive "birthday" message. She was starting to feel like Captain Ahab.

It was strange to only be looking at personal transmissions. The bulk of translating she did during her normal shift was made up mostly of generic military orders, requests for supplies, sightings of the enemy, all very short and businesslike. There was little humanity in it.

But looking at stacks of messages of a personal nature was almost enough to drum up some sympathy for the Germans and remind her that they were just people too. Or it might have been, if she didn't stop by the Bletchley mansion every morning to check the posted list from *The Times* of all the missing and dead British soldiers.

Everyone tried to keep a stiff upper lip. Cherry would hear comments like "So-and-so's bought it," and then they'd all go back to work. It wasn't that people didn't care. After all, every name on that list was someone's brother, someone's father, someone's sweetheart. But the work must go on. There was simply no time to mourn.

And so here she was, going into hour number three of scanning cards to find her white whale.

A noise behind her made her turn around to see Gilda approaching with an expectant look.

"I'm glad I found you. Hugh's managed to sweet talk one of the MTC girls out of her shooting brake and is taking us to the dance," she said breathlessly.

Cherry knew all about the dance. She'd been thinking about it since yesterday, when Gilda had mentioned that she'd found a ride. The RAF base at Chicksands held dances almost every Saturday, but Cherry generally didn't go because she often worked Saturday evenings and even when she didn't it could be difficult to procure a lift over there.

This morning, when Gilda had told Cherry her ride had fallen through, she'd been disappointed but reminded herself it wasn't significant in the great scheme of things and had resigned herself to another evening of index cards.

Normally there didn't seem to be much reason for Cherry to go to the dances. On the home front, the women outnumbered the men by a factor of ten. There was generally no shortage of women for the men to dance with at these events, they certainly weren't lacking for partners. Cherry didn't feel as though she were depriving them of anything by withholding her presence. At least generally.

But this dance was different. Not only was there a man she was actually interested in seeing, but she'd already offered to save him a dance. She was well-nigh contractually obligated to make an appearance if it was at all possible. And now it appeared that it was.

"Hugh?" Cherry asked, confused.

"Yes. He and Charles from Hut 3 are coming with us," Gilda replied.

"But why? What interest could they have in attending an RAF dance?"

Gilda pursed her lips. "You know Hugh. He's got an ego like Narcissus. He's probably trying to prove he doesn't feel inferior to the fighter boys."

Because this conversation was taking place in the Index both girls were keeping their voices low. But Cherry thought she sensed an urgency in Gilda's manner.

"Is everything all right, dear?"

"Yes, but Hugh did mention that if we weren't both ready to depart in five minutes he'd leave without us."

"You could have started with that!" Cherry exclaimed, a touch louder than she'd intended. She whispered an apology to the ladies sorting cards, and shot out of the building in the direction of the Cottage.

"How am I supposed to change?" Cherry called back to Gilda who, despite her much longer legs, was struggling to keep up.

"Grab your dress, you can change in the car," Gilda suggested.

They both managed to make it to the circle drive where Hugh was impatiently tapping his foot on the gravel by the car along with Charles and several women from Hut 3.

"I'd almost given up hope," he remarked. "Get in and we'll be off."

Cherry had her dress draped over one arm. It was her favorite dress for dancing, a crimson frock with a chiffon overlay that swirled as she moved. Fortunately for her, the shooting brake had plenty of room in the back for her to change. Hugh and Charles got in the front seat and the women loaded up in the back and they were off.

"Do you think your mechanic might be there?" Gilda asked, as they headed down the drive.

"I'm not sure. Do they invite mechanics to the dances?" Cherry asked, unbuttoning her blouse.

"A mechanic? Surely you can do better than that, Duck," Hugh called back from the driver's seat. Cherry hadn't realized he was paying any attention to her, but at least he had to keep his eyes on the road so he wouldn't catch her with her kit off.

"Oh, but you haven't seen this mechanic," Gilda teased, giving Cherry a wink. Cherry blushed as scarlet as her dress.

"I would have thought you'd be looking for more than just a pretty face," Hugh said.

"Maybe in Canada mechanics are held in higher regard than they are in Britain," Gilda offered.

"He's a Canadian mechanic?" Hugh asked incredulously.

"There's nothing wrong with Canadians, Hugh. Don't be a snob," Gilda replied.

Cherry was rather glad this exchange was all taking place without her, as it enabled her to slide her dress down over her head and slip off her skirt without anyone paying any mind. Like a number of people at Bletchley, including Cherry herself, Hugh had lived a privileged life before the war and his disparaging remarks about mechanics were not really an assessment of any individual man's worth, but simply a product of his upbringing. During her debutante years, Cherry would no more have been expected to date a mechanic than she would have been to become one herself. She was the granddaughter of the 5th Baron Fairfield and was expected to marry according to her station.

But war changed things. It showed the depth of a man's character. And if Hank's job really was fixing RAF planes and getting them back in the air to help defeat the Germans, then his work was as noble as that of any titled gentleman she'd danced with during her Season. It might take a little convincing to get her parents to agree with her but she was certain they'd come round.

Of course, all of this was premature. She had no idea if Hank would even be at the dance. Or if he'd remember her. She didn't consider herself to be in the same category of "memorable" as Gilda, for example. And a man like Hank would have no trouble finding a girl to share a dance, mechanic or not.

Cherry sighed. *Well, even if he doesn't remember me this is certainly a more enjoyable way to spend an evening than poring over cards at the Index. Even if I have to listen to Hugh all the way home.*

Chapter Six

Hank was sharing a drink at the bar with Dickie when he caught sight of Cherry and the rest of the dancing crowd disappeared. He'd been watching the door all night, hoping she'd turn up. As time went on he'd begun to lose hope. But there she was.

She wore a red dress and little red shoes. A barrette sparkled in her glossy brown hair, even in the semidarkness of the swirling colored spotlights overhead. Dickie turned to see what had caught his friend's attention and chuckled.

"So that's the mysterious chauffer, eh? Very pretty."

Hank started towards her, but Dickie grabbed his arm.

"Sorry, mate. That's not how it works."

"What're you talking about?" Hank asked, genuinely confused.

"We switch up partners. Don't worry, she'll come round."

Hank watched glumly as a young man in a RAF uniform tapped Cherry on the shoulder and led her on to the dance floor.

"If you want a chance to dance with her, you'd better queue up," Dickie remarked, propelling Hank toward the line of men waiting for a partner.

Hank stepped forward impatiently as each man ahead of him was paired up with a woman from another line. His height enabled him to keep his eye on Cherry as she spun around the dance floor, a flash of scarlet among a sea of brown and navy blue.

Hank finally made it to the front of the line and was presented with a very nice looking blonde in a sweater and skirt, but he was so distracted thinking about Cherry he barely noticed her. She craned her neck, taking in Hank's ample frame in his dashing uniform and beamed like she'd just won the lottery. He smiled politely and presented his hand which she grabbed with gusto and used to propel him towards the dance floor.

The next dozen songs were a whirl as Hank moved dutifully from girl to girl, half his attention always on the flicker of red through the sea of dancers. He did everything he could to make his way towards where he'd last seen Cherry, but the nature of swing dancing meant that people often moved quickly from place to place and he'd lost her in the crowd a few times. While he was tall, she was petite and her head barely reached the shoulders of the other male dancers.

"We hope you're all enjoying the music as much as we're enjoying watching you dance to it." The assembled throng turned toward the stage as the bandleader's voice came over the loudspeaker. "We've got just a few more songs for you before we take a break. And now, one of the band's favorites."

Hank looked desperately around, scanning over the tops of people's heads, hoping to see a red dress.

"Are you looking for anyone in particular?"

The tone was playful and the accent was crisp as an apple. He looked down to find Cherry standing right in front of him and a grin blossomed on his face.

"A new partner," he replied, holding out his hand as the drummer went to town on the opening bars of "Sing, Sing, Sing." The crowd wildly applauded their approval of the song choice. She placed her small hand in his larger one and he noticed she was wearing red nail polish. Cherry red.

Hank wasn't Fred Astaire, but he had done his share of swing dancing back in the States and he could hold his own on the dance floor. He was delighted to find that Cherry was an enthusiastic partner who floated in his arms like a dream. Some of the women he'd danced with that evening had been fighting him for control, while the better partners were able to read his signals and follow his lead.

Hank's strength and size was a definite asset in this style of dance, with spins, flips, and dips all combining in a mad whirl. He loved this song and he could tell that Cherry did too. She felt almost weightless as he flung her out to the side and pulled her back in towards him, spun her under his arm, around in front, and dipped her back over the other side in time to the music.

As the song hit a crescendo he brought one big arm around her waist, pitching her over his shoulder in a flip. Her gauzy red skirt swirled past his face and he caught the briefest glimpse of pale blue satin. She squealed as she came back down and he immediately stopped, terrified that he'd hurt her or done

84

something that had made her uncomfortable. She landed in front of him and looked up at him with twinkling eyes and a mischievous grin. He grinned right back and put his hands on her waist, tossing her legs out behind her, and then bringing her back against him so she was straddling his waist. Then he tossed her back out again, and brought her legs around his back, catching her by the knees with his opposite arm and returning her finally to her feet.

The song climaxed with a flurry of wild kicks, Hank and Cherry's legs crossing each other like a scissors. As the tune came to an end, Hank wrapped an arm around Cherry's shoulders and dipped her almost to the ground before returning her to an upright position. She looked up into his smiling face, laughing and breathless. He couldn't help it, even with no music playing he picked her up and spun her around in a circle, overcome with the simple joy of touching her. Now that he'd finally found her, he didn't want to let go.

The delicate strains of "Stardust" drifted down from the bandstand.

"Can I trouble you for another dance?" Hank asked hopefully.

"I'd love it." Cherry reached out to take his hand just as Hank heard a male voice from behind him.

"I believe it's time to change partners." The accent was decidedly British, although loaded with more hauteur than Cherry's.

Hank turned to find a slender man in a tweed jacket looking up at him disapprovingly.

Cherry glanced back and forth between the two men and pasted on a smile.

"Hugh, this is Hank. Hank, Hugh. Hugh and I work together," she added. Hank thought he caught an emphasis on the word "work."

Hank offered his right hand to Hugh, keeping the other on the small of Cherry's back. Hugh ignored it and held out his hand to Cherry instead.

"Duck?" he said.

"Cherry has agreed to another dance with me," Hank said evenly.

"It's not your place to come to England and start changing the rules," Hugh replied, with his characteristic distain.

"I think the lady can decide for herself who she wants to dance with."

As far as Cherry could tell, Hank hadn't moved an inch. His tone of voice was pleasant. But just the size and strength of him made Hugh take a step back.

"Now if that's a problem for you," Hank continued, "perhaps we should step outside and handle this like gentlemen."

Hugh sniffed. "Are you actually suggesting a round of fisticuffs?" Cherry knew Hugh well enough to see through his derision and sense a hint of fear.

"I said like gentlemen," Hank gently corrected.

"Pistols and swords, then?" Hugh challenged.

"Actually, I thought maybe we could talk. But if you're intent on violence—"

Cherry stifled her giggle as quickly as she could, but Hugh's face still reddened like mercury filling a thermometer. She could tell the minute Hank opened his mouth Hugh had deduced that this must be Cherry's Canadian "mechanic." The fact he was actually a pilot didn't seem to make Hugh any more deferential.

She knew she should probably intervene but Hugh was being an arse, and although she was perfectly capable of taking care of herself she was curious to see what would happen. The truth was that there were no established rules at these dances and Hugh could give a fig who Cherry danced with, he just couldn't stand to be challenged. Especially by anyone he felt might be intellectually inferior.

Hank was another story. His behavior felt like genuine chivalry.

What had made Cherry laugh was the idea that Hugh would volunteer to compete against Hank in any sort of physical altercation. One had only to glance at the two men to see who was almost certain to be victorious. Hugh was brilliant but he was a scholar, not an athlete, while Hank looked like something from the pages of a Viking pictorial.

"I'll agree to whatever challenge you're offering if you'll leave us alone to finish our dance." Hank's voice was still calm. He definitely wasn't trying to antagonize Hugh, but Cherry now sensed a bit of an edge in his tone.

"Very well." A slow smile spread across Hugh's features, a smile that made Cherry nervous. "How about a game of chess?"

Cherry looked up at Hank, who was clearly about to accept Hugh's challenge. He

88

could have no way of knowing that Hugh, like all the men at Bletchley, was a certified genius and had likely been playing chess since infancy. While Hugh would have little chance in a physical fight, Hank would be dreadfully outmatched in a chess game.

"Hank," she started, wanting to warn him.

"It's all right." He smiled down at her warmly. "I know how to play chess." He turned to Hugh and put out his hand again. "I accept."

Hugh took Hank's hand and gave a smile full of teeth. "Excellent. Can you make it to Bletchley tomorrow? We could convene at the Duck and Swan, and see if we can't get our own namesakes to appear."

"I'll be there," Hank replied.

"Five o'clock."

"Fine. Cherry?" Hank asked, holding out his hand to her. The band had wrapped up "Stardust" during the row and launched into a lovely rendition of "Someone to Watch Over Me." How appropriate.

Cherry placed her hand in Hank's and he swept her away from Hugh, all the way to the other side of the dance floor. His hand felt so reassuring on her back, his arms forming a frame that protected her and supported her.

She loved the way it felt to be held by this man. As though he already cherished her, even though they'd only just met.

Cherry had been overcome when she'd spotted him earlier that evening, all polished and gleaming in his RAF uniform. In dusty walking clothes he'd been enough to feature in her dreams. In uniform he was almost indescribable. His beauty was transformed into something noble and inspiring. His burnished hair glowed under the lights and the navy of his fitted coat rendered his eyes a deep, velvety blue.

She had been delighted to discover that Hank wasn't a mechanic at all, he was a pilot! While Cherry herself was not a snob and still believed that her parents wouldn't go so far as to overrule her choice of beau, an RAF pilot would be much easier to sell than a humble mechanic.

The dance was only half over when she felt a tap on her shoulder. Expecting to find Hugh standing there, she turned with a sigh but straightened up when she saw it was Gilda.

"What's wrong?" she asked.

"It's Hugh. He's threatened to leave you here if you don't come back with us now. Says 'your pilot friend can fly you home.'"

Cherry balled up her fists. It was just like Hugh to try and ruin her evening because of a petty quarrel. Sadly, she had little choice but to go along with his wishes. She turned back to Hank, who still held one of her hands lightly in his.

"I'm terribly sorry, but it looks as though I must dash."

Cherry would not have guessed that she had the power to make such a glorious man look so crestfallen. She was fairly certain a British chap would have simply adopted a wry smile, but Hank was the embodiment of dejection. His eyes scanned the venue for a moment, trying to ascertain if there was some way he could offer her a ride himself, and then, upon finding none, looked back at her with resignation.

"Are you really coming to the Duck and Swan tomorrow?" she asked.

"I gave my word," he said simply. "Will you be there?"

Cherry thought about the pile of cards waiting for her, in addition to her usual duties. Then again, this was war. The translations would always be there. Sometimes it was important to remember what one was fighting for.

"Of course," she replied, smiling brightly as she allowed herself to be dragged backward through the crowd by a determined Gilda. She gave a small wave as her view of Hank was quickly obscured by other dancers.

Chapter Seven

Cherry made her way determinedly back to the Cottage where Bertie would hopefully be at his desk. She'd been able to get an early start this morning, hoping to make it through some index cards before her shift started. (That was in part thanks to Hugh, who had been responsible for the previous evening ending much earlier than she'd expected.) There wouldn't be time for extra work after her shift if she was going reach the Duck and Swan by five. She was half expecting Hugh to requisition the shooting brake again so he'd have an audience for his victory.

The ride home after the dance had been rather excruciating. Hugh had been giddy with delight at the thought that he'd get to best an RAF pilot on his own terms. Cherry assumed he harbored some jealousy and she could understand up to a point. Pilots were revered everywhere they went, and rightly so. An RAF pilot drank for free in any pub in England. By comparison, while the work

93

Hugh did was invaluable to the war effort and Britain was much better served with him at Bletchley than out in a trench somewhere, the entire codebreaking operation was secret and therefore couldn't be discussed. Nobody could know the contributions Hugh and his team were making to the cause.

None of this meant that Cherry was looking forward to watching helplessly as Hank lost a wager to a pretentious fop. Maybe she could get there early and warn him. Maybe there was some way for Hank to back out without losing any honor.

Maybe she should try concentrating on the matter at hand and stop worrying about boys and their silly bets.

She'd only been at it for an hour this morning when she'd come across the message she'd been looking for. Her cry of joy had been such that Sarah had come over to reconnoiter. Cherry had made Sarah read the message back to her, just to confirm she wasn't hallucinating. But there it was.

"We shall have a party for my mother's birthday tomorrow. May she live a healthy life."

Cherry grabbed the card and hopped up, promising Sarah to bring it back as soon as she'd shown her evidence to Mr. Cross.

"Mr. Cross?" she called, finding him at his desk.

For as brilliant as he was, Bertie Cross always looked at sixes and sevens. As though he was perpetually searching for mislaid spectacles that were already on his nose.

There was a famous story about how he'd gone for a walk around the small pond on the BP grounds with a sandwich in one hand and a cup of tea in the other. He'd been watching a group of ducks on the pond and presumably intended to throw them the last of his sandwich, but instead he'd lobbed his tea mug into the water. Some people at Bletchley thought he was a bit mad, but Cherry reckoned his mind simply worked on a higher plane than the rest of theirs and he couldn't be bothered by trivialities, like which hand was holding the sandwich.

"Miss Spence," he replied, focusing on her.

"A word?" she asked.

"Of course," he replied, motioning towards the chair by his desk.

"I believe I've found something of interest. A possible code phrase that would indicate an upcoming attack." Cherry handed the two index cards to Bertie, who pushed his little round glasses up on his nose.

"Mother's birthday," he muttered, studying the cards. He looked back up at her. "You of all people know that we do receive messages of a personal nature from time to time, and although they sound remarkably similar, it's not impossible that it's a coincidence."

"Yes, of course," Cherry replied. "I'm not sure exactly how to say it, but there's just something odd about the messages. Even before there were two of them. Otherwise I never would have remembered the first one. Then, when it came up again, I had to go back and see if they matched."

"Close enough. It's possible they originally were the same message, and between all the steps it took them to reach us they got changed up a little," Bertie admitted. "But even if you are right, they don't contain enough information for us to be able to provide a warning to our forces. Did the original message fall on the day of or before a large scale attack?"

Cherry had thought of this, and checked the records. She shook her head.

"No. The first big attack following the message was two weeks later."

Bertie looked down at the messages, and then back up at her.

"You know the difficulties we experience convincing military leadership that our information is sound. We can't go to them with guesses and half theories." He sighed and gave her a sympathetic look. "If it makes any difference, I believe you. I believe that this is a code phrase. But because we have no further information on what it portends, to report it could be worse than doing nothing."

"Of course, I shouldn't have bothered you." She stood up, collecting the index cards from his desk.

"You never bother me, and when we win this war it'll be in part because of the work you're doing. Never forget that."

"I won't. Thank you, Mr. Cross."

"Thank you, Miss Spence."

Cherry hurried out of his office to her own workspace to copy the messages and dates before returning the cards to Sarah. She may not have enough to convince Bertie that this was a code foreshadowing an attack, but she knew in her heart it was. Now all she had to do was prove it.

"It's a good thing you're still in training, or you might have missed your duel this afternoon," Dickie remarked. He and Hank were on their way back to their quarters after another group training sortie.

"Is that right? What's the schedule for regulars?" Hank asked.

"You still get time off, twenty-four hours every week and forty-eight hours every three weeks," Dickie replied. "But even when you're not scheduled to fly there are alert shifts. And we're expected to be on-call in case of a large scale raid."

"Doesn't leave a lot of time for you to chase girls," Hank joked.

"That's why we have to make every night count. Speaking of that, who was the stunning blonde last night who fetched your little chauffeur?"

"Blonde?" Hank asked blankly.

"My God, you are smitten." Dickie shook his head. "I wonder if she might be in attendance this afternoon. That would be worth a trip to the pub. Perhaps I'll join you."

"To see me lose my honor to a fellow Brit?"

"Those government chaps can be clever fellows, I wouldn't wager anything you're not willing to lose."

Hank thought about what he could wager. He didn't have much of value, but then again he hadn't agreed to anything specific other than just showing up for a chess match. And the only reason he'd even done that was because he'd wanted to dance with Cherry. Not that it had worked out badly for him. It looked like he'd get to see her again that afternoon.

"I've got that cologne, if you still want it," Dickie offered.

"Sure. I'll take all the help I can get."

Hank had bemoaned the fact he hadn't thought to bring any Old Spice over with him, but Dickie said he had a bottle of Royal English Leather and Hank could borrow it.

"At the very least, you'll be the better smelling chess player. Here we are."

Hank followed Dickie into the other man's room. He noticed that Dickie had a few postcards of pinup girls on his bureau.

"I thought you liked them tall and slender," Hank remarked, picking up one of the cards.

"Those are just ideas for nose art, on a Spit," Dickie explained. "But they are appealing. Your chauffer looks a bit like a pinup. She looks like a Petty girl. In fact…" Dickie reached down beside his bed and pulled out a copy of *Esquire* magazine and paged through it, handing it to Hank with a smirk.

"Think that's what she's hiding under the dress and pearls?"

Hank stared fixated at the picture. In it a pert brunette winked at him as she posed provocatively and wound a phone cord around a dainty finger. She wore only a filmy black nightie and a smile. Every inch of her was visible through the sheer garment, from the tips of her full breasts, over her curvy hips and rounded bottom, past her shapely thighs and calves to her tiny feet.

The girl did bear a striking resemblance to Cherry, right down to the sparkling brown eyes, rosy cheeks, and full red lips. Hank couldn't speak for whether the rest of the drawing, which left little to the imagination, was accurate. But the facial resemblance was such that he felt a stab of guilt even looking at the picture. He snapped the magazine shut and slapped it irritably back into Dickie's hand, but the damage was done. That image of what Cherry was likely hiding under her modest clothing was now all he could think about.

Dickie laughed as he handed Hank the cologne. "Sure you don't want to borrow the magazine as well?" he asked.

"Are you trying to sabotage my chess match? Damn Brits," Hank grumbled, heading towards the door. Dickie's laugh echoed all the way down the hall to his room.

Chapter Eight

Hank and Hugh already had the chess board set up by the time Cherry arrived at the pub with Gilda. They could've walked the two miles from BP and probably gotten there earlier, but Cherry had elected to wait for the bus and turn up looking less melted. As it was, her waves and mascara were rather the worse for wear, but the smile Hank gave her when he saw her made her forget all about them.

She wasn't sure she would ever get used to the sight of him. He was in his RAF uniform again, minus the coat, one big arm propped up on the bar. Cherry was a little surprised the RAF was able to dig up a uniform that fit him properly, what with his proportions being larger than most Englishmen.

Cherry wore a dress in a vibrant blue bird print that she'd chosen especially for this event. She tried to be practical about her clothes, as she worked long hours in often uncomfortable conditions. But there were a few dresses in her wardrobe that brought her shape closer to the ideal silhouette of the day, tall and graceful, of which she considered herself to be neither. This one had a softly pleated skirt and lovely peplum that hid her hips. She flatly refused to wear shoulder pads like her modiste suggested. On her short figure they just brought to mind a boy in his father's coat.

She removed her gloves and hat and set them on a table next to Gilda's. As though he'd been waiting for their arrival, Hugh called the pub to order.

"So ladies, gents, an agreement has been made for a game of chess between myself, and my Canadian friend…" He turned to Hank, who raised an eyebrow at Hugh's formality.

"Hank Clarkson," he finally offered.

Hugh blinked at Hank's failure to include his rank in his introduction and opted to rectify it himself. After all, this entire exercise was, as far as Cherry could tell, an opportunity for Hugh to prove his mental superiority to an RAF pilot.

"Flying Officer Clarkson," Hugh finished. "What shall we play for?"

"I thought we were playing for honor," Hank replied.

"I suppose you don't have anything else of value," Hugh retorted.

Cherry's eyes widened. She would not have blamed Hank if he had plumped for a round of fisticuffs after all.

Instead, Hank just took a long hard look at Hugh and Cherry saw a muscle clench in his jaw. The pub quieted. Hank reached into his pocket and pulled out a silver pocket watch.

"If it makes you feel better to have a tangible trophy on the line, I offer this."

Hank set the watch on the table. Cherry could see that it was worn but very fine. It had lovely filigree carving on the cover and looked like something that must have been passed down to Hank from a past generation. Cherry desperately wanted to say something to Hank, feeling as though Hugh were tricking him into parting with an heirloom he must value a great deal. But everyone in the pub was suddenly interested in the goings on, so there didn't seem to be any way to warn Hank about Hugh without making it appear as though she doubted Hank's intelligence.

Hugh looked at Hank and smiled. "Let's see if I can match your wager," he said, reaching into his own pocket.

"You don't have anything I want," Hank stated flatly. "But I would wager for a picture of you."

The last bit was directed at Cherry. Hank's glance shifted to her and his tone softened. As she gazed back into those blue eyes she forgot to take a breath. It was only when he grinned that she remembered and sucked in a huge gulp of air.

"What do you say, Cherry?" he asked.

She wanted to say he could have her picture, her heart, and anything else he fancied. But she managed to murmur a quite composed sounding "Of course."

"Very well, then," Hugh barked, a bit put off at having his thunder stolen by an exchange not involving himself. "Shall we use St. George's Club Rules to start?"

"Don't be tricky, Hugh," Cherry chastised, turning to Hank. "He means the player who goes first has choice of color," she explained.

"Thanks." He smiled at her and took a seat.

The game began, and everyone in the pub turned to watch. Everyone, that is, except for Hank's dark haired RAF friend, whose attention seemed to be riveted on Gilda. Cherry didn't blame him. Gilda was looking quite fetching in a pale blue frock that set off her golden hair.

Although Cherry was familiar with the general rules of chess, she was by no means an expert. It was one thing to understand which piece could move where, but quite another to use strategy to determine what your opponent would do two, five, or ten moves down the line.

The crowd started off respectfully quiet but as the game continued and the players' pauses between moves lengthened, the buzz of conversation picked up. Hugh's face was the picture of arrogance as he abandoned proper chess etiquette to joke with the onlookers. Cherry wondered if he was trying to prove that besting Hank didn't require his full attention.

She wasn't sophisticated enough to know who was getting the upper hand. Both players had claimed a number of their opponents' pieces, and their remaining forces appeared to be equally matched. Hugh was the hometown favorite and it appeared he'd stacked the pub with colleagues from Bletchley Park. The mood in the place was light, nobody seemed to be very concerned over the outcome of the match. Perhaps they were assuming, as she had, that there was no way Hank could win.

By this point, Hugh had moved on to reciting bawdy limericks while he waited for his turn. In contrast, Hank's entire focus was on the board before him. It was impossible to tell if he was even aware of Hugh's trumpeting. He never looked up at his opponent's face.

Cherry took the opportunity to study Hank while his attention was elsewhere. She was so close she thought she caught a whiff of his cologne. His face was undeniably masculine, with a strong jaw and wide brow. But he had thick black lashes and a full bottom lip. His cheeks looked smooth, freshly shaven. There was a sweetness about him. A goodness, a pureness. As though the RAF uniform couldn't quite hide the farm boy beneath.

The thoughts Cherry had about him were not pure. She wondered if he would be shocked to know the things she imagined, this man who wanted her picture. Even in a crowd of people, she looked down at his strong hands and wondered how they would feel on her body. What he could do with those delicate fingers that plucked yet another piece from the board as he made his latest move.

"Checkmate."

It wasn't loud, but the whole pub went silent. Hugh stopped mid-limerick and turned his attention to the chessboard. Hank sat back in his seat as Hugh's confident smile transformed into a look of disbelief. Hugh looked down at the board and then up at his opponent.

Cherry held her breath. She had no idea what Hugh would do next. It would obviously be extremely bad form to make a disparaging remark, especially when he'd exhibited such poor sportsmanship during the match. But that didn't mean it couldn't happen.

Without speaking, Hugh pushed back his chair and stood up. He looked Hank square in the face and extended a hand. Hank looked back at him for a minute and then stood with a smile and took Hugh's proffered hand in a hearty shake.

"Good show," Hugh said.

"You never really had a chance. There was no way I was losing that picture," Hank joked. He turned to Cherry and winked. She blushed down to her navy pumps as Hank pocketed the watch.

"Can I buy you a pint?" Hugh asked. Cherry was fascinated by how solicitous Hugh had suddenly become. She wondered if it was because, while Hugh didn't particularly respect Hank's looks or position, he did respect intelligence.

"If it's all the same to you, I'd prefer to share a drink with the lady. If she'll have me." Hank turned to Cherry with a questioning look.

"I'd love you," she stammered. "To. One. I'd love one, thanks." She took a steadying breath. "A Pimms and lemonade would be lovely."

"Yes, well done," Hugh tittered at her, while Hank gave her one of his knee melting smiles. Was she incapable of talking to this man without reddening? Hank turned to fetch her drink, and Hugh was left looking after him.

"What do you know, Duck? You picked the only clever pilot in the RAF."

"You might have to reevaluate your view of Canadians," she added, attempting to regain her composure.

"Perhaps. But it appears his comrade has captured the Swan, and if he's Canadian, then I'm an Arab." Hugh motioned towards the bar where Gilda was indeed being entertained by the dark haired RAF pilot, this one decidedly more English.

Cherry watched Hank talk to the other pilot as he waited for his drinks. The two did seemed friendly. It would be nice if Gilda got on with the other pilot. Perhaps they would be keen on a double date.

Hank returned with her Pimms and Hugh faded into the background.

"You're almost as good at chess as you are at dancing," she remarked, taking the glass.

"Thanks. Not sure that either skill is particularly useful, but there should always be things in life besides work." He took a sip of his drink and grimaced. "I wonder how long it takes to get used to warm beer."

"I should think it would help to keep drinking," Cherry suggested.

Hank chuckled. "I'll give that a try."

"Where did you learn to play chess?"

"My mom taught me. There wasn't much to do for fun on the farm. We lived forty-five minutes from the closest town, so going to the movies wasn't an easy option. Dad played the harmonica, we played chess."

"I thought you were from Ottawa."

"Outside of there," Hank answered quickly. "Ottawa is the closest big city."

"Oh. Even so, just knowing how to play doesn't guarantee victory. You must have studied strategy."

"Not really," Hank replied. "Not formally, anyway. I just played a lot and watched to see how different moves came out. I have a pretty good head for pictures, understanding where things are in relation to other things. Can't really explain it, and it never seemed that helpful in practical matters. But it did make me decent at chess."

Cherry wondered if Hank knew how remarkable his skill actually was. She'd met people like him at Bletchley. They were usually put to work on some of the most challenging of the Enigma codes because they could see patterns where others couldn't.

"That must give you a pretty good head for puzzles," she remarked casually. "Do your supervisors at RAF know about this?

Maybe you should be working for Intelligence."

He barked a laugh, and took another drink.

"Intelligence," he repeated, shaking his head. She wasn't sure why he found the idea so comical. What he'd just said about how his mind worked was exactly the kind of thing the BP higher ups were always looking for in a codebreaker. Of course, she couldn't tell him that.

"Anyway, it was an impressive victory. I can't believe you went to all that effort just to get my picture. I would have given it to you even if you'd lost."

He looked at her and his face softened. "Then I'd have won either way."

Hank meant it too. He'd never had a girl give him her picture, not even back in Kansas. His previous experience with girls had been so unfortunate he was a little worried that his luck so far with Cherry was due to run out.

Hank felt that way about all of this. His job as a Spitfire pilot. The respect he was shown just because he wore the uniform. The fact that this smart, pretty girl liked him and actually thought he should be working for Intelligence. Him! What the folks back home would think if they could hear that. All those scrambled codes and messages. Shoot, regular books looked like a jumble to him. But nobody here knew that. It was as though he could reinvent himself, free from all the disappointment he'd caused back home.

Hank fingered the watch in his pocket. The one his dad had given him the night before he'd left for Canada. The old man'd surprised him with that one. When Hank had announced he was leaving to join the British Air Force, his father hadn't said a word. He'd just looked hard at his son and nodded. But that night, while Hank was packing, his father had brought him something wrapped in a cloth. He'd opened it up to reveal a silver pocket watch.

"This watch was given to me by my father," he'd said. "And I'm giving it to you. I know we haven't always seen eye to eye, and maybe you think I've been unfair. But everything I did was to try and prepare you for life, and I hope you'll remember that."

His father had handed him the watch and held out his hand.

"Good luck, son."

As Hank had shaken hands with his father he'd thought, maybe for the first time, about what it might have been like to have him as a son. And he tried to believe what Art had said, about his father just wanting what was best for him. Well, Hank knew what was best for him and this was it. This job, this country, and definitely this girl.

"Do you have dinner plans? Or would you like to get some here?" he asked her.

"That sounds lovely, but I came with a friend and I'd like to ask her about it first." Cherry looked over at the blonde who was now at the bar, laughing at something Dickie had said. Good for him.

"Of course. Maybe she'd like to join us, along with my buddy."

Hank led Cherry up to the bar, where it was decided that they would eat as a foursome. Everything went well until the waitress dropped off menus. Hank opened his up, gave it a token glance, and turned to Cherry.

"What's good?" he asked.

"I haven't had many dinners here, but I'd say any meat not out of a tin would be delicious. We humble secretaries don't get the fancy food they reserve for pilots," Cherry joked. "Perhaps you haven't been here long enough to become acquainted with the joys of rationing."

"Cherry is afraid to admit she has an embarrassing fondness for fish and chips," Gilda said.

"Don't be ridiculous." Cherry blushed.

"What's fish and chips?" Hank asked. The others looked at him, surprised.

"Fried battered fish with chips," replied Cherry finally, adding "Fried potatoes" when Hank furrowed his brow.

"Oh. What's wrong with that? I didn't eat a lot of fish growing up, but it sounds pretty good."

"It's perfectly fine food," Dickie explained. "It's just generally more popular with dockworkers and the like. But I'll state proudly that I've enjoyed my share as well." He grinned at Cherry, and she smiled back.

It was determined that Cherry would order fish and chips, not because it was her favorite but so Hank could try it. He was relieved he'd managed to get by without looking at the menu. He'd just waited until Dickie ordered prime rib and announced that he would have the same. Gilda selected a lamb chop.

As they waited for their food to arrive they shared stories of lives that were distinctly different, at least different from Hank's. He especially liked Cherry's and Gilda's tales of debutantes because the concept was completely foreign to him. Even Dickie seemed fascinated. Apparently these stories weren't the sort of thing they printed in the society pages.

"I'd just been on an extended ski trip in Switzerland," Gilda explained. "I arrived home shortly before the Season and my mother was rather appalled to discover that while my skin was snowy white from the neck down, on the top I looked a bit like a lobster." Everyone laughed as she continued.

"I was attending Queen Charlotte's Ball where we're all expected to wear silly white evening gowns to demonstrate our purity or some rubbish and the one my mother's modiste had designed for me left my shoulders bare. To make my face match my shoulders I was powdered up like a geisha. I looked ridiculous."

Hank and Cherry laughed heartily at her story but Dickie just gave her a tender smile. "I can't imagine you looking ridiculous under any circumstances."

116

Gilda blushed winningly at his compliment.

"I wish you'd been at the ball that evening. I don't think I danced with a single gentleman. I was so afraid I'd sweat and take all the powder off I spent most of the dance freezing out on the balcony."

"What about you, Cherry? Any scandalous tales of debutante life?" Hank asked, smiling over at his dinner companion.

"A number of them, but I think the most mortifying was when I was presented to the Queen at the start of the Season. I'd been sent to Miss Vacani's dance school to be instructed in the art of the curtsey to ensure there were no slipups. I'm a bit of a blunderer and mum feared I'd make a hash of it. And good thing too. It was quite a challenge. You remember, Gilda." Cherry turned to the other girl, who nodded solemnly.

"You had to place your left foot behind your right foot, bend your knee so it almost touched the floor while keeping your chin up and eyes straight forward. I was all right going down but coming back up I'd wobble terribly. It took poor Miss Vacani forever to teach me and even when I'd 'graduated' I'm sure I still wasn't doing it properly.

"Anyway, it turned out the wobble didn't matter. On the day of my presentation I'd been given shoes with heels so high I could barely teeter around while walking straight forward. They were supposed to add four inches and make me look statuesque, and I must say I've never felt taller, but when I tried to curtsey to the Queen my heel caught in my petticoat and I pitched forward quite spectacularly. His Royal Highness was half out of his seat to help me when an usher appeared and did it for him. I was mortified. But as this was the start of the Season, at least the gents' expectations for my dancing skills could be set suitably low."

Dickie and Gilda laughed, but Hank came to her defense. "I think you're a great dancer."

She smiled at him, and then her look changed and he realized he'd instinctively placed his hand on her knee and given her a squeeze under the table. He pulled it away quickly, but she smiled and took it in her own for a moment. Their food arrived just then and all hands were needed out in the open, but Hank found the whole incident very encouraging.

The dinner they shared was the most enjoyable one he'd had since arriving in England. The girls shared more stories of London high society and Dickie entertained them with hijinks from University, including the time his rugby team greased the railroad tracks the night before the rival team was to arrive by train. Apparently it took ten miles for the train to stop, and the opposing team was so exhausted from the walk back that they lost the match 45-0.

The only thing that dimmed Hank's pleasure was the fact that he had so many secrets to keep. He could talk about farm life, but not let it slip that he was an American. He could talk about school, but nothing about how he'd fared or how long it had taken him. As far as girls, there wasn't much to say at all. So he talked about flying.

"There was a town fifty miles west with the best ice cream you've ever tasted," he said, remembering exactly how it had felt on his tongue. "I was dusting crops one hot afternoon and decided I had a hankering for that ice cream so I flew over to get some. Unfortunately I hadn't planned on exactly what to do when I got there. Lucky for me the main road was wide and straight and pretty quiet for a summer afternoon." Dickie grinned at Hank, likely predicting what would come next.

"I brought Jenny in right down that main street, startling folks and scaring the horses. People came to their windows to see what all the commotion was. The plane wasn't real big and I'd cut the engine before landing so it was pretty quiet, but it wasn't every day someone dropped out of the sky on your doorstep."

Hank glanced over at Cherry, whose look of wonder seemed genuine. "I taxied that plane right up to Shoemaker's Ice Cream Shop and walked in. Bought my ice cream, ate it quick before it melted, and hopped back in my plane. Then I took off down the main street, just as easy as I'd landed."

"I thought I'd gotten away scot free, but I found out later I'd made the local newspaper. Art was the only one in the area with a plane so word got back to him and he near tanned my hide for making the side trip."

"Was it worth it?" Cherry asked, a twinkle in her eye.

"Best damn ice cream I've ever eaten," Hank replied with a grin. "Pardon me, ladies."

"I hate to cut this evening short," Dickie said. "But it appears we've worn out our welcome."

They'd long since finished their dinner and the bartender was giving signs he was waiting on them to close up. He'd already put up the blackout curtains.

Everyone looked glumly at their empty glasses. Cherry gasped. "Gilda, we've missed the last bus!"

"No worry on that account, I've got a car. We can run you ladies anywhere you need to go." Dickie placed a hand reassuringly on Gilda's forearm.

"And anyway, I owe you a ride home," Hank remarked, turning to Cherry.

"What do you say, dear?" Cherry asked Gilda. "If the military trusts them with their aeroplanes, I suppose we can trust them with a car."

"It's not the driving I'm worried about," Gilda teased, taking Dickie's proffered hand to help her to her feet.

"Why don't I get you girls settled while Hank here pays the tab?"

Dickie handed Hank a few bills and headed towards the door, a woman on each arm. By the time Hank reached the car,

Dickie and Gilda were in the front seat and Cherry sat alone in the back. Her little legs were tucked up beneath the blue dress and she seemed to be making herself as small as possible in the corner to leave him the bulk of the seat.

He bent down and climbed in next to her, torn between not wanting to crowd her and yet wanting to take advantage of the excuse to be pressed up against her.

"Are you okay?" he asked.

"I'm not the one who looks as though they were sitting in a car built for Lilliputians," she joked. "Here, would it be more comfortable…" She lifted his inside arm and placed it along the top of the seat, taking her place beneath it.

"Is that better?" she asked, looking up at him.

Her eyes were luminous in the moonlight. Hank could see her lips. They were slightly parted. It would be so easy to lower his head and kiss her. He wished he knew if she wanted him to kiss her.

Her silence made him realize she was probably waiting for him to answer her question.

122

"Yes, thanks." And it was better. Much better. She smiled and turned back around to face the front windshield. He'd missed his chance to kiss her, but maybe he could get a read on her feelings another way.

Ever so gently, he lowered his arm so that it was resting lightly on top of her shoulders. His fingers brushed the soft fabric of her dress. Rather than pull away, she snuggled back against his side. He tightened his hold a bit, his fingers now touching the warm, soft skin of her arm. She sighed and rested her head on his chest. A smile blossomed on his face and he hoped she couldn't feel his heart racing.

It turned out both Gilda and Cherry were staying with families just outside of Bletchley, Gilda in Stoke Hammond and Cherry in Aspley Guise. Hank wondered if it would take him longer to get used to the odd place names or the warm beer.

Although Dickie was driving, Hank had actually been the one to get the car from the motor pool. He'd volunteered a few hours to help the maintenance folks service the fleet and in return they'd told him he could borrow one when he wanted, as long as they had something available. Because Hank still wasn't used to driving on the left, and the blackout made any motor travel more treacherous, it had been agreed that Dickie would drive back to the aerodrome.

"So how will I find you to claim my prize?" Hank murmured. Gilda and Dickie were occupied in the front seat, navigating to Gilda's residence.

Hank could see Cherry smile and rummage around in her purse. She pulled out a pen.

"Have you got anything to write on?" she asked.

Hank reached into his pocket and pulled out a coaster from the pub. He'd snagged it on his way out as a souvenir of his evening.

"Will this work?" he asked, handing it to her. She took it and began scribbling.

"My penmanship is horrendous in the daylight, I shudder to think what it looks like in the dark. You may need Intelligence to decipher this," she warned, handing it back to him.

"Why don't you tell me the number, just in case? I've got a pretty good memory."

"Very well. It's Victoria, 1-5-9-7."

"Perfect. My brother's age, and my mother's birth year. I'm still keeping the coaster, though. Otherwise none of the boys will believe I actually saw a girl tonight."

Dickie pulled up into the circle drive of a huge brick house. Most of the lights were out, except for a few on the top floor.

"Will you be able to get in?" Dickie asked Gilda.

"Oh yes. I'm not the first girl who's crept in after the masters have gone to sleep," she replied. "Lovely to have met you." She put out her hand and Dickie took it in his and held it.

"The pleasure was mine, I assure you." Gilda climbed out of the car and glided silently towards a side door. Dickie didn't move until he saw her pale blue dress disappear into the structure.

"All right, punters. Anyone game to sit up front, or shall I play the chauffeur?"

"Drive on, Jeeves," Cherry joked, settling back against Hank.

"Yes, Ma'am," he replied, heading back down the lane. Cherry directed Dickie to the main road and on to her host family's home. Hank was feeling pretty good about things. He'd won the chess game and, apparently, the girl. Her number was locked in his head and the coaster would be proof for his wallet.

He'd carry it as a good luck charm until he had Cherry's picture to replace it. Pilots could always use a good luck charm.

He knew that the polite thing to do would be to give Cherry a friendly handshake and let her escape into the night as Dickie had with Gilda. But he didn't know when he'd get to see her again, and he was just dying to kiss her. He refused to try any of the lines that had been suggested to him, about his job being dangerous or not wanting to risk getting shot down without feeling her lips on his. They just cheapened things and sounded contrived.

Dickie maneuvered the car up another long drive to another old brick house, this one a bit smaller but more ornate, with vines creeping up it. Hank realized to his joy that he'd have to get out of the car himself to let Cherry out. And if he was going to do that, he might as well be a gentleman and walk her to her door. If she'd let him.

Once the car was stopped, Dickie went around to the passenger side and opened the door.

"Your stop, Madame," he said regally.

Hank clambered out, stretching his tall frame. He gave Dickie a look, and the other man smirked but returned to the driver's side. Hank reached down to offer Cherry his hand and help her out of the car.

"Thank you," she said politely, clutching her hat and purse in her other hand.

"May I walk you to the door?" he asked, offering his arm.

She looked up at the silent house, and back at him. "If you're quiet," she whispered with a smile, looping her hand around his arm.

"As a mouse," he replied. She led him around to the side of the house and pulled at a string next to the doorframe to reveal a key. She turned it in the lock, the sound impossibly loud in the still night. Upon hearing no response she returned the key to its hiding place.

"Thank you for a lovely evening," she said softly. She was looking up at him and he thought about how even in those fancy shoes she'd worn for the Queen she still would've been a head shorter than him.

Here it was. He might as well go for broke. As Dickie always reminded him, the whole country was full of women. But the only one he wanted was this one.

"Would it be okay if I kissed you good night?" he asked.

She placed her gloved palms on his chest and looked up at him. "If you can reach me," she teased.

Hank smiled and put a hand on her cheek, loving how soft it felt against his thumb. He bent forward, touching his lips to hers, delicately at first. Experimenting to see how she would react.

He had intended it to be a chaste first kiss, gentle and courteous. Cherry was from a privileged background and Hank didn't want her thinking he was some rough country oaf who couldn't be respectful. But there was nothing chaste about her reaction to his kiss.

She raised up on her tiptoes and her lips parted slightly, allowing him access. Her hands went up his chest and around his neck, pulling him closer. Hank was happy to oblige. He wrapped one arm around her waist and the other hand cradled the nape of her neck, arching her backward so he could feel her along the length of him. His tongue was in her mouth and it was glorious. She tasted like spice and oranges from those drinks he'd gotten her. She was as eager a partner for this kiss as she had been on the dance floor.

128

She sighed into his mouth and it brought him back to his senses enough to realize what he was doing. His left hand was still behind her neck, but his right hand had slid down and was cupping her nicely rounded bottom, pressing her against him where she could surely feel his—

"Oof," she said, as he set her down as quickly and gently as he could, trying to immediately create space between them. Cold air rushed in where her warm body had just been.

"Sakes alive," he whispered.

The sight of her was almost his undoing. Her curls were slightly mussed from where he'd had his hands. Her lips were full and swollen from his kisses, and her chest rose and fell as she caught her breath, the hardened tips of her breasts visible through the fine fabric of her dress. His fingers itched to hold her again.

"I'm sorry, that was… I hope I didn't take advantage, I mean…" What the hell did he mean? "I'm sorry."

"No need to apologize," she replied politely. "I rather enjoyed it."

She gave him a wicked smile, and he knew he was hooked. Whatever free time he got, he wanted to spend it with this girl.

They both noticed a light go on in the upper floor, directly above them.

"That's the room just next to mine. I've got to dash, thanks again for a lovely night!" she whispered, sliding swiftly through the door and disappearing into the dark house. Hank jogged back to the car, where Dickie was drumming his fingers on the steering wheel.

"Successful mission?"

"Hopefully the first of many," Hank replied with a smile.

Chapter Nine

"Here's the problem."

Hank pulled his head out of the Spitfire engine. "It's got a carburetor with a float. Any time the plane makes a sharp dive, the fuel all goes to the top of the chamber and none goes to the engine. That's why the engine stalls. The black smoke it kicked out must have been caused by the over-rich fuel mixture fed in once the gas returned to the bottom of the tank."

Hank put his hands on his hips and looked grim. "Worse yet, if the maneuver is held too long, the engine can flood and might make it impossible to start again." He turned to the mechanic assigned to the plane. "This is a serious flaw."

"You're bang on, sir," the other man replied. "These engines should really have fuel injection like the Huns."

"So why go with the carburetor?" Hank asked.

"Easier to produce, easier to repair. Pound for pound it's a more powerful engine. It's a trade-off, sir."

"So what do the other pilots do when the 109 they're chasing goes into a dive?"

"You'd have to ask them, sir."

Hank would definitely be doing that. Maybe if he inverted the plane before he dove he could keep the fuel in the bottom of the chamber. It was worth a try.

His thoughts were interrupted by the ominous howl of the air raid siren, kicking his pulse up into combat mode. Hank had never heard anything like it before touching down in England. It rose and fell like a wailing banshee, warning everyone in earshot that death would soon be raining down from the skies.

And the skies were where he needed to be.

Hank grabbed his life jacket and ran for the line of operational Spits. On the way he threw the jacket, affectionately known as a "Mae West" for what it did to one's silhouette when inflated, around his neck and fastened it in front. The ground team was already getting the props going and pilots were streaming out of the Dispersal hut. This was his first shift "at readiness" and he was keen to finally see some action.

Planes taxied past him towards the edge of the field, eager to get into the air and address the incoming threat. Hank reached his ship at a dead run and vaulted up onto the wing, swinging his parachute around him and snapping the front straps into place.

Pete, his mechanic, was in the cockpit priming the starter. When Hank had his helmet on Pete jumped out and Hank squeezed his large frame into the seat, quickly fastening the seat and shoulder straps. He slapped his oxygen mask on and released the brake.

"Give 'em hell, sir!" Pete called, as Hank gave him a thumbs up and took his place in the line of planes.

His takeoff was quick and before he knew it he was in the air, forming up into flights with his squadron. The squadron leader had given instructions that any time the group was looking for the enemy they were to stay in tight formation. If they sighted any Huns they were to report back with the location, but not head off to engage the enemy until the leader called "Break!"

Hank was in a section of three called a flight, with Dickie just ahead of him, and another pilot named Skip off Dickie's starboard wing. He could hear the squadron leader checking in with Control over the R.T. His squadron had been designated "Falcon squadron" for this sortie.

"All Falcon aircraft, patrol Colchester at angels one-zero, patrol Colchester at angels one-zero."

The squadron leader hit the gas and wheeled his kite over towards Colchester, climbing steeply to reach the designated altitude. The rest of the planes did likewise. Hank was careful to stay just off Dickie's wing, keeping one eye on his instruments and the other on his position in formation.

"Climb to angels one-five." Control's voice came through the speaker in his helmet. "Bandits approaching from the East!"

"All Falcon aircraft, full throttle! Full throttle!"

The squadron leader's voice sang out over the speaker and his aircraft pulled ahead of the others as he engaged his emergency thrust. Other aircraft followed in kind, including Dickie's. Hank jammed the emergency throttle lever down and his engine screamed with new power, shooting his craft forward like a bullet as he followed Dickie up into a steep climb.

Hank took a steadying breath and pulled the guard off his firing button. The button was painted red, a splash of color on his black spade grip. He turned the safety ring around from the "SAFE" position to the "FIRE" position and prepared himself to take another man's life.

"It's not complicated," Dickie had said earlier, when Hank had asked him about how he'd feel to shoot down a German plane. "It's us or them."

Hank had wondered if he'd feel conflicted when the time came. But as he craned his neck around beneath his bubble canopy and took in the immense sky, knowing attack could come from any direction, he was reassured by the feeling of the weapon at his fingertip.

Hank switched on his electric gunsight, which projected a little orange cross with a circle at the center onto his windshield. He was still working to stay on Dickie's wing, and again wondered how anyone was able to spot incoming enemy planes when they were expected to fly so close together.

He shouldn't have worried, at least for now. The incoming enemy was not hard to detect. What looked like a swarm of gnats appeared on the horizon. As they drew closer, Hank was able to see the gnats were actually German bombers. There must have been dozens of them. And swirling around above were smaller dots, the fighter escorts.

Hank had studied his opponent, its weapons and capabilities. The bitterest enemy of the Spitfire was the German Messerschmitt 109. A single seat, all metal fighter plane, equipped with two 20 millimeter cannons, one under each wing. While a superb aircraft, the Spitfire only carried Browning machine guns, eight in all, with three hundred rounds each. This gave him about fourteen seconds worth of bullets, to be expended in short one or two second bursts when a ship came across his sights. The machine guns were the main reason the RAF had its pilots fly in groups of three. An attack by three planes meant that all twenty-four machine guns could concentrate their firepower on a single aircraft.

The Spitfire's guns could be calibrated so they would converge on a single point. The recommended distance was 650 yards, but Dickie had advised Hank to set it at 250 yards.

It meant he'd need to get damn close to the target to get the most effective use of his weapons, but would mean the difference between just damaging a German aircraft and shooting it out of the sky.

Hank put a gloved hand over his pocket where he'd stowed the pub coaster with Cherry's number. He looked forward to calling her after this was over and his feet were back on solid ground. It was strange, a few weeks ago he hadn't had much to look forward to, and all he'd wanted to do was fly a real fighter plane. Now here he was, piloting the famous Spitfire, and he found himself wishing he were sitting in a drugstore across from his girl, sharing a malted. And sharing other things that weren't so innocent.

Hank thought about the way she'd looked, breathless and mussed from his kisses, and his insides tightened. He forced himself to concentrate, spare a glance over at Dickie's wing, check his instruments, then back up at the oncoming enemy.

Contemplating that massive cloud of incoming aircraft, Hank's first thought wasn't fear, but rather *where should we start*? But that decision wasn't up to him. As the leader of the three ship flight, Dickie would be directing the angle of attack, at least initially.

"Ignore the fighters as long as you can. Concentrate your firepower on the bombers. Let's teach that damned Austrian housepainter a good lesson."

The squadron leader's voice came through the microphone, calm and steady. This man had seen combat before. Hank had heard somewhere that if you could survive the first three weeks as a fighter pilot, you could survive six, and longer. Unfortunately, many men weren't able to make it that far.

Facing an enemy threat of this size should have made Hank's stomach clench up. He should have been terrified. But instead a strange calm came over him, steadying his hand and slowing his breathing. As his squadron neared the approaching enemy, the German fighters began to dive down from their position above the bombers in an attempt to target the Spitfires.

"Break by flight! Target the bombers!" The order came through his helmet and Dickie's plane broke starboard, heading for the closest bomber. Hank followed just off his wing.

He recognized the bomber as a Dornier, dubbed the "flying pencil" because of the skinny fuselage. Bombers were slow moving and relatively large targets, no challenge for a Spitfire to catch or hit. But they were well armored and thus required a lot of hits to take down. Dickie aimed his Spit to pass the Dornier on his port side.

Hank's dive at the bomber pushed him back against his seat and he tightened his grip on the yoke as the controls stiffened with the sudden acceleration. The Dornier rushed up at him until it all but filled Hank's windscreen. He heard the rat-ta-tat as Dickie fired his guns and peeled off to the right. Hank let out a burst of rounds as the bomber passed under him and felt his Spit vibrate with the force of the eight guns firing, although the sound was muffled by his helmet. He'd passed so close he could make out the bomber's serial numbers just next to the big black crosses on the wings.

And then the bomber was behind him. Hank knew he'd scored some hits, but he didn't have much time to track the bomber as the ominous buzz of 109s grew in his ears. He checked his rear vision mirror and saw four of them approaching, spread out in a line behind him.

"Bandits astern!" he called on his R.T.

"Break and engage!" came the reply from Dickie, as he pulled up sharply. Hank keeled his Spit to port, turning as tightly as the plane would allow. Once he'd completed his loop he hauled back on his spade grip, leaning forward and holding his breath as the grey tunnel closed in. His speedometer read 265 miles per hour.

The 109s had broken formation to engage his flight of three. Hank had successfully dislodged them from his tail, but he could now see that two had gone after Dickie while the other two had followed Skip. Hank continued his steep climb until he'd come around behind the pair pursuing Dickie's plane. They were turning sharply to starboard and he cranked his yoke, desperate to get one in his sights. The rear 109 passed in front of him and he let off a burst of gunfire.

Hank saw smoke and the Hun disengaged from his pursuit, diving down toward the ground. Remembering the issue with the carburetor, Hank pitched his yoke to the right, inverting the aircraft and shoved it forward as he followed the 109 into a steep dive. The flip gave the enemy craft a three second advantage, but Hank noticed to his satisfaction that there was no engine stall.

The 109 was trailing smoke but still pulling away. Hank opened the throttle and willed his Spit to catch up, holding his finger down on the firing button any time the other craft bobbed into the circle of his gunsight. He was finally rewarded when the plane listed to the side and begin a steep and uncontrolled dive towards the ground. A figure emerged from the flailing craft, and a minute later a white parachute blossomed into the sky.

Hank imprudently broke his attention for a moment to congratulate himself on his first official kill when a sound like hail on a tin roof made him reflexively pull his stick back to port.

Someone was shooting at him!

He checked the rear vision mirror but his view was obscured by the glare of the sun behind him. He knew he was dead if he spent more than ten seconds flying in a straight line, so he pulled up into a climb in an effort to shake his pursuer. He wondered if it was the other ship that had been chasing Dickie, and if so how his friend had fared. He hoped he lived long enough to find out.

There were some clouds ahead to port, and Hank made a dive for them, attempting to find some cover. Having reached the fluffy refuge he immediately changed direction, hoping his pursuer would lose his trail. As he came out the other side, he noticed his controls were a little sluggish. It wasn't his speed, he was only going 200 and the air was thinner up here. That second 109 must have hit something. Thinking he'd better get his plane back to the aerodrome before it fell apart under him, Hank made one last sweep for enemies and headed towards Chicksands.

His Spitfire quickly joined a number of planes on the ground. The landing had been a bit rocky with the elevator controls all but useless, but he'd managed to wrestle it down. As he climbed off the wing, Pete ran up to greet him.

"Looks like you saw some action, sir. Good to have you back in one piece! Get any Huns?"

"One 109 for certain, got in a few rounds at a Dornier too. Pretty sure my elevator controls are shot. Know anything about how we did?"

Pete filled him in on what he knew while a gasoline truck roared up to refill the Spit and get it ready for action. When Hank turned to look at his plane he was surprised to see holes all along the side of it. He knew he'd been shot at, and knew the controls had behaved strangely, but to actually see where someone had hit him made the whole thing infinitely more real. He was in it now.

Hank joined the rest of his squadron to brief the Intelligence officer about how he'd fared. It turned out the squadron had done quite well even though they'd been badly outnumbered, with several confirmed victories including Hank's, several probably destroyed, and even more damaged. The full extent of the harm done by the Germans would take a while to ascertain. A number of planes were still unaccounted for. Hank shook every man's hand as they all shared their stories, but was dismayed to see that he was the only one from his flight who had returned.

Skip was still missing, as was Dickie.

Chapter Ten

You behaved like a complete trollop, Cherry thought to herself. *No wonder Hank had to push you away. He was probably afraid of being eaten alive.* Her cheeks flamed just thinking about how eagerly she'd responded to his kiss. He must think her quite the tart. She wondered glumly if he'd phone her at all, or if he was now concerned she'd devour him like an anaconda.

The truth was Cherry had little experience in the art of lovemaking. There had been some furtive kisses with a few chaps at deb events, but they'd all been so heavily chaperoned it had required elaborate strategy simply to slip away undetected, and nobody wanted to get caught in a compromising position. But those few stolen moments with boys at dances and teas hadn't come close to the pulse jolting, sensual riot that was Hank's kiss.

Cherry self-consciously raised her fingers to her lips, feeling the ghost of his searing caress even in the stuffy silence of the Cottage. She imagined Hank's hands on her and wiggled in her chair as her mutinous body kindled a warmth between her legs, wanting…. She didn't know. Maybe she should see if she could get her hands on another copy of *Lady Chatterley's Lover*.

Cherry sighed as she looked down at the paragraph in front of her, the garbled German requiring more concentration than she was apparently capable of providing. She'd read it a dozen times, and as sometimes happened, missing letters or possibly misheard Morse code meant that she would have to do some creative translating to get the true meaning of the words.

The worst part was that the message seemed important. It appeared to be a notice regarding preparation for an event or attack. There was just one word that didn't—

"Eagle Day!" she crowed triumphantly. Gilda turned around in her chair at Cherry's outburst. "I have 'Adlertag' again."

The odd expression had started showing up a few days ago and nobody yet knew what it meant. At least nobody in the Cottage. She jumped to her feet and headed for Bertie's office.

"Knock, knock boss." She peeked her head through the partially open doorway. Bertie was studying some papers, but he waved her in.

"Yes, Miss Spence," he said.

"I've got another message about Eagle Day." She showed him the transmission tape and her best guess at what the proper translation was. Bertie took it and sighed.

"Do you think they're planning some sort of large scale attack?" she asked.

"That's a question for a different office," he said absently, still studying the message she'd handed him.

"Is it possible this Eagle Day is what the 'mother's birthday' messages are signaling?"

"You know I appreciate your insight as much as anyone," Bertie replied, peering at her from behind his small round glasses. "But we have a specific job to do here and it's translation. I'm afraid you're too valuable for me to consider any transfer to analysis."

Cherry knew him well enough to take that for the compliment it was and politely excuse herself.

"Thank you for bringing this to my attention, Miss Spence," he called as she exited. She was heading back to her desk when the door opened and Walter entered looking a bit grim.

"There's a skirmish over Colchester. Quite sizeable. RAF has dispatched several squadrons to engage."

News like this wasn't unusual. BP was a hub of intelligence of all kinds and was generally kept in the loop regarding military actions so that it could provide the most helpful and timely information. In the beginning, Cherry's heart had raced any time she'd heard that British men were in danger. Since then her concern hadn't waned, but she'd discovered that one could not maintain a sense of impending doom at all times and still be effective at one's work.

Now there was fresh reason to worry. Hank could be up there at this very moment, risking his life against the Germans. It had always been "somebody's somebody" fighting these battles, and it was impossible to see the lists of missing and dead in *The Times* every morning and not feel sympathy for those left behind, but Cherry was learning it was altogether different when one of those up there was hers.

When had she begun to think of him as hers? Possibly around the time his tongue had entered her mouth.

She cast a look over at Gilda, wondering if her colleague was having a similar reaction to the young man she fancied being in peril, and saw that the actress looked concerned but managed to give her a tight smile.

"Let's keep calm and carry on, shall we?" Gilda suggested, and Cherry nodded and returned to her seat.

Thoughts of Hank continued to distract her, but they had taken on an altogether different tone. Now it was images of him being targeted by some monstrous German Messerschmitt, miles above solid ground, running for his life in the cover of the clouds while cannon fire screamed around him.

She renewed her efforts working through the ever present pile of transmissions, knowing that every message she translated brought England one step closer to discovering Germany's plans. Gave them one more hour of preparation. Perhaps even gave Hank a better chance at survival.

The afternoon dragged on endlessly. While the battles in the sky were generally short, owing to the German planes only having enough fuel for a brief skirmish if they wanted to make it back to France, it could be quite some time before word of the outcome reached Bletchley.

Towards the end of her shift, news arrived that the battle had ended and there had been some losses, although as per usual the Huns had lost more. Not that the German people would hear about it. Cherry's father was fond of saying that if the RAF had half as many planes as Hitler claimed to have shot down England would have already won the war.

She considered staying late, hoping to find another mention of "Adlertag" or maybe even another message about mother's birthdays, but her nerves were wearing thin and she had difficulty focusing on her work. When she closed her eyes all she saw was the image of Hank's Spitfire crashing into a field somewhere. Life had certainly been drearier before she'd met him, but this constant worrying was going to take some getting used to.

It was likely she wouldn't know how he'd fared until she checked *The Times* lists tomorrow morning. Unless someone had found her number among his belongings and thought to inform her of his fate. That happened sometimes. Cherry never imagined she'd be on the receiving end of that phone call. The one that began with "It's my sad duty to inform you..."

She finally made it back to her lodgings and popped into the kitchen to make herself some tea. Mr. and Mrs. Ponsonby, the lovely elderly couple who owned the house, had been nothing but kind to her and she counted herself lucky to have been provided with such pleasant accommodations. It was likely a result of her father's title, which, although occasionally a burden, came in handy at times. Mrs. Ponsonby was in the kitchen, speaking with the cook about upcoming menus, when Cherry walked in.

"You look all done in, lovey. I'll put the kettle on," she said.

Cherry sat gratefully at the table.

"By the by, you've had a telephone message, about an hour ago. There's a note in the hall."

Throwing decorum aside, Cherry jumped up and ran into the hallway, heading for the small table with the telephone. She stared down at the folded piece of paper, terrified of what it might contain.

It's probably from mum, she thought to herself. *Reminding you to wear your pearls inside your clothing so they don't lose lustre, or keep your legs crossed at the ankles when sitting.*

She took a deep breath and opened the note. The first words her eyes lit on were "Flying Officer Clarkson" and her heart stopped. Then she read the rest of the message and it slowly began beating again.

In Mrs. Ponsonby's careful script read the following:

Flying Officer Clarkson would like to know if you are available for luncheon this Saturday. You may dial the following number to make arrangements.

Relief took her knees out from under her and she sank to the floor, the note still clutched in her hand.

Hank was in the Officer's Mess when he heard the commotion outside. Knowing it could be a damaged plane limping back to the aerodrome, he ran out to discover if another one of his squadronmates had returned at last. There were no planes in the sky or on the airfield, besides those being serviced and repaired after the recent battle. The cause of the hubbub was a lone figure on a motorbike approaching the building. Once the bike drew close enough for Hank to see it was one of the large black models favored by the British police, he could also make out the rider.

Dickie.

Hank breathed a sigh of relief and jogged over to where his friend was parking the bike.

"I thought you'd kicked off," he said, pulling the other man in for a fierce hug. Dickie hesitated for a moment, unaccustomed to such an un-British display of affection, before giving Hank a hearty slap on the back.

"Can't get rid of me that easily, mate," he said, stepping back as Hank released him. "It did look rather grim there, for a moment. I'm afraid I've duffed my plane."

"What happened?" Hank asked, as the other men surrounded Dickie to hear his story.

"I couldn't seem to shake the 109, and when my engine started to smoke I was sure I was done for. The Spit pitched forward and I managed to get the cockpit open and slide down the wing before it completely conked. I popped the chute and landed in a field where I was greeted by a farmer with a shotgun who was convinced he was being invaded. It took some doing to persuade him I wasn't part of the Hun army, but it helped that once I'd managed to establish where I'd landed I realized I knew the local butcher.

"He was sent for and upon arrival verified that I wasn't a Jerry and deserved of a shot of whiskey rather than lead. To my delight he took me back to his shop, provided the drink, and sent for the constabulary. One showed up, good lad, and lent me his motorbike which, although knackered, is in a sight better shape than my kite. And Bob's your uncle."

Dickie received slaps on the back from the men assembled and people began to wander back to their duties. Hank looked over at his friend.

"Skip?" he asked. Dickie shook his head.

"He'd gone for six before I took my brolly hop. Left a crater south of Sudbury. Never had a chance, poor devil."

It was strange to be in Skip's room, going through his things and knowing he'd never need any of them again. Hank hadn't really known Skip, other than to say hello over eggs in the morning.

"Were you close?" Hank asked, as Dickie opened the dead man's locker.

"We went through pilot training together. He was a mate," Dickie replied, pulling out a stack of comic books and a St. Christopher's medal. "Lot of good it did you in your bunk, you silly sod," he said softly, shaking his head.

Dickie had explained that when a pilot "bought it," one of his friends would go through his belongings and help get them back to his family. Hank had asked if he could help. Looking around at the room he got a sense of the comrade they'd lost.

Skip came from a nice looking family, had a pretty sister. He was apparently interested in fishing, there were several books on the subject. Kept a small stash of candy bars and some model airplanes. Extra socks. Shoe polish. Victory throat lozenges. Some sketches of planes. A flower pressed in a field handbook.

Hank suddenly thought about what would happen if he bought it. He'd given the RAF an address in Canada of a friend of Art's, who would get the word back home if he was killed.

"Dickie, can I give you a number to call, if anything happens to me?"

Dickie turned to him. "Righty-o," and pulled a small notebook out of his pocket. Hank gave him Cherry's number. He didn't know how much it would matter to her, but he didn't like the idea of just disappearing without letting her know.

"I don't want her to think she's the kind of girl a guy would leave in the lurch," he explained. Dickie nodded and tucked the notebook back in his pocket.

"By the way, I believe I owe you a pint. It was you who shot the 109 off my tail, wasn't it?" Dickie asked.

"I got lucky," Hank replied.

"Either way, against one I lived to tell the tale. I wouldn't have stood a chance against two."

"You would have done the same for me. I'm sorry about Skip," Hank said. Dickie had been cavalier about the whole thing. Hank knew he'd already lost closer friends than Skip, but that didn't mean it was easy.

"Well," said Dickie matter-of-factly, "he'll have lots of friends to greet him where he's going."

Chapter Eleven

Hank spotted Cherry the moment she came through the door at the Blue Bird Café and jumped up, so happy to see her his chair tipped back dangerously before righting itself. Even in the dim recesses of the dining room she couldn't help but notice him standing there, waving and grinning like an idiot.

Down boy.

She looked so pretty in her bright green dress with little white shoes and matching hat that a wave of proud possessiveness swept over him as she made her way to the table.

"Hi," she said, almost shyly.

"Hi," he replied, smiling at her. Then he realized she was probably giving him credit for being a gentleman, so he rushed around the table to pull out her chair and replace it once she'd sat down.

"It's good to see you hale and hearty," she said politely as he took his seat. "I was very relieved to get your message. We'd heard about the skirmish over Colchester."

Colchester. Oh, right. Tuesday. Hank had been on so many sorties and alert watches since then, Tuesday seemed like a distant memory. He was only two weeks away from becoming an "experienced" pilot.

"That was a squeaker but most of us pulled through. I'm feeling much more comfortable in the cockpit now with a few patrols under my belt."

"I trust Dickie fared as well?" she asked carefully.

"Oh yes. Spitting mad he hasn't gotten a Jerry yet, but otherwise swell."

"Splendid. I will be sure to pass that along to Gilda," Cherry replied cheerily, then looked disconcerted, as though she may have spoken out of turn, and fished around for a change of subject. "Have you gotten a chance to study the menu?" she asked.

Shoot, that would have been a good idea.

"No, I arrived shortly before you did. Let's take a look."

They both glanced down at the cards set before them. Hank couldn't ask her what was good here, he'd suggested the place. It had been recommended by one of the fighter boys, but Hank now kicked himself for neglecting to ask after the pilot's favorite dish.

"Hankering for fish and chips again?" he teased, attempting to distract her while he willed the letters before him to hold still long enough to untangle them.

"Heavens, no." She blushed. "I don't have that very often, Gilda just likes to chaff me about it."

"Well I thought it was very good. I'm not much of a fish guy myself, but I definitely understand why you like it. Especially with the malt vinegar."

He turned back to the menu and was plotting how to fake his way out of the situation when the waitress appeared to his rescue.

"'Ello loves, what can I get you?"

Hank stole a glance at Cherry, who murmured "I'd like an egg and cress sandwich, please, with veg," and handed the waitress her menu.

"Anything to drink?" she asked.

"Tea would be lovely, thanks."

"This is my first time here. What do you recommend?" Hank asked.

It was probably an odd request for a modest luncheon shop. The waitress peered at him askance for a moment so he shot her a brilliant smile and the corners of her mouth

158

quirked up. Dickie claimed the RAF uniform opened every door (and skirt) in England, and while Hank didn't want to use something like that to his advantage, he felt the favor here was relatively minor.

"The roast beef sandwich is good, sir. Served with juice on the side for dippin'."

"Sounds great. I'll have that," he said, handing her his menu.

"And tea, sir?"

"Have you got any coffee?"

"I believe so, sir."

"A cup would be great, thanks."

"A pleasure, sir," she said, and headed back towards the kitchen.

Hank returned his attention to Cherry whose brows were furrowed, but they relaxed when he smiled at her across the table.

"Where were we?" he asked.

"You were discussing the air battles," she replied, refraining from reiterating that Gilda had worried after Dickie's well-being.

"I'm more interested in hearing about you," he said. "How has your week been?"

"Likely not as exciting as yours, my feet were firmly on the ground at all times."

He'd noticed at the pub that Cherry didn't seem to want to discuss her job. She'd been free with her stories about growing up and her family, but when he'd asked her anything about work she'd avoided the question or given a vague answer. He couldn't tell if she didn't want to talk about work or just didn't think he'd find her job very interesting. The truth was, he was interested in everything about her.

"No Messerschmitts in range of my desk, thank goodness. It's interesting," she mused, "the Messerschmitt family must have been in the weapon making business a long time. Their name means 'knife forger.'"

"You speak German?"

Hank was surprised. He'd assumed someone like Cherry would speak a fancy language, like French. Of course, the only German he'd ever heard had been spewing out of Hitler's mouth on a newsreel so it didn't sound very pleasant. Certainly not something he could imagine anyone wanting to learn.

"Yes. I studied it in school and then lived in Munich for a year. It's sad, you know it's actually quite beautiful there. I very much enjoyed my time in Germany and would have stayed longer, but I was sent home under, shall we say, unfortunate circumstances."

Cherry took a dainty sip of tea and lowered her lashes. Hank shook his head.

"I don't suppose you think you're going to get away with not telling the rest of the story," he remarked.

"Oh, all right," she relented. "My friends and I arrived in Munich before actual war had broken out, but the Nazis were in force in the city and we found them odious and were determined to rebel in any way we could. We began by refusing to return Nazi salutes, but because we were just girls, and foreigners at that, they didn't think much of our rebellion.

"We decided to escalate. There's a nasty little publication called Der Stürmer, full of hateful anti-Semitic Nazi propaganda. Copies were displayed all over the city in glass cases. At night my friends and I would skulk about near our lodgings, breaking the glass and tearing up the papers. We almost got caught once, but the Stormtroopers wore those slippery jackboots and we all had trainers and ran in different directions so we managed to elude them."

"You were chased by Nazis?" Hank was incredulous. "Did you get caught?"

He was in awe of her bravery. Even as a schoolgirl, Cherry had not only traveled to a foreign country but actually fought the Nazis on their home turf.

"Eventually," she replied with a grin. "After several nights of our vandalism they started covering the papers with wire mesh instead of glass. This necessitated the use of wire cutters, which we managed to obtain, but it took longer to get the paper out and one night we were apprehended. The Stormtroopers had imagined they were fighting an uprising, but when it turned out to be schoolgirls they simply contacted the Home Office and sent us back to England in disgrace. It was just as well. Things were getting heated there and my parents would have summoned me home anyway."

"I don't think I have a story that can top that," admitted Hank.

"I find that hard to believe. Look at where you are, what you do. You came all the way across the ocean to fight in a war, and I suspect you've faced danger every day since I saw you last," she insisted.

He gazed at her earnest face, so determined to believe the best about him. It had been a long time since anyone had come to his defense, even to himself.

"If you insist on painting me as the hero, I suppose I'd be a fool to try to talk you out of it," he replied with a smile.

"You are a hero," she said quietly.

"You wouldn't be so quick to think so if you'd known me growing up." For some reason, he couldn't stop himself from dispelling her illusions about him. Apparently he was a fool.

"How about you tell me about your childhood and let me judge for myself?" she asked.

He didn't want to tell her about his childhood. Everything he could think of was either humiliating or boring. But she'd been so generous sharing her own stories, he felt he owed her something in response.

"You know I grew up on a farm, there isn't much to tell."

"What did you grow?"

"Mostly wheat, but we also had some livestock. A few cows and pigs. And horses, of course. And dogs, and a few cats that wandered in and out. And some chickens. A few rabbits. And even a goat, for a few years. Until it ate all the laundry off the line, that was the last straw."

Cherry was laughing. "What, no lions or tigers?"

"They would've eaten all the other animals."

"Sounds like quite the menagerie."

"Most of them were for practical purposes. Cows for milk and butter, pigs and chickens for meat, cats to kill the mice, horses to get around, and dogs for protection. On a farm, everyone has a job." He stopped to think. "Except that goat, he was a freeloader."

"I can't imagine, with all that going on, that there weren't interesting moments."

"Well, there was the time my pop and uncle tried to make moonshine and blew up the basement. But most of the time, life was pretty simple. For fun we listened to the radio, played football or baseball, horseshoes. Went into town every Sunday for church and groceries. Went to the county fair. There were dances in town, and free outdoor movies on Thursday nights.

"My brother and I grew watermelons one summer. Man, that was great. We picked them in August, and I can tell you there's nothing that tastes better after a long hot day of farm work than a big, juicy slice of

164

watermelon. You bite into that pink flesh and the sugary juice rolls down your chin."

Cherry's lips parted and she could feel herself actually start to salivate just listening to Hank describe a piece of fruit. She looked at his bottom lip, having to fight the urge to bend across the table and nip at it. They were leaning so far towards each other she was almost close enough to do it. What was it about this man that made her forget all sense of propriety?

Fortunately for her, the waitress arrived just then with their sandwiches. They sat back in their chairs and Cherry tried to get her breathing in order. She found herself suddenly wishing her tea was dosed with something a little stronger. Like Hank's father's hooch.

She tucked her napkin back in her lap and tried to think of something clever, or at the very least related to what Hank had been saying.

"I hadn't realized it got so hot in Canada," she breezed, taking a delicate bite of her sandwich.

Hank looked up at her, startled for a moment, and then replied "Oh yeah, hotter than you'd think, in the summer," and took a long drink of his coffee.

It was so strange, when Cherry asked Hank about life back home he always seemed reluctant to discuss it. Once he started talking he'd relax, but then if she asked him anything specific he'd button up again.

Cherry was, by nature, a trusting person. She tended to give people the benefit of the doubt and not ascribe ulterior motives to anyone without some sort of proof. But her time at Bletchley had put her on her guard. They were under strict orders never to discuss anything done at Station X, but also to always have their eyes and ears open for any whiff of espionage. Churchill was convinced that a "fifth column" of Nazi spies was already operating in England.

It was preposterous to imagine that Hank Clarkson, RAF pilot, was a Nazi spy. There was absolutely nothing about him that hinted at German roots. But he also didn't seem quite like the Canadians she'd met. Perhaps it was his rustic upbringing that gave him an open, genuine quality. And that was what was so strange, that in most respects he lacked the artifice of even other British men of her acquaintance. But for these occasional hints of secrecy. She couldn't imagine what he might be concealing, or why.

Her suspicion was soon forgotten and the rest of the meal was a continuation of the warmth and familiarity of the pub dinner they'd shared, with the added delicious intimacy of dining as a couple. Once she'd managed to convince him that she was genuinely interested in farm life, Hank was more than happy to share stories about 4-H activities, community dances, and odd contests his neighbors had made up for cheap amusement. She, in turn, shared tales of pranks played on governesses and how she'd fallen off her horse during her first hunt.

"To be fair I was never a gifted horsewoman, but I'd adopted all of the hunting dogs and my concern for what the foxes might do to my pets overcame my sense of balance and I toppled to the ground. It would probably not happen today, as I've found I'm much steadier astride. And now I leave the dogs to fend for themselves."

As with all of her stories, Hank gave a wonderfully genuine laugh and insisted he couldn't imagine someone of her grace and bearing falling from a horse.

"My father still keeps a stable full of horses, perhaps we could go riding sometime," she suggested hopefully, adding, "I promise to keep my seat if we do."

"I would love that," he replied enthusiastically.

"It would require a bit of a drive, but if you get a couple days off in a row it's quite manageable. You'd be welcome to stay there overnight of course, the house has got loads of space."

The waitress arrived to clear the dishes away and return Hank's change. Cherry looked down at her watch and was surprised to see they'd been at the table for almost two hours.

"My goodness, I had no idea so much time had passed," she remarked. Hank's face fell. For as dodgy as his answers seemed sometimes, his face was delightfully expressive regarding his feelings.

"Are you needed somewhere?" he asked.

"Oh no, I was just surprised at how quickly the time had gone. I've very much enjoyed talking to you," she said.

"Would you like to continue our conversation? I wouldn't mind stretching my legs a little." He stood and offered his hand.

168

"A brisk walk might be just the thing," she agreed, taking his hand and getting to her feet.

Hank kept her hand in his as he weaved past the other tables and held the door for her as she exited. On the sidewalk, he proffered his arm and she wrapped her gloved hand around it.

"The summer weather here sure is nice," he remarked as they strolled down the thoroughfare. "Even in these uniforms it's pretty comfortable."

"We should have a picnic," she suggested.

"That's a great idea. I could get a car," Hank offered.

"And I can pack the food. I'm sure the Ponsonby's have got a hamper they'd lend me."

"Fine with me, but I'll bring dessert. It's a treat from home. My mom sent me a package with some candy bars in it. No offense, but all the chocolate here tastes like the kind you cook with."

Cherry smiled at his offer, but then frowned when she realized what he'd just said. Something was wrong.

Candy bar?
Hot summers.

Football and baseball.

She shrieked with delight.

"You're an American!"

The words had hardly left her mouth when Hank put two strong hands on her upper arms and hauled her around the corner into a mews behind a greengrocer. He set her up against the wall, planting his palms on either side of her, pinning her in place. His eyes were wild with fear.

Hank's heart was hammering in his chest. His breath came in and out in great gasps. The moment he'd dreaded was upon him. His secret was out. The one that could bring the life he'd created here crashing down. He was more than willing to leave his past behind him. Part of him didn't care if he never saw Kansas again. But he was desperate not to jeopardize his future.

He looked down at Cherry's astonished face and thought about everything he'd lose if they sent him back now. He loved flying for the RAF. Being a member of his unit had given him a sense of purpose. For the first time in his life, he felt as though he was making a difference. Doing something useful, something noble. Something he was good at.

170

People looked at him with admiration, and he was starting to believe he might actually be worth something.

And he wouldn't just lose his position as a pilot, he'd lose Cherry too.

Maybe Dickie was right. Maybe the whole country was full of women who would love to be with Hank. But looking down at Cherry's face, he'd happily swear off all those other women if only he could be assured of not losing the one in front of him. The spunky debutante who'd thumbed her nose at Nazi Stormtroopers and sat enthralled at his tales of livestock.

A denial was on his lips, probably the safest course of action at this point, but Hank found he couldn't lie to her. Didn't want to. He was tired of lying, it wasn't in his nature. If he wanted Cherry to be a part of his future, he was going to have to trust her.

He took a deep breath.

"You can't tell anyone, Cherry. Not anyone. I lied to come here. If they find out where I'm actually from they could send me back, or even put me in prison." His voice was rough as he admitted his greatest fear. But the words were honest and Hank felt a sense of relief as he said them.

She looked up at him with those wide brown eyes, absorbing the enormity of what he'd just told her.

"You've nothing to fear from me," she said softly. "I would never do anything to risk losing you. For Britain," she added weakly. But he could see in her eyes she'd meant exactly what she'd said.

Hank had never had a girl look at him the way Cherry was looking at him now, her eyes a mix of longing and admiration. He'd never had a girl come to his defense or call him a hero. He didn't know what to say to her, or how to respond to her admission, so he answered her the best way he knew how. He kissed her.

He kept one hand braced against the wall and leaned down to reach her. His other arm went around her waist and drew her against him. And just like last time, what had started with his lips gentle on hers soon became a crushing embrace. His body covered her and pressed her back against the brick wall of the building. Her little gloved hands wrapped around his neck, pulling him closer, as his hand on her back lowered to cup her rounded bottom and hold her against him. He ran his palm down her hip over the smooth fabric of

172

her dress, lifting her soft thigh and cradling himself in the warmth between her legs.

She returned his kiss with abandon, her hands on his chest, tugging him towards her by his collar. Her mouth opened to allow him access to her sensitive places.

He was going too fast, pushing too hard, but Hank couldn't stop himself. Forgetting where he was, forgetting his fear, forgetting everything except his feelings for her. This girl who admired him, who thought him a hero. He wanted her for who she was, but also how she made him feel about himself.

He couldn't get enough of her, couldn't pull her close enough. He wanted to feel every inch of her soft skin against him. He wanted to be inside of her. He was mindless with desire, kneading her thigh and thrusting himself against her, trying to will away all the clothes that formed an infernal barrier between them.

It was the delicate gasp when his fingers cupped the softness of her breast that brought Hank back to himself. Through sheer force of will he wrenched his mouth away from hers. They were both breathing hard. Her eyes were wide and her lips parted.

Hank was fairly certain Cherry hadn't anticipated being mauled in an alley when she'd accepted his invitation for lunch. As gently as possible he lowered her leg but his hands refused to leave her waist, not wanting to lose the touch of her.

He shook his head. "What is it about you that I can't keep my hands to myself?"

Cherry didn't know how to tell him that she didn't want him to keep his hands to himself. She wanted to feel those strong hands all over her body. Even on the parts that had never been touched by a man. Maybe especially those parts. Girls like her weren't supposed to harbor secret desires, weren't supposed to crave the feel of a man's hand on their bums, or thighs, or breasts. But she did.

She'd loved every moment of his passionate kiss, wanted more of it. For all that she'd tried to play coy, to undo some of the damage she'd done in falling so eagerly into his embrace the other evening, she'd melted into him again.

She was overcome with relief. The concerns she'd had about what he might be hiding had completely evaporated. Now she knew the truth. The glorious truth that Hank, her Hank, had risked imprisonment to come to the aid of her homeland. If possible, it made her love him all the more.

There was a sound from the mouth of the alley, and a little boy in short pants with a toy balsa wood plane came swooping past, imitating the sound of a propeller. He stopped short when he saw Hank.

"Oy, are you a pilot?"

Hank stepped away from Cherry and approached the boy with a smile, crouching down to better converse with him.

"Sure am. What's your name?"

"Tommy, sir."

"My name's Hank. Is that your plane?"

"Yes, sir," the boy said politely.

"Can I see it?" Hank asked.

"Yes, sir." The boy handed his plane over to Hank, who studied it intently.

"This is quite a craft you have here, very sturdy," he said, turning it over in his hands. "Did you put this together yourself?"

"Yes, sir." The boy was looking at Hank with something akin to reverence.

"Would you like to be a pilot someday?" Hank asked, returning Tommy's plane.

"Oh, yes sir."

"A fighter or a bomber?"

"Fighter, sir. I want to fly the Spitfire." Hank laughed and stood up, tousling Tommy's hair.

"Good boy. Make sure you tell 'em to give you one with fuel injection."

"Yes sir!" Tommy ran off in the direction from which he'd come, presumably returning to his mum. The rather darling exchange had provided Cherry with an opportunity to put herself back together, righting her hat and smoothing her dress. Once little Tommy had seen Hank, he'd had no use for her.

Cherry tried not to allow herself to be distracted by thoughts of what might have happened if Hank hadn't stopped kissing her. As difficult as it was for her to believe, he seemed to want her with the same hunger that she had for him. It had never occurred to Cherry that she could inspire that kind of desire in a man. Even as a debutante, she had never seemed in peril of having her virtue sullied by an overzealous admirer. Neither her form nor her face seemed to encourage that level of zeal. To have a man like Hank seem irresistibly drawn to her was surprising, and also quite marvelous.

Hank turned to her and smiled. "We'll have to find someplace a little more private for our picnic. That is, if you're still willing to come with me after all that."

"Of course! Dare I say I am more enthusiastic than ever. I haven't had real chocolate in ages," she joked, taking his outstretched hand. They turned the corner and continued down the sidewalk. There had always been an easiness about Hank, but something in his manner seemed even lighter now that he'd admitted his true citizenship.

"Oh my goodness, I almost forgot!" She stopped suddenly and rummaged around in her purse. "Your prize."

Cherry pulled out a small photograph and handed it to Hank. She'd had professional photographs taken on occasion, most recently during her Season. She tended not to like the way she looked in photographs. The photographer always encouraged her to assume a demure smile, like the Mona Lisa, which Cherry felt made it look as though she were grimacing. Her genuine smile was a little too broad to be ladylike, apparently. Showed too many teeth. But this photographer had at least managed to make her look pleasant, and not like she was trying to swallow something distasteful.

Hank cradled the photograph in his palm as though it were a treasure of great value.

"Thank you," he said, still looking at it. Then he tucked it carefully into his inside jacket pocket. "I'll keep it with me for luck."

"You don't seem to need luck," she remarked. "It sounds as though you've acquitted yourself quite well in the air."

"Ah, but you forget I had the coaster for luck."

"The what?"

Hank reached back into his pocket and removed an object that on closer inspection turned out to be the pub coaster she'd written her telephone number on the other evening, looking quite worn and tattered. He handed it to her and she smiled.

"I thought you'd memorized the number," she teased.

"I did. Like I said, the coaster was for luck."

She handed it back to him and he returned it to his pocket. They continued down the street and Cherry thought about how many lies Hank must have had to tell to keep his homeland a secret.

"Where are you from, really?" she asked softly, leaning towards him to avoid eavesdroppers.

"Kansas," he murmured, holding her hand tightly in his. "I didn't like lying about it, but there didn't seem to be another way."

"And nobody else knows?"

"Nobody in this country."

"But why? If I may ask, why did you come all the way here, and risk imprisonment just to fight in another country's war?"

"Because Hitler must be stopped," he replied simply. He seemed to want to say something else, so she waited. He looked down at his shoes for a moment, and then back up. "Because maybe dying for a good cause isn't the worst thing that can happen to a man."

Cherry wondered then if Hank's citizenship wasn't the only secret he was keeping.

Chapter Twelve

Hank gave Dickie a wave as the other man entered the Officer's Mess. The sun was just coming up and both pilots were on dawn readiness. The sky was so beautiful at this time of day, dark purple fading to red. It made Hank think about waking up back on the farm.

He'd seen countless sunrises while taking care of his chores before school. It was strange to think that his family back in Kansas would be watching the same sunrise several hours from now. By the time they'd started their day, he might've already shot down an enemy plane. Or been shot down himself, he supposed, but he was feeling optimistic this morning.

"Smiling for any particular reason?" Dickie asked, setting his plate next to Hank's.

"Just looking forward to another day in this man's RAF," Hank replied with a grin.

"And how is the lovely chauffeur?" Dickie asked.

"We met for lunch on Saturday. She invited me to meet her family."

"That bodes well. Know anything about her kin?"

"I get the impression they're well off. She mentioned that her dad keeps horses. Something tells me it's not the same kind of horses my dad keeps," Hank replied, finishing his toast.

"Probably well-connected, too, since she was a deb."

"And what about Gilda? Have you seen any of her?"

"Not enough, my boy. Not nearly enough." Dickie winked at Hank and dug into his breakfast.

Hank drank the last of his coffee and felt a sense of contentment envelop him. He'd been in good spirits ever since his lunch with Cherry, and he was certain it was in large part because finally someone knew where he was really from. Even if it was just one person in the whole of England, he could let his guard down and be himself when he was with her. He was counting the days until their picnic date the following Saturday.

"Cherry gave me her picture," Hank remarked to Dickie.

"Spoils of the chess match, eh? Come on, let's have a look then."

Hank pulled out his pocket watch and opened the clasp. He'd cut the corners off the picture so it would fit in the cover of his watch. That way he could have it with him and know it was protected.

"She does look quite fetching," Dickie agreed, after viewing the photo.

"I'm going to keep it with me for luck."

Dickie shook his head. "You've brought down three Jerrys and not lost a kite. Precisely how much luck does one need? A few more sorties like we've done and I'll be asking to borrow the picture."

"Not on your life," Hank retorted, returning the watch to his pocket.

"That's what I'm afraid of," Dickie joked.

The men cleared away their dishes and headed out of the Officer's Mess. A jeep was waiting to take them to the Dispersal hut where they'd serve their alert watch. As they neared the vehicle there was a droning from overhead that made them both look up.

An ominous shape appeared on the horizon, dark against the red sky. Hank recognized the shape as a German Heinkel bomber. It was only a few thousand feet up, there was no way the crew could have looked down and not spotted the aerodrome. Hank braced up on the balls of his feet, ready to throw himself on the ground if the bomber released its cargo. As the plane sailed silently by overhead, Hank turned to Dickie, confusion on his face.

"He's going to turn and drop his lot on the way back," Dickie guessed.

"Come on!" Hank made a run for the Jeep and slapped the driver on the shoulder once Dickie had jumped in next to him. "Go! Go!"

The driver hit the gas and careened towards the airfield, laying on the horn as the jeep approached the guard post. The sentries saw them coming and pitched the barricades out of the way to allow the vehicle through.

"Dammit, if we'd been out of the Mess five minutes earlier we'd be in the air now!" Hank was furious at the thought that this bomber, gliding lazily by overhead, was about to do serious damage to his own aerodrome, endangering his fellow pilots and crew.

Just as the jeep reached the Dispersal hut, Dickie turned to trace the path of the Heinkel.

"He's dropped it, then!" he called.

Hank turned to see that the bomber had indeed released his deadly cargo several miles away. A blaze was already evident in the western sky where the last stars were just disappearing.

"What's over there? What was he aiming for?" Hank asked. He couldn't think of anything in that direction that would have been a better prize for a Jerry bomber than an RAF airfield. Dickie just shook his head.

Aspley Guise, where Cherry lived, was west of the airfield. Hank hoped the fire wasn't anywhere near her house. "Come on, let's get that damn Jerry," he called as he ran into the hut.

He and Dickie grabbed their helmets and parachutes, forgoing pilot suits in order to be in the air that much quicker. The mechanics on the line had heard the jeep roar up and had already started the Spitfire engines. Both Hank and Dickie were airborne in minutes but the Heinkel had disappeared.

Hank radioed in to Control, which had apparently also lost track of the bomber.

"But we've got two contacts, bandits dead to port at angels three-zero."

Hank figured maybe they were the bomber's escort. He hadn't seen any 109's with the Heinkel, but fighters tended to fly at higher altitudes as a tactical advantage. Hank was about to head in that direction when Dickie's voice came over the headset.

"Red Two, my engine is having some difficulty. I'm going to have to abort and return to the aerodrome."

Hank could hear the disappointment and frustration in his friend's voice, but with the damage toll borne by the fighter planes it wasn't unusual to pull some sort of trouble. Better for him to head back now than risk having to bale out over water.

"Copy, Red One. I'm after those bandits," Hank responded.

He wheeled his Spitfire around to port and scanned the ever lightening sky for enemy aircraft. It wasn't long before he spotted them, two 109s flying next to each other, a half a mile or so in front of him. Considering their location and heading it was likely they'd been escorting the bomber that had just left a fire blazing west of the aerodrome. Hank's pulse kicked up with adrenaline and more than a little anger.

He was closing quickly but just before he had them in range, the port 109 broke to port, and the starboard broke starboard. Without thinking, he turned after the starboard ship and kept his spade grip pulled all the way to the right as he followed the 109 into a tight turn.

Hank managed to get off a few quick bursts when the 109 drifted across his gunsight, but too late he wondered after the other plane. There was a *"Powp! Powp!"* from behind him and his Spit jerked in the air.

Stupid, stupid!

He'd let the other 109 get behind him, and he pulled sharply to port to evade the cannon fire. Looking below, Hank saw only open water below him. This would not be a good place to go down. He reflexively tapped his finger on the pocket where he kept the watch with Cherry's photo. *Come on, sweetheart. I could use some good luck right now.*

Hank twisted in the air to avoid becoming easy prey. Although he would have loved to take another swipe at the planes that had threatened his home station, Hank decided the smartest thing to do was to head back to Blighty. These 109s probably didn't have much fuel left for pursuit after escorting the bomber as far inland as Chicksands. He hit the emergency thrust lever, but instead of feeling the surge of power there was a sputtering and smoke began pouring into his cockpit.

Better smoke than fire, Hank thought to himself. With the Spitfire's engine being just in front of his feet, there was always the danger of a cockpit fire and pilot burn injuries were common.

Although he was able to breathe all right with his oxygen mask, the smoke was making it impossible to see what was in front of him or even his instrument panel. He could tell there was at least one 109 still behind him because whenever he stopped juking for a moment there was a blast of cannon fire just off his wing. Hank reached forward and hauled the canopy back on its rails. The roar of the wind was incredible but the smoke immediately dissipated, and when he unclipped his harness and stood up he could see that the coast of England was within sight. If only he could reach it.

His engine was still sputtering, and he was having to veer wildly back and forth from his standing position in order to keep out of the 109's gun sights. The coast grew blessedly nearer as the engine made a sound he knew well. *Radiator's overheating.* Even knowing that this foreshadowed the engine seizing up completely, he grinned at the recollection of happening upon Cherry's broken down bus with the same problem.

Hank's Spit crossed the border of land and sea just as the engine conked and his plane became a glider. He'd had the foresight to point his craft towards an open field before the propeller stopped turning. The ground rose up to meet him, just like that day he'd almost bought it while dusting crops. At least then nobody had been shooting at Jenny.

He pulled the lever to release the landing gear and was hardly surprised when nothing happened. He tried the flaps and airbrakes and managed to slightly slow his descent before touching down. Taking his seat, he swiftly clipped his harness in and braced himself for impact. The belly of the Spit hit the ground with a jolt and plowed a furrow into the hard earth, the propeller chopping up the dirt in front of him, before finally coming to rest.

The silence was immediately interrupted by a buzzing from the sky. Hank looked up from his cockpit and watched the 109 that had been pursuing him glide by overhead. He'd heard stories about German pilots shooting down parachuting airmen, so he

188

didn't put it past this one to take a few parting shots at his downed plane. Unclipping his harness, he jumped out onto the wing and jogged a little away from the plane, hoping to make himself a smaller target. The 109 just circled once and headed back towards Germany.

Hank took a moment to examine his craft, which he could now see was riddled with holes. Everything hit him at once and he toppled over, landing on his back in the grass. Some birds flew by overhead and he reflected on how pastoral the scene was, but for the wounded fighter plane just next to him. He reached into his pocket, pulled out his watch, and opened it.

"Thanks for the luck, sweetheart." The photo of Cherry smiled back at him, and he couldn't help but kiss her.

"Not joining in Rounders, Duck?" Hugh asked. "You know how I love to see those little legs of yours engaged in sport."

Cherry was watching over the fence near a grassy area on the BP grounds where the codebreakers liked to play games. Someone had scrounged up a broom handle and ball at the beginning of summer, and if the weather was nice there was usually a match after lunch. Cherry played on occasion, although she didn't consider herself to be very gifted at the game. It did serve to provide a brief respite from the hours of demanding translations. Codebreaking work required perfection in order to be useful. Any error made anywhere along the chain could render the information worthless to the British war effort. The pressure to be accurate wore one down if they didn't take occasional breaks from it with games and other diversions.

"I shall chalk up that remark to wounded pride resulting from your loss at chess," she replied tartly. It had been over a week since the infamous chess match, but Cherry hadn't seen much of Hugh and could easily believe that he was still nursing his tarnished self-image.

"Despite what some may believe, my ego is not that fragile." He leaned back against the fence next to her, arms crossed over his chest.

"No, knowing you I'm sure it is still securely in place." Cherry looked over at him. "Does it gall you so because you were beaten, or because you were beaten by an RAF pilot?"

Hugh was silent for so long that Cherry thought he might not answer. Finally he said "My younger brother is a pilot in the RAF, you know."

"I didn't know," she replied, surprised. "Where is he stationed?"

"Tempsford in Bedfordshire."

"That's not far from here. You must see him often."

"Not really. We… aren't close. And his job keeps him busy, just as mine does."

"What does he do?"

"He drops supplies into occupied France."

"My goodness. That sounds quite dangerous."

"Indeed. He is the soul of bravery." Hugh's voice hadn't changed much, but Cherry thought she sensed a hint of sarcasm.

"You must worry after his safety." She guessed perhaps Hugh's odd tone stemmed from his concern over his brother's wellbeing. Some people found the fear so overwhelming they tried to ignore it or minimize it.

"My parents certainly do." Hugh hadn't looked at her once since he'd begun talking about his brother. His attention seemed to be focused on the Rounders match. But a muscle jumped in his jaw when he spoke of his parents.

"Are you jealous of him?" she asked.

"Jealous?" he barked a laugh. "God, no. The work we're doing here is vastly more consequential than his job. He's just one man in a plane. The codes we break here, the information we provide, change the course of the war."

"Of course, nobody knows that," she said softly.

He was quiet again, and she looked back at the men and women laughing and joking as the teams switched sides at the end of the inning.

"It's not easy, Duck." His voice was gentle, in a tone she'd never heard him use before. "People assume I stay here in my tweeds with my books because I wasn't brave enough to join up. And I can't do a ruddy thing to correct them. My father is just short of handing me a white feather."

"I'm sure that's not true. There are lots of people who stayed here for the good of the war effort. Everyone knows that."

"Everyone says that, but in their hearts they see people like me and wonder why we're not doing our duty. Even those who know us."

"Well, you know better. It's not important what people think of us, so long as we know we're doing our part."

"I wish it were that easy for me."

"I don't think you're a coward," she said. He finally turned to face her.

"That almost makes up for it, then." He gave her a look that, if she didn't know better, might have been tenderness. "Now be a good girl and fetch me some tea." But of course, it couldn't last.

"So sorry, must dash. Back to shift you know." She headed off toward the Cottage, annoyance quickening her pace. "And you can get your own ruddy tea," she muttered to herself.

For a minute she'd thought Hugh might actually be deserving of her sympathy. She knew it wasn't easy for the men at Bletchley, never being able to discuss the importance of their work or justify their failure to join their chums in uniform. And for all that he'd denied it, she felt certain that Hugh feared for his brother's safety.

Cherry, herself, had been in a near constant state of worry over Hank's fate. The

German Luftwaffe had stepped up the frequency of their raids such that it appeared as though Britain was under near constant attack. Some might have thought this an exaggeration, but for the fact that information flowing into BP tended to be more accurate even than what was stated in the newspapers and on the radio.

She still didn't know what "Adlertag" meant, although she was convinced it was a code word denoting some sort of large scale attack. The Germans were building up to something and she was desperate to find out when it would happen. Upon reaching the Cottage she said a quick hullo to Gilda and Walter, and sat down at her workspace.

Concentration wasn't something one could spare while doing the type of work Cherry did. She emptied her mind of all pleasant thoughts of Hank and cross thoughts of Hugh, and slid the next document over to translate. The letters read:

UUUEI NSEIN SNULD RFIKK
EISEL EKKVO DVONF DUUUO
STING XXXSO FORTU MFANG
DOVKA RBEIT HERGE BENNM

Looking down at it she could understand why it must appear as nonsense to most people. But she'd been doing this job long enough to recognize that it was actually German, albeit specialized German with odd abbreviations and no punctuation. There were even typographical errors, as the Enigma machines that the Germans used to encode their messages didn't include a backspace key. Nor did they include punctuation or spaces so they sometimes used letters to indicate these characters, such as "X" for a space, "J" for a quotation mark, and "Q" for the two characters "CH."

Following her usual routine, Cherry first divided the odd five character combinations into readable German text. After a bit of puzzling the above letters became:

[An] U-1103 "(Eisele)" von F.d.U. Ost Ingenieur: Sofort Umfang Dockarbeit hergeben. (NM)

Cherry had discovered that the idiosyncrasies of the Nazi transmissions were such that the translation from letter combinations into readable German always took the longest. There could be no mistakes.

Numbers came up frequently in the messages and were always spelled out, as Enigma machines had no numerals. U-boat U-1103 was a specific vessel and it mattered that it was not confused with U-1102 or U-1104. The Admiralty kept track of as many vehicles as possible in order to keep the shipping lanes clear.

Once she'd managed to unmangle the letters into readable German, the translation to English was generally quite simple. This message read *"[To] U-1103 '(Eisele)' from Comsubs East Engineering: Give extent of [needed] dockyard work at once."* She filled in words that were required to make sense of the message and placed them in brackets to indicate her addition. Cherry carefully printed out her translation and moved on to the next message.

The afternoon wore on and she was beginning to despair of finding anything that might provide information about an impending attack when a word caught her eye. "Onkel." Uncle. The entire message read:

"There will be a celebration for my uncle's retirement in three days' time."

Cherry pushed back her chair and thought for a moment. She'd pored over hundreds of transmissions looking for the initial "mother's birthday" message, and she knew she'd seen at least one that had mentioned an uncle's retirement. Maybe this was it! A second indicator of an attack. A way to confirm her theory.

She plucked the message off her desk and headed toward Bertie's office. Gilda and Walter both looked up from their work, wondering what might have gotten her so excited.

"Uncle's retirement," she announced as she breezed by. Neither of them said a word, they just nodded and turned back to their translations. They were used to her non-sequiturs and assumed that she'd explain when she came out.

Fortunately Bertie agreed with her.

"The actual timeframe specified in the message is probably meaningless. It would be the code word itself that signified the impending attack," she remarked. "We've seen them use multiple code phrases before, to allow them to keep the timetable flexible."

Cherry knew as well as Bertie that it was not good strategy to plan aerial attacks well in advance, as British weather tended to be unpredictable and planes required clear skies for bombing raids.

"I tend to agree, Miss Spence. I believe it would be helpful to locate the other message regarding 'uncle's retirement,' as well as any transmissions pertaining to relations celebrating momentous events. With any luck we'll be ready for the next one, and perhaps it will give us a clue as to what they signify."

Cherry sighed, anticipating more long hours in the Index poring over cards.

"I wish I'd thought to pull them all out the first time round."

"Well, you needn't worry about it. You're too valuable to waste your time doing bumph like that. I'll have one of the Index girls do it."

"Oh. All right. But I'd like to see any other messages she finds, so I know what to look out for in future."

"That can be arranged. Thank you again for bringing this to my attention."

Cherry stood and left his office. She felt slightly vindicated, although if this new message meant that the Germans were that much closer to "Adlertag," there was little reason to celebrate.

Chapter Thirteen

The weather was perfect for a picnic. The sky was a bright blue, dotted here and there with fluffy clouds. Not a good day to be flying, as 109s liked to come out of the sun. Hank much preferred cloudy days that kept the blinding rays out of his rear vision mirror, leaving a clear view of what was behind him. But he was determined to keep all thoughts of air battles out of his mind today.

He had picked up Cherry in a jeep he'd borrowed from the motor pool. The top was down and the warm breeze ruffled his hair as he propped one arm on the open window. He finally felt comfortable driving on what he still considered "the wrong side." Even so it was unlikely they'd encounter any other vehicles on this dusty country road. Cherry's picnic basket was in the back seat along with a blanket. And next to him sat Cherry herself.

She looked pretty as a picture, with a flowered scarf tied neatly over her hair and another brightly hued dress, this one a vibrant teal. Hank loved the way she wore cheerful colors, not like some of the other British women who seemed to favor browns and drabs, even in the summer. She was generally dressed more formally than the girls back home but that didn't bother him. She clearly didn't mind a little horseplay, even in her fancy clothes. He grinned, glad to finally have some time alone with her. His fingers itched to touch her but he kept his left hand firmly on the wheel and dutifully followed her directions to the chosen spot for the picnic.

"You been out here before?" he asked, turning off onto a side road that cut along a stone fence bordering a farm.

"Oh yes. I did some bicycling when I first arrived to acquaint myself with the grounds. There's a charming little pond just past those trees." She pointed a gloved hand towards a copse of elms up ahead.

Hank drove along until the pond became visible and then turned off the road and parked the jeep near a grassy knoll. It was indeed a very pretty setting. He liked that there were a lot of trees in England, at least the parts he'd seen. Kansas didn't have many trees, it was mostly just bushes and other vegetation low and close to the ground. The elms here formed a nice shady spot overlooking what he would've called a swimmin' hole.

He came around to the other side of the jeep and pulled the door open for her just as she was starting to climb out.

"You've got to at least give me a chance to be a gentleman," he joked.

"I'm sorry, it just seemed silly to perch there like a princess when I'm perfectly capable of opening the door. I'd be obliged if you'd carry the hamper, though."

Hank hoisted the large basket out of the back seat and grunted comically. "Are we having a boat anchor for lunch?" She laughed.

"Well, I wasn't sure what you'd like, and you do appear to be someone who requires a certain amount of food to maintain your…"

Hank had started up the hillock to the shady spot but he turned around to face her as she trailed off. He was amused to see her cheeks flush a becoming shade of pink.

"Yes?" he prompted with a grin.

"Size," she finished weakly.

"I'm a country boy, farm fed. Maybe I could do with a bit of slimming." He patted his trim stomach with one hand.

"Oh no," she insisted. "I find you to be just the right size."

His smile broadened as her face reddened.

"You do, do you?" He took mercy on her then and turned away, chuckling to himself and setting the basket at the top of the rise overlooking the water. "Is this all right?" he asked as Cherry made her way up with the blanket.

"Yes, perfect," she replied, having managed to compose herself. He took the blanket and spread it out on the ground.

"Shoot, I almost forgot." Hank ran back to the jeep, grabbing a bag he'd brought with him.

"Is that the promised 'candy bar?'" she asked when he'd returned, emphasizing the phrase that had given his secret away.

"I believe it's called a 'chocolate bar,'" he replied deadpan. "And yes, among other things."

Hank watched for a moment as Cherry knelt on the blanket and pulled off her gloves and scarf before busily removing items from the basket. Apparently she'd brought an entire table's worth of accoutrements. He observed, fascinated, as she laid out two sets of silverware and cloth napkins, plates, bowls, cups, even a vase with several slightly wilted flowers.

"Don't forget to leave a spot on the blanket for me," he said. "Keeping in mind my considerable size."

She smiled up at him but continued her task, pulling out a thermos and producing a variety of food. There was bread, cheese, several cooked sausages, a jar of fruit preserves, some kind of salad, crackers, several slices of ham, and even two eggs.

Hank was touched. This looked like more than a week's worth of rations. He'd learned that civilians were only allowed one egg per week so Cherry had either saved up or borrowed an egg from someone else.

"That's quite the spread," he remarked.

Cherry looked up and laughed. "It's possible I overdid it. I just threw in anything I thought you might like. And I'm not quite finished. I saved the best for last." She reached down into the basket and removed two bright red apples and a small cake. Hank knew that fruit wasn't rationed, but it was hard to get.

"The apples are from my mother. They have a tree on the property and with a week's notice I was able to have some sent down. As far as the treacle sponge, I know you said you'd bring dessert, but Mrs. Ponsonby insisted. Her son is in the Army and she said if she can't bake for him, she'll bake for you and hope that someone else's mother makes him a lovely pudding."

"It looks delicious. Thank you," he said genuinely, taking a seat next to her on the blanket. He reached for the thermos to pour their drinks and was surprised when he opened it and caught a whiff.

"Coffee?" he asked.

"Yes." She sounded pleased. "I remembered that you liked it. And it's not rationed, so it wasn't hard to find."

"But serving coffee to company? Can't you lose your British citizenship over something like that?" he teased.

"I won't tell if you won't." She glanced down at the food spread before her. "This looks like what we used to eat at home for a midnight snack. Sometimes we'd arrive late from a social visit or the theater and we'd raid the larder. My mother used to call it 'hodgepodge.'"

"I like it," he said, reaching for some bread and cheese. "We always ate pretty well on the farm, even during the Depression. We were lucky. Our area wasn't hit as hard as some farms further south. We had a few bad years for crops, but there was always enough food. You don't get to be my size by starving yourself." He winked at her as he took a bite of sausage. She laughed.

"I'm not going to live that down, am I?" she asked, spreading preserves on a slice of bread.

"If it helps, I find you to be just the right size as well." She blushed charmingly and took a bite of bread. "We grew lots of stuff on the farm, fruits and vegetables. You heard about the watermelons. We also had a peach tree in the front yard. My mom used to make pies. I think we must've had peach pie every week for the entire month of July."

"I love peaches. I haven't had a ripe, juicy peach in ages. Mmmmmm." She closed her eyes and smiled, evidently recalling the last peach she'd eaten, and Hank's breath quickened as he thought about tasting that peach on her lips, licking the juice as it ran down her chin. He swallowed hard.

"The tree should still be in our yard. Maybe when this is all over I'll take you back there and you can try one."

"I'd like that," she replied with a smile. Hank wasn't sure exactly what he'd intended when he made the suggestion, or what she'd interpreted it to mean. But the fact that her presence made even Kansas life seem desirable had a strong impact on him. Somehow Cherry seemed to make everything better.

They enjoyed their fill of the food she had brought, including both eggs. Afterwards Hank watched her pack the things away in her basket as he unbuttoned the top button of his shirt and rolled up his sleeves, sitting back on the blanket and stretching his long legs out in front of him.

"I thought of a story to tell you, although it's not going to paint me in the best light."

"I'm intrigued," she said, her eyes bright with interest. "Do go on."

"I've always enjoyed fiddling with engines, trying to get cars and trucks up and running. A friend of mine back in Kansas managed to get his hands on a couple of old clunkers when I was still in school. They were all rusted out and the engines didn't run, but one summer I managed to get 'em both in mostly working order.

"We used them to get around from place to place, but being foolhardy boys we also invented contests with them. We'd race them on country roads, and so on. One night my friend got the brilliant idea to drive around a field where the wheat had already been harvested. He wanted to do it in the dark, with no lights on, to see if we hit each other." The smile had left Cherry's face, and she scooted closer to him on the blanket.

"Did anyone get hurt?" she asked, concern in her eyes.

"No, but no thanks to us idiots. Fortunately, even after my tune-ups the engines were loud enough that we could hear each other coming. But he was going pretty fast and there were some near misses. Sometimes I wonder if he wanted us to crash."

Cherry placed a hand delicately on his arm. "Everyone has youthful indiscretions."

"But to spit in the face of death like that for no reason…." Hank shook his head. "Good men lose their lives every day fighting this war, and it galls me to think about how we were ready to just throw ours away."

"I would say you've more than made up for it, wouldn't you?" she asked gently.

Hank looked into her face. Her lovely, understanding face. He kept telling her his most terrible secrets, and she somehow made them okay. It was intoxicating, as if she was slowly removing all of the humiliation and shame he'd kept buried for so long, bringing it out into the light and showing him he wasn't really a failure after all. That he was a good man, the kind of man he'd always hoped to be.

He put his thumb on her chin, tilting her face up towards his, and leaned over to plant a soft kiss on her lips. She tasted like marmalade, sweet and familiar.

God, he wanted her.

Hank's hand wrapped around her delicate neck, drawing her towards him. His tongue eased past her parted lips and he felt her melt against him like butter. Her hands went up his chest and over his shoulders, twined in his hair. He wound a strong arm around her back, reclining her as he traced a line of kisses down her throat and kissed the soft pulse throbbing there. She sighed softly and turned her head away, exposing more of her satiny skin to his ministrations.

He felt awkward with his legs out in front of him, so without releasing her he brought his legs around, coming up on his knees and pulling her against him. His lips had made their way back to hers and she whimpered into his mouth as he claimed her with a building urgency.

He wanted to eat her like a juicy peach. He wanted to fill his palms with her soft breasts, squeeze her round bottom. His hands strained to roam free over the lush contours of her body. He'd sworn to himself he would behave like a gentleman at this picnic, with lots of longing looks and sweet kisses, but the moment he got his hands on her, his lips on her, he lost all self-control.

"Sweet Lord," he breathed, tearing his mouth away from hers. "What is it about you? You're like my Spitfire. Before I know it I'm going four hundred miles an hour."

Cherry smiled at his remark, deciding it was a compliment. Being kissed by Hank swamped her senses and she took a moment to gather her wits.

"Spitfire would be a good nickname for you, but I'm afraid the association would leave me too distracted during patrols," he mused, settling back on the blanket. "Say, why does that guy you work with call you Duck?"

Cherry blushed, for possibly the hundredth time that afternoon, and replied matter-of-factly "Because I work with Gilda, and because of the pub."

She decided that even when confused, Hank was alarmingly handsome.

"The Duck and Swan pub," she clarified. His puzzlement deepened.

"Gilda is the Swan," she added. Incredibly, he still seemed baffled. The further she had to elucidate, the deeper her mortification became.

"But why are you the Duck?" he asked finally. She took a deep breath and the next bit came out all in a rush.

"Because she's tall and lovely while I'm short and plain."

The words sounded petulant but her voice was unemotional. Cherry had long ago accepted the reality of her appearance. Hank paused to process her words and then shook his head.

"Then he can't see you at all, can he?" he asked softly.

"I'm sure he sees me the same as everyone else does. It doesn't bother me, I'm quite content with my appearance. I don't begrudge Gilda her beauty."

"She is pretty, in a bland kind of way," Hank agreed. "But you're a firecracker. Honestly Cherry, I think you're the most beautiful woman I've ever known."

If he'd written the words to her she would have dismissed them out of hand. Sadly, she was too familiar with her own looks to believe it might be true. But looking into his earnest blue eyes she could almost imagine he meant it.

"What rubbish," she blushed. "Oh! I'd almost forgotten your chocolate bar," Cherry exclaimed in a naked attempt to change the subject. She reached for the bag he'd fetched from the jeep and peered into it. To her surprise, there was a book along with the chocolate.

"*When I Was King and Other Verses*, by Henry Lawson," she said, removing it from the bag. She looked at him quizzically and he shrugged, giving her a sheepish grin.

"I keep some poetry books in my bunk. I grabbed one of them along with the chocolate. It seemed like a good idea for a picnic." She paged through the book, stopping here and there to study a verse. "You want to read something?" he asked.

"Would you like me to?" Cherry looked up at him. She'd never had a man ask her to read anything before. Well, other than professors. She'd never thought there was anything particularly appealing about her voice.

But Hank replied "Very much," and seemed sincere.

"All right. Do you fancy any verse in particular?" she asked.

He stuttered for a moment, seemingly lost, and then said simply. "They're all good."

One of the poems had caught her attention as she'd paged through. She went back and found it, thinking about how it rightly suited both of them. Then she cleared her throat and read it aloud.

The fields are fair in autumn yet,
and the sun's still shining there,
But we bow our heads and we brood and fret,
because of the masks we wear;
Or we nod and smile the social while,
and we say we're doing well,
But we break our hearts, oh, we break our hearts!
for the things we must not tell.

There's the old love wronged ere the new was won,
there's the light of long ago;
There's the cruel lie that we suffer for,
and the public must not know.
So we go through life with a ghastly mask,
and we're doing fairly well,
While they break our hearts, oh, they kill our hearts!
do the things we must not tell.

We see but pride in a selfish breast,
while a heart is breaking there;
Oh, the world would be such a kindly world
if all men's hearts lay bare!
We live and share the living lie,
we are doing very well,
While they eat our hearts as the years go by,
do the things we dare not tell.

We bow us down to a dusty shrine,
or a temple in the East,
Or we stand and drink to the world-old creed,
with the coffins at the feast;
We fight it down, and we live it down,
or we bear it bravely well,
But the best men die of a broken heart
for the things they cannot tell.

213

Hank was quiet for a moment when she'd finished. He lay on his back, looking up at the sky, hands clasped behind his head making his arms strain against his sleeves. She would have given a lot to know what he was thinking. She, herself, should probably have been thinking about the deeper meaning of the poem, and how secrets had led Hank to lie about his background and her to lie about her job. And how those secrets could stand between them, if they were allowed.

But all she could think about was how big his arms looked in that position.

"Would you do something for me?" Hank asked.

"Of course," she replied, a little too quickly.

"Say 'break our hearts.'" He looked over at her.

"Break our hearts," she dutifully repeated. He chuckled.

"Are you chaffing me?" she asked, genuinely curious. He looked over at her quickly and propped himself up on one arm.

"Am I what?" he asked, confused.

"Having a laugh?"

"No, not at all," he insisted. "It's just, I could listen to you read the telephone directory with that voice of yours."

Cherry gave an undignified giggle and reflected on the hours she'd spent in elocution lessons. She wondered if Hank would be dreadfully disappointed to discover she'd actually been a complete failure at pronouncing many of her vowels properly. She'd given up on ever sounding truly posh, but she supposed to someone from another country she could pass herself off as the real thing.

"I think it's mostly because of the way we pronounce our R's," she replied.

"Your 'ahhh's'?" Hank asked.

"Our *arrr's*," she responded, doing her best exaggerated American accent.

Hank gave a look of surprise and fell back on the blanket, laughing uproariously and holding his stomach with both hands. She watched entranced, completely delighted by his spontaneous fit of mirth. It was another first. She'd never made a man laugh like that before, at least not on purpose. Not without some sort of physical mishap. It warmed her inside.

"Would you like to read something?" she asked. His wonderful laughter stopped and she was immediately sorry she'd spoken.

"No, thanks, my voice isn't nearly as pleasant as yours."

"I beg to differ," she countered. "I very much enjoy the sound of your voice."

Hank turned his head to look at her and there was heat in his eyes. Gazing at him, lying there on his back, Cherry wanted to straddle him like one of her father's horses.

But she was distracted. She sensed that she'd missed something significant. Part of her job at Bletchley was putting together disparate pieces of information, and it often took a while for the pattern to emerge. Only when she caught a glimmer of meaning did the pieces finally come together. Her logical mind now began assembling pieces that revealed a pattern.

She thought back to the first day she'd met Hank, as he had looked over the RAF papers in the bus. She'd noticed at the time that while he was ostensibly reading, his eyes had jumped all around the page. She'd thought it a bit queer at the time, but allowed he was in a foreign country and must have become so familiar with the information he'd

216

memorized it. Since then he'd never done more than glance at a menu, preferring to ask others for a recommendation. He'd memorized her phone number rather than read it from the coaster.

When she mulled it over, she realized she'd never actually seen him read anything in front of her. But certainly he must know how to read. He had finished school, the RAF wouldn't have taken him otherwise. So what was it then? Some sort of difficulty?

Cherry had some experience with that type of thing. Not herself, but other codebreakers at Bletchley. The type of work they did attracted individuals whose minds worked in different ways. While they all were extremely intelligent, brilliant in fact, some of them had accompanying deficits in other areas. Many of them were socially awkward to the point of eccentricity. Some were a wonder at word puzzles but abysmal at maths, some were the opposite. Hank was clearly gifted at chess and sorting out the inner workings of machines, but must have difficulty with printed letters.

The fact that he had gone to such great lengths to hide his trouble made her want to discuss it with him, to let him know it was nothing to be ashamed of, but she wasn't sure precisely how to start.

"When did you know?" she asked gently.

"Know what?" His tone was casual, but his body language changed. Became slightly defensive. He seemed to sense immediately what she was referring to.

"That you had trouble with words."

All six plus feet of him went rigid.

"I can read," he said gruffly. He'd probably said it a thousand times.

"I know."

"I'm not stupid." He'd probably said that a thousand times too.

"I never said you were. In fact, I'm quite certain of the opposite."

Hank finally turned to face her but didn't seem to know how to respond to her comment. It clearly wasn't what he was expecting and was possibly something he'd never heard before.

"I work with the most brilliant people in all of England, and some of them have minds like yours." It was the closest she'd ever come to violating the Official Secrets Act, but she said it anyway. "They just process things a bit differently."

Hank sat up and looked at her. He seemed to want to believe her. There was hope in his eyes. Cherry wondered if it was possible he'd never spoken to anyone about his problem, at least no one who had understood it.

"What is it like, when you look at words on a page?" she asked.

He didn't answer right away, as though he were deciding whether to trust her enough to finally admit his difficulty, as vulnerable as that would make him.

"The letters seem to jump around," he said finally. "I can't get them to sit still long enough to work them out. I know how to spell, I can spell out loud just fine. But when I try to put them down on paper they get all jumbled up."

Cherry considered this. Her life was words. Her mission, her work, her hobbies, her skills. She thought about what it would have been like not to be able to read. Or at least, only to read with great difficulty. She knew a little about the source of shame it was for some of the men she worked with who dealt with similar deficits.

"But you keep poetry books?" she asked.

"A man who doesn't read wouldn't keep poetry books," he replied simply. His response told her much about the lengths to which he'd gone to hide his deficit.

She ached as she realized how often Hank would have been expected to read in day-to-day life, not just in private but in public, and how he must have had to compensate for fear he'd be discovered. What kind of perseverance it would have taken to complete schoolwork. The fear that must have been ever present, and must still be so. She was astounded at his persistence, his courage.

"It must have taken great determination and fortitude for you to complete your studies," she remarked. "It's a shame so many people equate reading ability with intelligence, when it's clear that there are many different types of intelligence. Your memory for spatial relationships, for example."

They were simple words, but they seemed to have a great effect on Hank. The way he looked at her as she spoke told her for certain that no one had ever said anything like that to him before.

He took a breath, and Cherry waited expectantly. But instead of speaking he reached for her and pulled her down on the blanket next to him, framing her face with his hands.

"What did I do to deserve you?" he asked softly.

Hank's lips came down on hers before she could reply. He kissed her gently, reverently, as though she were very fragile. It made Cherry feel cherished but also stoked a hunger rising in her. She wanted him to kiss her long and deep, like he'd done before. She took a handful of his shirt in her fist and pulled him on top of her. Obligingly he moved and settled over her, careful to prop up his bulk so as not to crush her. She wrapped her arms around his big body and hugged him tightly to her, wanting to feel more of his weight on her. Wanting his hands on her body. Wanting all of him.

Cherry had no idea how to get what she wanted, so she let her body do what came naturally. Hank groaned into her mouth as she parted her legs, pulling him down between them. She could feel his maleness, hard and full against the inside of her thigh. She supposed she should have been scandalized, but in truth it made her feel powerful. Desirable. A tangible sign that this incredible man wanted her.

His mouth was urgent now, desperate on hers. He was still propped up on one elbow, but the other hand skimmed along her bare arm, leaving gooseflesh in its wake. It drifted down to her ribcage, his touch feather light as his fingers explored her body. They were everywhere but where she wanted them. With shameless boldness she captured his hand in hers and placed it squarely on her breast. Hank abandoned her lips for a moment and pulled back, looking down at her with a question in his eyes.

"Please," was all she could manage. Hunger replaced his hesitancy, and he bent his head to leave a trail of fiery kisses along her collarbone.

The warmth of his hand cupped her breast, stroking it tenderly. She gasped when his finger brushed her nipple, teasing it into a hard peak. Her eyes closed in ecstasy with his continued ministrations. She'd never experienced anything like this. Never known her body was capable of this kind of physical response. There was a fire burning between her legs, molten and simmering. A nameless need, a desperate hunger that drove all thoughts of modesty from her head.

Hank groaned again and slid his hand down from her breast to her knee, raising her leg up and pressing his body into the hollow of her splayed thighs. His hand slid up further, past the top of her stocking where it encountered bare flesh. He paused for a moment, and then his fingers slid up the satin of her knickers to tenderly cup the source of her warmth, and–

"No!" He let out a strangled groan and pulled back his hand. "I may be a country boy, but I refuse to take you right here on this blanket."

There was a hazy moment as the trees and sky retook their proper forms around her. Cherry supposed she should have been glad that at least one of them was capable of thinking clearly. She, herself, was in no position to stop what he was doing. There was an immediate and severe sense of frustration. She'd felt as though she were on a precipice, about to experience something new and wonderful, wanting to fling herself off but unsure of where she would land. She just knew that she wanted Hank to be with her when she jumped.

Hank had moved his big frame over to her side and occupied himself with righting her clothing. He slid her skirt back down into place, taking an extra moment to run his hand down the back of her leg, tracing the seam of her stocking all the way to her ankle.

"You are not the kind of girl who gets a tumble in the woods," he said gently. "There should be candlelight and champagne. And a ring on your finger," he finished, looking up at her.

Her eyes widened. Was he going to propose to her?

"Come on," he stood up and held out his hand to her with a smile. "Let's get out of here while we still have everything we came with."

Cherry didn't often find herself speechless, but she seemed oddly unable to summon an appropriate reply to his comment. While he hadn't actually said the words, it did seem quite promising that a proposal from Hank was in her future.

She was docile as he grabbed up the blanket and hamper and led her back to the jeep, carefully helping her up into it. Quiet as he drove back down the country lane.

She was in love with this man. She was certain of it.

Cherry wanted him to propose more than anything she'd ever wanted in her life. She looked over at him and he smiled back at her, the beautiful warm smile she remembered from that first day when he'd appeared out of nowhere, as if an answer to her prayers.

And he was an answer to her prayers. She'd always dreamed of finding someone to love her, cherish her, share her dreams and her life. During her Seasons she'd made a genuine effort to find someone suitable for a husband. She'd known it was her duty. And really, how hard could it be? But the boys she'd met had been just that, boys. They'd been silly and superficial and playing at being men.

Hank was a man. For all that he was only a few years older than the prospective matches she'd met as a debutante, he was a man in every sense of the word. He'd worked hard and struggled for everything he'd accomplished. He'd bravely risked his citizenship and his freedom to come to England and defend it. Once here, he'd risked his life in the skies above to keep evil at bay. He'd struggled with a challenging handicap that had likely made him a target of ridicule, and persevered. The fact that he still went to such lengths to hide his difficulty told Cherry all she needed to know about how hard it must have been for him in his youth. And yet here he was, a celebrated pilot in the RAF.

She had no doubt he would be a good husband to her. No doubt that he would care for her. Cherry had never in her life felt beautiful, but Hank brought her closer than any man ever had. And even all the daft, awkward things she'd done he seemed to find quite charming. He'd seen more of the real "her" than any man she'd known, with the exception of her father. And the more he'd learned, the stronger his fondness for her seemed to grow. If he cared for her with even half the depth of feeling she had for him, she knew they would be happy together.

"I've got a full schedule of flying coming up, but I have two days off next week. You'd mentioned visiting your parents. Is that offer still on the table?" he asked, looking over at her, seemingly perplexed by her silence.

And suddenly the solitary problem loomed before her. Not her parents, she was still certain they could be convinced of Hank's merit.

His job.

"Oh, yes, of course," she responded absently. The thought of her Hank being sent up day after day to fight the Luftwaffe was suddenly unbearable. Doubly so because she knew there was some sort of large scale attack in the offing and she was helpless to stop it. Helpless to even warn him it was coming.

She turned to him and opened her mouth. But what could she say? Tender your resignation? Refuse to fly? Depending on what type of attack was planned, he might be in just as much danger on the ground at the aerodrome. It was all beside the point anyway, she couldn't say a thing.

"How about we plan a visit to your folks? I'd like to meet them," he said, a smile on his lips, oblivious to the anguish she was experiencing.

She glanced down at his strong hand, gently cradling hers in it. She hadn't donned her gloves, preferring the touch of his warm skin. She tried to imagine seeing his name in *The Times* list of lost soldiers posted at the mansion. Tried to imagine giving a resigned "Oh, he's bought it then," and returning to her translations with a stiff upper lip. The thought alone made her heart ache, and this was with Hank sitting strong and vigorous next to her.

"Oh, God," she whispered.

"What, having second thoughts?" he asked, mildly concerned.

"No," she assured him, finally giving him her full attention. "I'd be so pleased to introduce you to my family."

"Good," he said, returning his attention to the road. "I'll be counting the days."

As will I, Cherry thought to herself. *Until this war is over and I know you're truly safe.*

Chapter Fourteen

Hank had been engaged once before. To say it had not ended well would have been an understatement. It might have been enough to put him off the idea of marriage altogether, had it not been for Cherry. He had no concerns that this situation would end up as that one had.

Proposing to Irene had admittedly been a mistake, although it had seemed like a good idea at the time. He'd known he wanted a family, a wife. She had been willing to give him those things. And she had seemed to love him, but looking back now he realized he'd only seen what he'd wanted to see.

Hank told himself he'd always intended to reveal his problem to Cherry, at least before she made the decision of whether or not to marry him. To have a family with him. But he'd been scared to lose her. It wasn't a matter of trust, she'd already proven she could be trusted with the secret about his citizenship. But as much as he didn't want it to come out that he was an American, there was no shame in it. Not like the other thing. Hank had hoped to make her love him before he told her. And then she'd surprised him by figuring it out on her own.

Never in his life had anyone reacted the way she had. In the past it had always caused ridicule, or disappointment, or at the very least, sympathy. Even Art had been perplexed by it, although he didn't bother Hank about it as long as it didn't affected Hank's ability to do his job.

But Cherry thought it meant he had determination and fortitude.

Hank had always believed the best he could hope for was to find someone who would love him in spite of his flaws. It had never occurred to him that he could find someone who would love him because of them.

He was practically floating as he entered the Officer's Mess the next morning.

"Morning, Dickie," he called cheerily to his friend, who was reading a paper by the fireplace.

"And a fair morning to you as well. How was the picnic?"

"I'm going to marry that girl," Hank replied with a smile, adding a piece of bread to his plate.

And he was too. Heck, he would have asked her right there on the blanket, but with Cherry he wanted to do everything right. Hank was going to get her father's blessing when they went for the visit so she would know he was serious. Wouldn't have been proper to ask something like that with his hand up her skirt. She might have gotten the wrong idea.

"I say, take a look at this. Your girl's in the paper," Dickie called over, his eyes still scanning the page.

Hank was intrigued. He grabbed up his toast and wandered over to the fire.

"What does it say?" he asked, hoping Dickie would just tell him about it rather than handing him the paper.

"It appears your girl is a lady," Dickie responded, still studying the article.

"I could have told you that," Hank replied, taking a seat next to him. "But why is she in *The Times*?"

"Not a lady, an Honorable." Dickie was starting to frown, but Hank still didn't understand what he was talking about.

"Her grandfather died," Dickie continued. "Her grandfather being the Fifth Baron Fairfield."

"Her grandpa died? She didn't mention it." Hank wondered if he and Cherry had been close.

"Regardless, his death makes her father the Sixth Baron Fairfield, making Cherry the Honorable Miss Charity Spence." Dickie turned to Hank and there was pity in his eyes.

"All right," Hank said slowly. Clearly there was something he was still missing.

"You said you were going to marry her," Dickie said.

"Yes." Now Hank was getting worried.

"I'm afraid that's impossible."

Hank's brows furrowed. "What are you talking about? How does Cherry being an 'Honorable,' whatever that means, determine whether or not I can marry her?"

"She'll be married off to one of her peers. That's the way it's done in England."

"That can't be right. This is 1940. She should be able to see whoever she wants."

"See, yes. Marry, no."

"But that's ridiculous. She's a grown woman."

"That's not the way it works, mate. They have different rules."

Hank couldn't believe what Dickie was saying could possibly be the truth. He thought things like arranged marriages had died out generations ago. "But Gilda was a debutante too. Don't you have the same problem?"

"Gilda's an actress, not an aristocrat. She and Cherry aren't in the same class."

Hank raised an eyebrow.

"It's not a measure of value," Dickie assured him. "I daresay my flaxen-haired beauty would measure up against any woman alive. It's simply a matter of title. Perhaps you have to be British to understand."

Hank tried to absorb what Dickie was saying. While it was true that they spoke the same language, for the most part anyway, he was still in a foreign country. It was easy to forget that. But he had a hard time believing that in the modern world, people were still restricted as to who they were allowed to marry. He didn't want to believe it. The thought of Cherry marrying somebody else, even kissing somebody else, made his stomach lurch. He was glad he'd only eaten the toast.

Dickie took note of his dejection. "Buck up, mate," he said, coming to his feet and slapping Hank on the back. "Let's go get some Jerries."

"We're weeks into this bloody fight and I still haven't downed a Hun. Yet you're the one who looks like someone spit in his ale," Dickie remarked, gulping down the last of his beer.

Hank sat glumly across the table at the pub. He didn't know why he'd let Dickie talk him into coming out for a drink. He wasn't in the mood to be around people, to pretend his world hadn't come crashing down. It didn't help that Dickie couldn't seem to understand why Hank was so upset. Perhaps it was the three pints Dickie had just finished that had dulled his friend's wits. It had certainly made the fellow harder to understand.

Hank was lucky they hadn't gotten close to any German planes during today's patrols. Only half of his brain had been devoted to keeping his Spitfire aloft. The rest was busy trying to reason his way out of losing Cherry. There must be some way for him to prove his worthiness.

"What if I work my way up in the RAF, become a celebrated pilot, earn the Victoria Cross or something. Surely her father can't object to a man defending his homeland," Hank argued. Dickie shook his head sadly.

"It's not about proving you're a good man, mate. I know you're a good man. I'm sure the Honorable Miss Spence knows you're a good man. Her father, unless he's a complete wanker, would probably find you to be a good man as well. But you saw the houses Gilda and Cherry were staying in. She grew up in a house like that. Likely much more grand, with servants, and dozens of rooms, and grounds and property. That's the kind of life she'll have when she marries the son of Viscount What's-his-name and goes to live on his estate."

"Maybe Cherry's not the kind of girl who's hung up on things like servants and property."

Dickie raised an eyebrow. "Have you ever known a girl to choose a pauper over a prince when she had the choice?"

"But why would she be spending time with me if she knows she's going to end up marrying somebody else?" Hank asked.

"You're a charmer in a rustic, strapping kind of way. I don't deny that. Maybe she considers you a 'just for now' bloke. Or perhaps the lady is fooling herself into thinking it would work out. But I haven't known it to happen. Just the opposite, I'm afraid. A chum at school lost his heart to a gel he met at a dance and they spent a summer together before she went off and married some toff, leaving him brokenhearted. I'm trying to spare you from meeting the same fate."

Dickie's attention turned to Hank's empty glass.

"Downed another one, eh? Now how are you still so glum? You have an astonishing tolerance for someone whose country outlawed spirits not a decade ago."

Hank could barely focus on what Dickie was saying, and when his friend headed for the bar Hank couldn't muster up the energy to stop him. But when Dickie returned a minute later with two girls in tow along with the drinks Hank knew it was time to leave.

"This is the chap I was telling you ladies about," Dickie remarked, smiling at the blonde and brunette he'd brought with him. "Downed four Huns and not lost a plane, jammy bugger. And might I say, quite easy on the eyes."

Hank nodded politely to the girls and turned back to his friend.

"It's getting late, Dickie. We should head back to the drome. Dawn readiness is going to come mighty early." As a reflex, Hank pulled his watch out of his pocket and snapped it open. Cherry's lovely face smiled back at him. His chest tightened.

"She's pretty," the blonde said, looking over his shoulder.

"She is," he agreed.

"Who is she?"

"My sweetheart," Hank replied, sliding out of the booth and heading towards the door.

Dickie caught up with him at the corner. "You realize I just left two full pints on the table? That's not nothing on a pilot's salary."

"I'll pay you for the drinks," Hank countered. They walked in silence for a while and Hank got the impression that the other man was studying him.

"You really love this girl," Dickie said, his normally tight British accent slurring slightly.

"Yes, I do," Hank replied sincerely.

"Then think of what's best for her. You know the type of life she's had. Even if she was willing to throw it over for you, do you want to be the one to take that all away from her?"

Hank's shoulders sagged.

"I'm not saying this to be cruel," Dickie insisted. "I'm trying to spare you the pain of getting your hopes dashed as her father explains it all to you during your visit next week, if that's still on."

It was true that Hank would never be able to give Cherry a big mansion, with servants and lots of property. But he loved her with his whole heart and would do anything in his power to make her happy. That should count for something.

"I'm not going to make any assumptions until I hear from Cherry that she doesn't want me," he said with resolve. "I'm going to fight for her."

Dickie's glum face broke immediately into a wide grin and he threw his arm around Hank's broad shoulders.

"That's the spirit, mate!" He took a deep breath and broke lustily into a verse of an old RAF drinking song.

"Oh, if by some delightful chance,
When you're flying out in France,
Some Bosche machine you meet,
Very slow and obsolete,
Don't turn round to watch your tail,
Tricks like that are getting stale;
Just put down your beastly nose,
And murmur, 'Chaps, here goes!'
It's the only, only way,
It's the only trick to play;
He's the only Hun, you're Hank the Yank,
And he's only getting the wind right up—"

The echoes of Dickie's clear voice rang down the lane as Hank clapped a hand over his comrade's mouth.

"Jesus, Dickie," he hissed. The other man looked startled, both by the speed and intensity of Hank's reaction. Once Hank was assured that he had Dickie's full attention, he removed his hand. "How the hell do you know that?"

"Give me a little credit, surely," Dickie replied, indignant. "I've spent quite enough time in your company to ferret out your big secret."

At least one of them, Hank thought to himself.

"Don't look so stunned, I'm hardly Sherlock Holmes. Your mother's letter, which you read to me, included a home address. The envelope was lying on your bureau."

Hank swore silently.

"And if I may say so, you have a quality about you that I find refreshingly carefree and not at all servant of the empire." Dickie looked carefully at Hank, and his face sobered. "You needn't worry about it, you know. Nobody here would dare to turn you in. We all know we're safer when you're flying with us."

Hank was moved by his friend's words. Despite the news about Cherry, which had hit him like a death, his heart lightened a bit with the knowledge that he had apparently proved his worth to his fellow fighter boys, and at least someone else in his life knew his real background.

"Come on, let's get back." He put a steadying arm around Dickie's shoulder and headed down the street.

All the way home Dickie had continued his campaign to convince Hank to find a new girl, going so far as to hint rather ominously that certain members of the aristocracy had actually disowned rebellious children who had married against their parents' wishes. Hank knew Dickie meant well, and he let his friend ramble on about it because he was afraid of who might overhear them if Dickie instead chose to dwell on the topic of Hank's country of origin.

After he'd ensured Dickie had successfully managed to stumble into his bed for the night, Hank headed for his own bunk, but he couldn't shake Dickie's words. He wasn't willing to take something so important on Dickie's authority alone, so he headed to the Officer's Mess and gathered up every old copy of *The Times* he could find. He brought them back to his room and spent several hours painstakingly making his way through the Society pages. It was a good thing he wasn't searching for sports scores, those sections had been almost ripped apart. But the level of interest in the goings-on of British society was apparently so low that the pertinent pages had remained virtually untouched.

It was arduous work for Hank, parsing out the small print in the dim light of his lamp, but he made his way through every marriage announcement, birth announcement, and obituary, searching for mention of some member of the peerage who had married a commoner. There were none.

He realized his sample size was rather small, only checking the papers from the past few weeks, but it did seem to confirm Dickie's assertion that Cherry would most likely marry someone of her own station. He angrily brushed the papers off his bed and pulled out his pocket watch, studying Cherry's picture as if it could provide him with answers.

He refused to believe that she was using him as some sort of plaything. What had Dickie called it? A "just for now" bloke. She wasn't like that. So what then? Did she plan to leave her estates and money behind to marry him? What kind of a person was he, if he let her give all that up?

But did he love her enough to let her go?

"I thought we'd seen the last of you," Sarah joked as Cherry entered the Index. "The last girl Mr. Cross sent chasing 'daughter's christenings' and 'cousin's weddings' was someone else entirely."

"Yes," Cherry replied. "And she did a bang-up job. That's why I'm here."

Toward the end of Cherry's shift, a young woman had come to the Cottage and handed her a packet of small slips of paper. "Mr. Cross said you wanted to see these," the woman explained. "I gave the originals to him, but copied these out for your use."

They were the texts of transmissions that had included some mention of what Cherry had come to think of as "relation's celebrations." She looked them over.

"Did you locate these yourself?" she asked.

"Yes," replied the blonde.

"Well done," she said. "I know how tiring it can be, combing through those card stacks." The other woman smiled and departed.

Cherry scanned through the pile, dismissing most of the messages as incidental mentions of family rather than deliberate use of code words. She was gratified to come upon the previous "uncle's retirement" message, but the only other "relation's celebration" that smacked of code to her read:

"I have word my nephew celebrates his graduation this spring."

As she'd told Bertie, "this spring" was most likely a throwaway, meant to distract from the use of the words "nephew's graduation." Just as the "mother's birthday" messages hadn't really signaled any action the following week.

Chronologically, the nephew message was the third in a series, assuming Cherry hadn't missed a message predating "mother's birthday." And if her hunch was correct, that would make it the closest in time to the attack it signaled. The nephew message had been sent and intercepted on June 2, 1940. Therefore, it might be helpful to know whether it had immediately preceded some sort of large scale assault.

Cherry was certain that Bertie had passed along the information to the analysts, and there was very likely someone in a different office sorting through calendars, trying to determine which previous attack had been signaled by the code words. At least, she hoped there was. But even if everyone at Bletchley followed her logic, it would be a different thing altogether to convince the RAF leadership that she was correct.

Oh well. No use trying to solve problems before they manifested. She'd cross that bridge when she came to it. In the meantime, she was a great believer in having as much information as possible so she could be as useful as possible, and part of that would be knowing what type and scale of attack might be coming.

Thus, Cherry once again found herself paying a late night visit to the Index after her normal shift had ended. She was on mid-shifts this week, working four in the afternoon until midnight. It was strange how once she managed to slog on past ten o'clock her fatigue vanished and she found herself quite wide awake. The four cups of tea she'd drunk had probably helped as well.

"This evening I'm in search of dates of attacks, Sarah," Cherry continued.

"Can you be more specific?"

"Yes, I can," Cherry smiled. "I'm looking for aerial assaults in early June, 1940."

Narrowing down the attack to the Luftwaffe had been a simple matter. Each of the different branches of Hitler's military used a different Enigma encryption. The codebreakers at BP had named them after colors and things to help keep them straight; "Red" and "Brown" for Luftwaffe, "Dolphin" and "Shark" for naval codes, and so on. She knew that the messages involving relation's celebrations had all come from the Brown

Enigma cypher, which directed Luftwaffe attacks.

"Well, that's awfully straightforward for you, Miss Spence," Sarah teased. "I'll show you where that information can be found."

Sarah wound her way past tables of cards and led Cherry to a section containing boxes labeled by date.

"Hmmmm, naval, land, and yes here you are, aerial."

"Thank you, Sarah," Cherry replied, taking a seat.

"Care for some tea?"

"I'd better not, I'll be bouncing off the rafters as it is."

"Righty-o. Best of British to you."

Cherry turned her full attention to the cards. Or rather, tried to wrangle her full attention. She'd been flowing hot and cold like an unreliable tap ever since the picnic with Hank, vacillating wildly between memories of his fiery kisses and icy terror at his continued peril.

One minute she'd be floating in the clouds, picturing how proud she'd be to introduce him to her parents, and how handsome he'd look in his RAF uniform at the wedding.

How he would gaze at her on their wedding night, love in his eyes as he took her in his arms and made her his own. The joy of coming home to him every day, with his gentle nature and ready smile.

When she was with Hank she felt beautiful, cherished, even clever. All the things she'd longed to feel as she'd fancied up for every event during her Seasons, only to return home heartbroken yet again.

She was still a bit incredulous that he appeared on the verge of a proposal. Cherry hadn't quite resigned herself to a life of spinsterhood as she'd joked to Gilda, but the idea that such a considerate and honorable man was smitten with her seemed just short of a miracle, and the fact that he was also a brave and dashing RAF pilot provided the icing on the cake.

Unlike some of the girls of her class, Cherry had never wanted for love. Her parents were affectionate and involved in her childhood, and she had always been encouraged to pursue her own interests. Such was not the case with all noble families. Her parents had modeled a marriage based on love and mutual respect, and that was what she sought in a husband. She had witnessed the sad results of marriages where her peers had settled for the trappings of luxury rather than holding out for someone who would value them for themselves.

Cherry had no interest in a marriage like that, regardless of the finery it entailed. She had no fears that a marriage to Hank would be like the empty, isolated affairs to which some of her friends had sadly resigned themselves. No, with Hank there would be wonderfully genuine smiles, the warm intimacy of the marriage bed, and the even the occasional bout of helpless laughter.

And love.

Just when Cherry had completely lost her train of thought, her eyes would stray to the cards and she'd see "infantry regiment" and "slowly forwards" and her attention would rivet back to the letters before her. That is, until she got word that there had been yet another aerial incursion by the Luftwaffe and RAF pilots were no doubt being sent to counteract.

It was a blessing and a curse to work in what was essentially a central hub of information about the goings-on at the front. It would have been easier to carry on oblivious, perhaps, had she been assembling aeroplanes at a factory or doing work on a farm somewhere with the Women's Land Army. But in her current position, she was unable to hide from the realities of the war.

Cherry tried to tell herself that it could have been worse. She could have fallen in love with an infantryman who'd been taken prisoner in France or even killed on the beaches of Dunkirk. At least Hank was relatively safe at Chicksands, close enough to visit when they were able. The fear she felt over his occupation was not enough to drive her away from him. That was unthinkable at this point. She would simply settle for as much time together as they could steal and continue to pray for his safety.

And the best way to ensure his safety was to help prevent or at least prepare for an attack that was almost surely coming soon. If only she could get a clue as to what it would be.

"April, May, June. Here we are." She thumbed through the cards, past small skirmishes in southern France, until—

"Oh, no," she breathed, her trembling hand clutching a card with the heading:

June 3, 1940 – Operation Paula.

Operation Paula had been an attack by the Luftwaffe with the express purpose of decimating the French Air Force, leading to the total conquest of France.

For this attack, the Germans had unleashed over 1,100 planes.

Chapter Fifteen

"Morning, Pete." Hank slung his parachute straps over his shoulders as he jogged over to his plane.

"Mornin', sir. Thought you had leave today."

"I did, but I switched with a buddy. My head's already in the clouds, might as well get some flying done."

"Out for a patrol, then?"

"Guard duty. A convoy in the Channel." Hank tugged his leather helmet snugly down over his hair and secured it under his chin.

"I've been messin' with the longitudinal controls but it's still a wee bit touchy. Should be up to scratch for your flight, though." Pete slapped a grease stained hand lovingly against the Spit's battle worn fuselage.

Although he couldn't admit it openly, Hank felt a kinship with his Irish mechanic. Pete's family had moved to England several years earlier and he did what he could to support the war effort although Ireland, like

America, was a neutral country. He also took excellent care of Hank's plane. Pete's speech was peppered with a mix of RAF slang and Gaelic dialect so that it occasionally took a minute to catch his meaning, but when it came to engines they spoke the same language.

Being a mechanic himself, Hank had a better understanding than most pilots of what it was like to know a vehicle inside and out, to labor over it and almost think of it as a living thing.

"I know she's your plane, Pete. It's nice of you to let me fly her on occasion." Hank grinned.

"Just bring her back in one piece, sir. And yourself as well," the other man added with a smile.

Hank hopped up into the cockpit, connected his radio and oxygen, and started the engine.

"Give 'em what for, sir! Slán!" Pete called, just before the spinning prop drowned out his voice.

Hank taxied forward and glanced to his right, where Dickie and Novi, a Polish pilot from his unit, were also readying to head out. The three would be forming a flight to guard a convoy of supply ships heading to the port at Ipswich.

It was RAF strategy to send only the minimum number of planes necessary for any particular mission because airpower had to be split between defending the coast and defending the shipping lanes. This meant that the British force was often outnumbered, but as of yet the tactic had also helped to minimize losses.

Once in the air, Dickie took the lead with Hank and Novi just off his wingtips. Hank's pulse always kicked up as his plane shot into the clouds, never knowing what the sortie might bring. Thus far fate had been good to him, at least with regards to his flying.

His heart was another matter. He should have known things couldn't be simple and straightforward with Cherry. It had been too easy. He should've known there would be a catch. Hank flatly refused to believe that she was just toying with him, so he'd come to the conclusion that it was her intention to throw away a life of privilege to be with him. It was cruel irony that he would have to be the one to turn her away, even though she was easily the best thing that had ever happened to him. But if he was the hero she thought he was, he'd be willing to sacrifice his heart for her happiness. At least, that's what he was beginning to think.

And there was too much time to think during this patrol. His flight circled endlessly around the convoy, watching out for enemy planes in the skies above. Since his first engagement with the Huns, Hank had learned that only new pilots sought cover in the clouds where you couldn't see a thing. Experienced fliers flew with the sun behind them, making it almost impossible for their prey to spot them until it was too late.

They'd been out for three-quarters of an hour when Dickie requested permission to head back to the aerodrome. They hadn't spotted any Jerries and were getting short on fuel. Control came back on the R.T. and instructed them to continue the patrol.

Hank was following off Dickie's wing for another pass when he saw a plane dive into the clouds two miles off his port side. When the craft reappeared Hank got on his radio.

"Bogey dead to port," he said.

Dickie swung his ship around and Hank and Novi followed on his wing. Two more planes dropped out of the clouds and Hank immediately identified them as German

Junkers 87s, better known as Stuka dive bombers. They were very effective against ground targets but generally made easy prey for Spitfires due to their lack of speed and maneuverability.

"Prepare to engage." Dickie's voice came over the R.T. and Hank could practically hear his friend salivating at the thought of dropping his first Jerry.

Hank flicked on his gunsight and set his trigger ring to "FIRE," eager for a little target shooting to take his mind off his girl troubles. He instinctively tapped his pocket with the watch for good luck. The flight of Spits was accelerating down at a steep angle of attack towards the Stukas when Hank spared a glance in his rear vision mirror and was horrified to notice a cluster of at least eight 109s descending from a few thousand feet above, gaining rapidly on his formation.

"Look out behind!" Hank bellowed over his radio. "109s behind!"

Hank broke sharply to port to avoid becoming an easy target, but both Dickie and Novi headed inexorably on towards the Stukas as though they hadn't heard his warning. The leading 109 opened fire and Hank watched tracer rounds blaze past his canopy. He pushed the stick down, bringing the Spit into a steep dive that caused a grey tunnel to form in his peripheral vision. As his speedometer crept towards four hundred he leaned forward, tensing his gut muscles and pulling forward on his harness, willing himself not to black out.

He came out of the dive and oriented his ship in the direction from which he'd come, hoping to get a bead on Dickie and the other planes. The two Spitfires were nowhere in sight, but a Stuka was tumbling down towards the water with great gouts of flame erupting from the cockpit and a trail of smoke in its wake.

So Dickie finally got one, Hank thought with a smile. He caught sight of several planes off to his right and wheeled in that direction. It turned out to be a Spitfire engaging three 109s.

Hank set his sights on the rear-most Jerry and fired the minute the plane skittered across his gunsight. It was quick but it must have been a lucky shot, the 109 immediately pitched over towards the water, smoke trailing from its engine.

"I was wondering where you'd got to," Dickie's voice came across the R.T., calm as though they were back at the Mess.

Hank grinned. "Couldn't let you get all the glory for yourself."

Powp! Powp! Powp!

He pulled hard right on his spade grip as the sound of gunfire raked his Spit. There was a hard tug at his yoke, and for a moment he seemed to lose control of the plane. Hank dropped several thousand feet before the spade grip came alive again, but he quickly discovered that it was stuck in a right hand turn. The attack must have damaged his rudder. He tried to pull up but had to go in a full circle to continue his heading.

Hank hauled back with all the strength he could muster, grabbing for altitude to get back to Dickie. The clouds parted to reveal the trio of planes he'd just left. Dickie's Spitfire was pumping bullets into the lead 109, while the second 109 was flat on his tail. Before his plane turned again, Hank saw the lead plane go down, followed almost immediately by Dickie's Spitfire in a long uncontrolled dive. He was helpless to do anything but watch as his friend's plane tumbled into the ocean below.

It had fallen from at least twenty thousand feet, plenty of time for the pilot to get out if he was still alive.

There had been no chute.

Hank circled the wreckage of the Spit as low as he dared, but saw no movement. His low fuel warning light blinked on and part of him yearned to stay and conduct a vigil over Dickie's resting place until his own propeller stopped spinning. But his thoughts turned to all the other pilots who had already been lost, how it would be a betrayal of their legacy, their fight for survival, for him to just give up the ghost like that.

There would be time to mourn for Dickie later. As it was, he was going to have a fight to get back to land. His kite would still only turn right and his fuel tank was almost dry.

He tried to raise Control but got no reply and guessed his R.T. had been shot out along with his rudder. He circled around to head back towards shore and came almost immediately face to face with the remaining 109, blazing right at him.

Hank had no tricks left up his sleeve. He tapped his lucky pocket for possibly the last time and headed right for that Messerschmitt.

This one's for Dickie.

Chapter Sixteen

"Is it… No, that's *neben*."

Cherry shook her head and mentally chastised herself for her carelessness. Ever since she'd plucked out the card at the Index informing her that the previous attack had been Operation Paula, she was seeing nephews in every message. Or rather, "Neffe," the German word for nephew. The problem was there were so many German words that looked like Neffe that any time a word came close she wondered if perhaps a wireless operator intercepting German transmissions had perhaps misheard the Morse code and the attack was in fact being signaled. It helped that she was also looking for the word for "graduation," which was "Graduierung." That should be distinctive enough not to mistranslate and was perhaps why the Germans chose it for such an important purpose.

She was feeling a bit perplexed after a phone call from Hank that morning. He'd called quite early to ask if she would be available to meet for dinner. Hank had the day off, but Cherry, unfortunately, was still on mid-shifts at four so dinner would have to wait. He'd sounded overly formal and she'd briefly set her hopes up that he might be planning to pop the question, but his quelled tone seemed indicative of something less celebratory.

She had become so accustomed to Hank's lively manner that it concerned her to hear him so subdued. But once she thought about it, she realized that he must simply be exhausted and his nerves worn. She knew that the RAF squadrons were operating at all hours, just as BP was. The pilots must be burning the candle at both ends to keep up with all the flying. She'd heard they were doing as many as seven sorties a day. It made her wonder how long they would be able to keep up that pace, and how the beleaguered forces would fare against a large scale assault.

"Miss Spence?"

Cherry jumped at the sound of her name. Part of the reaction was guilt for letting her mind wander, but a sense of icy panic washed over her as Bertie poked his head out the door and asked "Would you please come into my office?"

Every face in the Cottage swiveled around to look at her. It wasn't unheard of for someone to be called to see the boss, but it was almost never good news. As Cherry stood and smoothed her skirt she tried to reassure herself that he probably just wanted to discuss something about the "relations' celebrations" timeline. She'd told him about Operation Paula and he'd confirmed that there was, indeed, another office looking into what the code words might be foretelling but he would inform them of what she'd found.

Bertie motioned her into a chair and took his seat across the desk from her, appearing for all the world as though he'd rather be anywhere else. He couldn't even look at her. She knew women in general made him nervous, but this was something else.

"Is something wrong?" she prompted. Better to find out why she'd been summoned than sitting there conjuring up worst case scenarios.

"Yes, Miss Spence. I've been informed, that is, I've been asked to inform you…" He removed his glasses and nervously began cleaning them with the handkerchief from his pocket.

Cherry's pulse quickened. A lump formed in the pit of her stomach.

"What is it, Bertie?" At her use of his given name, he finally looked at her.

"Your young man," he said softly, putting his glasses back on. "They found a body. I'm sorry."

No. Her brow furrowed. "But he wasn't scheduled to fly today. How do they know it was him?"

"They found your name and information in a notebook in his pocket."

She wouldn't believe it. She shook her head.

"That doesn't mean anything, it could have been someone else."

Bertie gave her a look that conveyed exactly what he thought of the idea that she was carelessly giving out her name and personal information to random men. In truth, she had no explanation for why her name was in some notebook, but she knew that she'd written it down for Hank on a coaster from the pub. This must be something else. Someone else.

"Cherry," Bertie said softly. "He had your picture in his pocket."

There was a roaring in her ears. Her eyes stung and she shut them tightly against the unbearable sympathy in Bertie's eyes.

"No," she whispered.

Her traitorous mind conjured up an image of Hank grinning over at her from the picnic blanket, brimming with more life than any man she'd ever met. It couldn't be true. That he was, at this moment, lying cold and still on a table in a room somewhere. Not her Hank.

"You have my deepest sympathies. You may, of course, take the rest of your shift if you like. Do you need someone to see you home?"

"Home?" she asked, the word suddenly sounding strange to her.

Her room at the Ponsonby's, as nicely furnished as it was, was not home. Her grandfather's estate, which had only just passed to her father, was no longer home.

Somehow Hank had become home to her. The home she'd built in her mind, where he came home to her every day and held her every night. A welcoming, familiar warmth, knowing that she was loved for herself. If

Hank was truly gone, she might never go home again.

Like a woman in a trance, Cherry felt herself being led out of the Cottage and helped into a car. She was dimly aware of trees, fences, and fields passing by her window. The car pulled into a long drive and stopped in front of a familiar stone house. The Ponsonby's house. The sudden lack of motion roused her from her brown study. She turned away from the window and was mildly surprised to see Hugh behind the wheel.

"Hullo, Duck," he said softly.

"How did you get stuck with chauffeur duty?" she asked.

"I volunteered."

"I'm sure you had more important things to do than drive my sorry self home."

"Not today."

She managed a small smile. "No clever remarks for me then?"

He shook his head. "Not today," he said gently. Too gently. It was enough to summon up the crushing blow of Hank's loss and she fell against Hugh's shoulder, sobbing into his jacket.

The loss was a physical, tangible thing. Her chest ached. Her mind didn't know where to turn. She couldn't bear to think about him, couldn't bear not to think about him. In the brief time they'd spent together he'd become a part of her heart, always in her thoughts even when out of her presence. Hank had made her feel loved, and that love was now gone. It had left a gaping hole in its wake.

"There, there," Hugh soothed, patting her head like a child.

Cherry sniffed and sat back, suddenly aware that she was soiling Hugh's jacket with her dripping face.

"I'm sorry," she said, pulling off a glove and dabbing her cheeks.

"No trouble, this coat was due for a good washing," Hugh joked. He looked at her then, a long look that Cherry was at a loss to explain. But inevitably the smirk returned. "Now then, best be off. I've got consequential work to do."

"Yes, of course," she replied and stepped out of the car. She slammed the door shut and watched the blackout-dimmed taillights of the car disappear down the drive. She supposed she should go into the house. Wash off her makeup, pin up her hair in curls, and prepare for tomorrow's shift.

Tomorrow.

She didn't want to walk into the main house at Bletchley, to see Hank's name listed there in *The Times* with all those other poor souls who would fight no more. That would make it real somehow. Right now it was just the absence of him, which didn't seem as final.

Even though Cherry had always known it was possible, and how could she not when it had happened to so many other young men, she had utterly failed to prepare herself for it. Hank was so full of life and vitality, it seemed impossible that his could be snuffed out so quickly.

And it wasn't just that she'd lost Hank. She'd lost her future. His death had robbed her of the life they would have had together. The bright future of happiness and love that she'd been building since the first time he'd held her in his arms. He was irreplaceable.

She turned resignedly and headed for the house as though approaching her executioner. There was no use avoiding the reality. The dawn would come tomorrow, even in a world without Hank. There would be another shift, more messages from the Germans. Another code. Another attack. More men killed.

It suddenly all seemed so futile. All this loss. A generation of young men.

Cherry had been blessed, she hadn't suffered many great losses in her life. There was the recent death of her beloved grandfather, god rest his soul, but he'd been eighty-eight years old and had lived a full life. He had been ready to pass on and was with Grandmama now. Cherry knew that she would be far from the only girl in England crying into her pillow as she fell asleep tonight. But that didn't make it any less painful.

She reached the door and pulled the string, finding the key and remembering that this was where she and Hank had shared their first kiss. She could still feel his hands on her body, the heat of him against her. A memory of his embrace was all that she had left to warm her. It was unbearable.

She could not continue like this. Could not function with thoughts of him dominating her mind. She tried to return to the numb trance-like state she'd experienced on the ride home, to empty her mind of all painful thoughts of Hank. There would be time later to remember. To cherish. For now, she simply needed to do her duty, to translate messages and prevent more death.

Somehow she made it up to her room. Somehow she cleaned her face, pinned her hair, stripped out of her clothing and into a nightgown. Somehow she peeled up her counterpane, slid between her sheets, and laid down to sleep.

For a bed that had never known the presence of a man, it somehow still seemed emptier without Hank.

Cherry didn't remember falling asleep, hadn't thought it was possible. But she was aware of waking up to a sound in the night. A light tapping sound. It was intermittent. As she slowly swam towards consciousness it came again. Two taps close together. Then a pause, then another tap.

She blinked her eyes open and waited to see if the sound came again so she could locate its source.

Tap.

Tap tap.

It was coming from the window. She pulled aside the covers and stepped onto the rug, her bare feet padding silently across the room.   Absently, she grabbed her dressing gown and slid it up over her bare shoulders. She cautiously pulled the curtains aside to pinpoint the origin of the sound.

The moon was almost full and it bathed the side yard in a cool glow. She could see that there was a man standing just under the alder tree, tossing pebbles at her window. He wore no hat and no coat, but she couldn't make out any other detail of his clothing. His arm dropped to his side and he looked up at her.

A cloud obscured the moon, turning the world dark for a moment. When it passed she was able to see the man's face.

It was Hank.

Chapter Seventeen

The German pilot must have thought he was suicidal. Hank's actual intent was much more homicidal. He'd decided if his plane was going down he was taking that 109 with him. Also, by this point he had very little control over where his plane was headed.

As the two ships careened toward each other Hank pumped all his remaining ammunition at the 109, but it didn't seem to have any effect. His malfunctioning rudder pulled him right at the last minute and the 109 sailed by almost close enough to touch. Even though Hank hadn't brought him down, the near-collision was apparently enough to spook the Hun, which looped and made a break for the Fatherland. One problem down.

The Spit's engine began to sputter, prompting Hank to flick the switch accessing his reserve fuel. This would buy him a little extra time, but there were still no guarantees. He was close enough now to see the coast but wasn't entirely sure how to reach it. Every time he aimed for dry land his rudder would force a right turn. Eventually Hank determined that he could travel forward by making a series of right hand turns, proceeding in a looping pattern that left him north of where he started.

He was finally able to make landfall at Southwold. He had to ditch in a farmer's field, but at least he wasn't greeted with a shotgun like Dickie.

Dickie. A sharp pang struck Hank as he realized he'd never see his friend again. It was incredible that after all the death he'd witnessed, all the funerals he'd attended, it was still a shock to lose Dickie.

He couldn't think about that now. He had to get back to the aerodrome.

While Hank's landing may have received a warmer greeting, he wasn't so fortunate as to find a friendly cop to lend a motorcycle. Instead he hitched rides and walked back in the direction of Chicksands, an odd sight with his helmet and parachute in tow. He was lucky his patrol had set off in the morning. As things were, it was nightfall by the time he'd reached Cambridge. He stopped in to a pub and got a bite to eat. He'd really only gone in to find his next ride, but the bartender had taken one look at him and told him to pull up a chair for some food. Hank hadn't realized how hungry he was. Hungry and exhausted.

If the patrol had provided too much time for his thoughts to wander to Cherry, the hours spent walking were even worse. He couldn't bear to think about Dickie quite yet, but Hank already knew what his friend would say if he were there. He'd already said the words.

"Think of what's best for her. You know the type of life she's had. Even if she was willing to throw it over for you, do you want to be the one to take that all away from her?"

The truth was, no Hank didn't want that. He wanted Cherry to have everything her heart might desire, and he was enough of a realist to know he couldn't give that to her. But even if he were selfish enough to want to try, he had another problem.

Hank couldn't prevent his own death any more than he could prevent Dickie's. He was worrying about what kind of life he'd be able to give Cherry after the war, but the truth was he probably wouldn't live that long. How many close calls did he need before he admitted that all he could offer her was fear?

272

That blowhard she worked with had a better chance of making it through the war than Hank did. Pilots had to live for today. It wasn't the kind of thing you could build a future on.

Despite this, had Hank been given the opportunity to leave the RAF he wouldn't have taken it. The work he did was too important, even considering how small his contribution was in the grand scheme of war. Every 109 he shot down was one less plane the Huns could send against his comrades. Every bomber he shot down meant fewer buildings destroyed, fewer people killed. The combined efforts of all the RAF pilots were going to help win this war. He'd resigned himself to his fate, knowing that those RAF wings were, as one of the fighter boys had put it, a "one way ticket." But part of that sacrifice was letting Cherry go to find someone who could give her what he couldn't. A future.

His resolve grew with every step he took, and he decided rather than heading straight to Chicksands he needed to see her one last time, to inhale the sweet scent of her, and hold her in his arms.

To say goodbye.

It must have been close to two in the morning when he finally reached her place. Cherry looked like an apparition as she emerged from the house. She was wearing a filmy dress and the way it billowed behind her in the gentle night breeze made it look as though she were floating. She had a scarf tied over her hair and her little feet were bare. They made no sound in the wet grass as she walked towards Hank. She stopped some distance from him and looked at him strangely.

"Are you really standing there?" she asked. He thought he heard her voice catch.

"I'm sorry to come here like this in the middle of the night," he replied. "I hope I didn't scare you."

Cherry didn't respond, she just continued towards him like a woman in a trance. As she got closer he could see that the dress was actually a fancy nightgown, pale aqua with cream lace, and some kind of gauzy wrap over her shoulders. Even in his exhaustion, Hank's eyes traced her body hungrily, pausing briefly at the dark outlines of her nipples, visible through the delicate fabric of her gown. His breathing quickened as his body gave an instinctive reaction to her state of near undress, with one organ in particular lobbying to drop his original plan. But he steeled himself, determined to do the right thing no matter how weak his willpower might be.

When Cherry reached him, she threw her arms around him and hugged him fiercely. The force of the embrace was so unexpected it took a moment for Hank to recover, and then he wrapped his arms around her and held her close.

She felt so good, all warm and soft against his body. Even through her scarf, her hair smelled like flowers. He knew he was filthy, first from the morning in a blazing cockpit and then from the hours spent on the road. But she clung to him like ivy on a tree, seemingly oblivious to the dirt and stink. He held her in his arms, trying to memorize every facet of the experience, knowing this would likely be the last time he'd get the opportunity.

Cherry's face was buried in his shirt and Hank realized she was crying. He stepped away from her, putting a finger under her chin and tilting her face up towards his, and was concerned to see the tear streaks.

"What's the matter?" he asked gently. She sniffed and wiped her cheek with the back of her hand. Her face was fresh and clean, making her look even younger than her twenty-one years.

"They told me you'd been killed," she replied.

"What?" Hank was bewildered. *Who had told her that? And why had they thought to contact her at all?*

"They found a body. My name and number were in a notebook. My picture was in the pocket."

She was looking at him as though she still expected him to vanish at any moment. She seemed afraid to let go of him, keeping his shirt tightly clutched in her hands. At least now he understood.

"Dickie," Hank said roughly, the pain hitting him like a blow. He'd seen the man go down, but only now did he realize that he'd been harboring a small hope that his friend had somehow survived. That hope was gone. "Apparently your picture is only good luck for me."

Hank thought back to the last time he'd seen his friend alive, heading out of Dispersal and towards his plane.

"Ready for another go, mate?" Dickie had asked, pulling his Mae West over his shoulders.

"A piece of cake," Hank replied, glad to have something to occupy his thoughts besides Cherry.

"Decided to give up the knitting, then?"

Of all the nicknames RAF pilots had come up with for girlfriends, that might have been the strangest.

"Looks that way," Hank replied, in his best attempt to be nonchalant. Dickie had picked the one topic he'd rather not dwell on.

"I suppose you don't need her picture, then," Dickie remarked. Hank looked at him warily.

"What's it to you?"

"Well, it seems to have brought you good fortune. I thought maybe you'd be willing to spread it round to a fellow pilot, that's all." Now Dickie was the one playing at nonchalance.

"Are you serious?" Hank asked.

He had no concerns at all that Dickie had any romantic designs on Cherry. RAF pilots were the most superstitious folks he'd ever come across. It was completely believable that Dickie had begun to think of Cherry's picture as some kind of good luck charm.

"Look, the way I see it, I'm down a kite," Dickie explained. "Jerry got me and I haven't returned the favor. I owe the RAF a 109 at the very least. And seeing as how you've got four Huns to your credit I thought you might be willing to part with your talisman."

Hank considered Dickie's request. There was no practical reason for him to deny it. Likely as not they would both be back on solid ground within a few hours, he could get the picture back then. Either Dickie would have shot down a plane, in which case he'd no longer need it, or he'd have shown Dickie the picture had no effect on his chances.

He looked at Dickie's face. There was a whiff of desperation shading his fellow pilot's normally impassive face. He knew how fixated Dickie had become on the fact that he had yet to shoot down a plane. Nobody in the squadron cared how many planes he'd shot down, as long as he kept going up and doing his job he had their trust and respect. But Dickie just couldn't seem to let it go. This was something Hank could do for his friend.

"Why not?" he breezed, pulling out his watch and removing the photo. He ran a thumb over Cherry's sweet face, savoring every detail of her smile. "It's not like I'm going to forget what she looks like."

Dickie plucked the picture out of Hank's outstretched hand and slid it smoothly into his pocket.

"Cheers, mate. Now let's see if it's as lucky for me as it has been for you."

Dickie, if I could go back in time and keep the damned picture I'd do it in a second.

Hank watched Cherry process the explanation, the loss, although it was plain to him that the emotion she was experiencing most strongly was relief.

"Then I'll give you another one," she said, looking up at him.

She was so beautiful, gazing at him through the tears that were still streaming down her cheeks. Her face was in his hands and he had to fight the urge to kiss her. He'd already made the decision about what to do, but standing there, looking at her in the moonlight, he was having a hard time actually going through with it. It helped to glance up at the hulking manor house behind her and think about how that compared to the humble farmhouse he'd been raised in.

"No, I don't think you'd better," Hank said softly, forcing his hands down to his sides after swiping away one last tear with his thumb. She looked confused.

"Why not?"

"Cherry, I came to tell you that you'd be better off without me." His voice broke. Hank knew he'd have to keep this short, just say what he'd come here to say, or else he'd lose his nerve and do something stupid, like propose to her.

"What?" Any relief she'd felt at discovering he was alive had been replaced by confusion.

"You know why, even if you won't admit it to yourself. I'm a nobody. I make five pounds a week. I'll never be able to give you a house like that." He motioned toward the massive structure behind her. She didn't even turn to look at it.

"If I wanted a house like that, I'd already have one," she replied, sniffling.

"It's easy to say that now, but you don't know what you'll want after this war is over, when things get back to normal. I can't offer you the kind of life you deserve. I can't even offer you a future."

Hank thought about Dickie, who'd never get to see his future. About Skip, and Red, and Shorty, and all the pilots who'd already come and gone. He had no reason to believe he'd last longer than any of them. His number would be up any day now.

"Cherry, I'm a fighter pilot in a war that's taking the lives of half of us. And it's likely going to get worse before it gets better. That feeling you had, when you heard I was dead, that's all I can offer you," he said dully. "You need to find yourself someone who can give you a future. A future with the kind of life you grew up living. I care about you too much to let you throw your life away on me."

Hank saw the confusion on her lovely face, watched it start to crumble. The knowledge that he was hurting her was unbearable. Wordlessly, she reached out for him and he took a step back, away from her.

He should stay. He should stand there and tell her how incredible she was. Tell her all the things he loved about her, so she would know that he wasn't rejecting her, he was trying to save her.

Tell her he would love her for the rest of his life, however long it was.

But Hank knew if he stayed too long, dwelt too much on the kind of girl he was giving up, he'd never be able to go. Unable to bear the anguish on her face any longer, he turned like the coward he was and fled into the night.

Chapter Eighteen

The following day was Cherry's last on midshifts. She went in early, having failed utterly to get any sleep after Hank's nocturnal visit. Since she was of no use to anyone at the Ponsonby's in her current state, she reckoned she might as well go in to work where she could do some good.

Or should have been able to do some good. Her eyes were bloodshot from crying and she was nearly cross-eyed with fatigue. Hank's rejection had come so quickly on the heels of his presumed death she hadn't been given any time to enjoy his return from the beyond before despair had set in again.

When she'd glimpsed him standing outside her window she'd been sure he was a hallucination brought on by her fervent desire to see him one last time. And then when she'd touched him, smelled him, held him in her arms, she'd realized that he had been miraculously returned to her. It was fate. They were meant to be together.

Until he'd ripped her heart out again by declaring he was throwing her over for her own good.

It made no sense, he'd seemed so keen. What had changed in the few days since the lovely picnic to make him question his suitability? If that truly was the reason for his actions.

Hank had spoken about not being able to offer her a future. Perhaps Dickie's death had struck such a blow that it was causing him to make rash decisions. She'd heard that some soldiers dealt with the harsh realities of war by severing ties to spare their loved ones anguish later when they were killed. But it must be detrimental to their wellbeing, to risk their life every day with no one to support them, no one for them to come home to.

"That feeling you had, when you heard I was dead, that's all I can offer you."

Hank's bitter words echoed through Cherry's head and prompted a glance at Gilda, obliviously plugging away at a pile of translations without any notion that her world was about to change.

Gilda was on the day shift and would be finished at four. Cherry was taking it upon herself to inform her friend that Dickie had been killed and planned to tell Gilda when she went off shift. Cherry knew Bertie would have been willing to give Gilda the rest of her shift off, just as he'd done for Cherry, when he found out it was the other woman who had lost her beau. But Cherry could not bring herself to break the news quite yet. She wanted to give Gilda one more afternoon, one more hour blissfully ignorant of Dickie's fate. Cherry didn't know how close the two had become, but she knew they'd seen each other a handful of times since the first dinner at the pub and believed the news would deal a blow.

At four o'clock, Cherry took Gilda for a walk round the small lake on the BP grounds. Gilda seemed a bit curious, but Cherry knew Gilda had heard about Hank and she believed Gilda would assume the outing was connected to her own loss.

Cherry waited until they'd done a half circuit and then paused to watch the ducks on the water. It seemed like a peaceful enough spot, and there was never going to be an ideal place to give news like this. She gently explained that it hadn't been Hank whose plane had been shot down, it had been Dickie. Gilda took it gracefully, as she did everything. No noisy sobbing on anyone's shoulder, just a few glistening tears. She dabbed at them delicately with a handkerchief.

"It's quite silly of me to be crushed, I suppose," she said. "We only went out a few times."

"Good heavens, Gilda, when I heard about Hank I went into a coma."

Cherry felt her own eyes well up and tried to drive all thoughts of Hank from her mind. She was determined not to let herself fall apart. This moment was not about her own situation, she wanted to be there for her friend.

"There is no right or wrong way to react to the news that a dear friend has been killed," Cherry said softly. "I'm so sorry."

They continued their walk around the lake for a while as Gilda tremulously recounted the enjoyable evenings she'd spent in Dickie's company. He'd been thoughtful and amusing, and Cherry suspected Gilda may have harbored hopes of a future union, just as she herself had hoped for with Hank.

As Cherry comforted the other woman, she reflected on how lucky she was not to be in Gilda's position. The news of Dickie's death helped Cherry put her own situation into perspective. Dickie was lost forever, but

286

Hank was alive. And as long as Hank was alive, there was still a chance for them to find happiness together.

One might have predicted that experiencing the shock of Hank's supposed death would have made Cherry balk at any future relationship with him. But in fact it had done the opposite. It had highlighted the importance he had in her life. The way that her happiness depended on him.

Her goal should be to spend every moment with him that she could, precious as they were. Rather than crying into her pillow, she should be formulating a plan to win him back. She had to find some way to bring Hank round to the idea that there was no one better suited for Cherry than him. She was supposed to be quite clever. Surely there was some stratagem she could devise that would convince him they were meant for each other.

If only men's hearts were as easily deciphered as German transmissions.

Between her lack of sleep the previous evening and the emotional talk with Gilda, Cherry should have been in utter shambles by the time her shift ended at midnight. But she found that her determination to recapture

Hank's heart had reinvigorated her with a sense of purpose. The more she thought about it, the more hopeful she became.

He hadn't truly rejected her. He'd simply withdrawn his suit because he felt somehow he wasn't deserving of her. There was gallantry in that, something her father would have respected. He was way off-beam, of course. But she was confident that she'd find some way to bring him round. She just needed to convince him that she couldn't give a tinker's curse about what size house she lived in.

As for the other thing, none of them had any guarantees on life. The way this war was going, they were all on borrowed time. That didn't mean anyone should put their lives on hold. If anything, it meant they should cherish the time they had together. And she intended to do just that.

A plan began to coalesce the next morning when Mrs. Ponsonby mentioned in passing that she and her husband were taking the small household staff to a relative's lodgings in Clacton-on-Sea to assist them in preparing a house for sale. They would leave her a housemaid, of course. But they'd be gone for the better part of two days. She hoped it wasn't too much of an inconvenience.

An inconvenience? Cherry thought to herself. *It's an answer to a prayer.*

Hank sat in the cockpit of his Spit, monitoring the darkening skies above him for the glow of a flare gun. He was on cockpit alert, which meant he sat in his plane until orders came in to scramble. Then he had thirty seconds to get his kite in the air. It was the most intense type of alert watch, so pilot shifts were only two hours long. Then he'd get two hours off, before another two hours on. It was tiring to remain at a state of readiness, never knowing whether you'd be expected to hustle to address some threat. It also didn't leave you with much to occupy you besides your thoughts. Hank had had altogether too much time to think the past few days.

He still believed he'd done the right thing by letting Cherry go. It hadn't brought him any pleasure to do it. To be honest, it had brought him nothing but misery. Losing both Dickie and Cherry in such a short time had been a body blow. Normally he would have been able to lean on one to weather the loss of the other. But now he had no one to lean on but himself.

That wasn't entirely true, he had his squadron. And he had been very relieved to finally make it back to Chicksands and discover that Novi was still among the living. Hank had asked him why he'd ignored the warning about the 109s and Novi said he'd never heard it. He'd still had his R.T. in "transmitting" mode and suspected that Dickie had done the same. It was a common enough issue with pilots.

Due to Dickie's loss, Hank had been promoted to flight leader. The cause of the promotion robbed him of any joy it might have otherwise brought him. But he did take his responsibility seriously and intended to do whatever he could to keep his fellow pilots alive. Many of them were virtual strangers to him. He'd only been in the squadron for six weeks, but that already made him one of the "old men" of the group. Of the twelve original members, only five remained. The rest had either been killed or wounded to a degree that they were kept off the operational roster.

The pace of battle was beginning to wear Hank down. Between patrols and alert shifts, the days and nights had run into each other until they were almost indistinguishable. There was no Tuesday, no Friday, no weekend. And with the ceaseless clashes in the air, there was no sense of "winning." There was only the acknowledgment that he hadn't died that day. Hank didn't know how he'd managed to survive when so many better pilots had been shot down. It hadn't been skill or courage. Probably just dumb luck. He wished that Cherry's picture had been as lucky for Dickie as it had been for him.

He wasn't sure why he'd been hit so hard by the loss of his friend. It shouldn't have come as a surprise. Not with the rate of attrition of RAF pilots. Looking back, Hank couldn't think of anything he could have done to prevent Dickie's death, but that didn't make the loss any easier to bear. He'd been the one to go through Dickie's things, gathering up items of value to send back to the man's family. There had been the usual stuff, some gramophone records, pictures, books, magazines.

He'd even stumbled upon a notebook with a few scribbled verses dedicated to Gilda, of the flaxen hair and alabaster skin. Hank had kept the book, hoping to find some way to deliver the poems to the object of Dickie's affections. It might comfort her, to know she'd been in Dickie's thoughts.

Hank had elected to keep the *Esquire* magazine with the pinup that looked like Cherry. He didn't think Dickie's family would mind, and after losing Cherry's picture it was all that Hank had left of her. Well, that and the coaster with her number on it.

He touched his pocket where he'd placed the coaster once again. He couldn't bring himself to throw it away. No reason to believe it couldn't still bring him luck, even if he wouldn't be phoning the number anymore. Apparently he was just as superstitious as the rest of the fighter boys. Or maybe he just couldn't bear to sever the last tie he had to Cherry. Holding it in his hand, looking at the dainty handwriting, made him feel a connection to her.

The sky burned red with the glow of the flare as it shot up over the aerodrome. Hank switched on his engine and prepared to take to the skies once again.

So he'd lost his best friend and his best girl. He still had his life, his wits, and his Spitfire. That was more than a lot of good men who had come before him. He'd do what he came over here to do. Blow Jerries out of the sky.

Two hours later, Hank flopped down on his bunk, exhausted. The scramble had been a false alarm. By the time Hank and the other two Spits in his flight had gotten airborne the bandits had disappeared. They'd flown around for a while, following Control's directions, but eventually it had become clear that it was a lost cause so he'd been instructed to land. The rest of his alert watch had been uneventful, and after a quick bite and shower he should've been ready to hit the hay. But the truth was he was restless.

He couldn't seem to shut off his mind and relax. He turned off the light and closed his eyes, but all he saw behind his eyelids was his gunsight. He hallucinated signal flares. Instructions shouted on the radio. *Patrol Colchester at angels ten! Bandit dead astern!*

He's on your tail!

I can't shake him!

He'd never get to sleep like this. And he needed all the rest he could squeeze in. Tomorrow would be another day, with more sorties and more bandits. Drowsiness in the cockpit could get you killed.

Hank tried to occupy his mind with happier thoughts, and then laughed humorlessly at the futility of that idea. His happiest thought would soon belong to someone else.

But that didn't mean he couldn't dream about her.

Hank clicked on the light next to his bed and reached down under his mattress where he'd stuck the *Esquire* magazine. After confiscating it from Dickie's possessions he'd felt too guilty and self-conscious to actually look at the pinup. But now he flipped the magazine open to the picture that resembled Cherry. She smiled back at him, her eyes full of promise and invitation. Hank's breathing quickened as he imagined Cherry giving him that same warm smile. He ran his thumb slowly down the pinup's delicate shoulders, tracing the lush contours of her full breasts, clearly visible through the filmy negligee. Up one shapely leg to the top of the tantalizingly short skirt, and over the juicy roundness of her bottom.

He'd never had the opportunity to run his hand over the smooth skin of Cherry's bare breast, but he'd cupped its fullness in his hand, teased her delicate nipple into a hard peak with his finger. Hank closed his eyes and let his mind linger on the memory of how Cherry's supple form had felt beneath him. The excitement of running his hand up her inner thigh to cup the warmth at the top. The sweet scent of her feminine response. He imagined how it would feel to come down on top of her naked body, to press her warm, soft skin along the length of him. Feel her arms around his neck. Her lips on his. Her tongue in his mouth.

His breathing quickened and he snaked a big hand down into his boxer shorts and touched himself, imagining Cherry taking him gently in her soft hands. He groaned aloud as a pang of deep satisfaction surged through him. He hadn't been with a woman since… Well, it had been a long time. His body ached for the touch of a lover. Not just any woman, but someone who meant something to him.

As an eligible man of marriageable age, especially as an RAF pilot, Hank was aware that he could have engaged in any number of dalliances with local girls. And if he hadn't been aware, Dickie's joking remarks on the subject would have enlightened him. But a shallow affair held no appeal for Hank. He wanted more than just a warm body to lay with. He wanted something meaningful, a real connection with someone who knew him and wanted him for what he was, not what he represented. He'd found that with Cherry. She'd made him feel like the kind of man he wanted to be. And there was nothing more gratifying, more appealing than that.

He longed to hold her against him, look down into her eyes as she told him she wanted him. To take her nipple in his mouth and tease it with his tongue. To run a hand down her stomach and feel her tremble beneath him as he opened her folds and stroked the sensitive bud there. He wanted to worship her body. To bring her the pleasure of sweet release, just before he claimed her as his own.

Hank's hand moved faster now, caught up in the intoxicating images of burying himself deep in Cherry's soft warmth. He imagined the sounds she might make as he drove into her, imagined her pink lips open, eyes closed, arms and legs around him, holding him tightly.

I want you, Hank.
I need you, Hank.
I love you, Hank.

His climax hit him with the force of a tidal wave, washing over him again and again. He gave a hoarse cry as he pumped his seed out onto his chest. It took a moment for him to catch his breath and regain his bearings after the most intense sexual release he could remember. And Cherry hadn't even been in the room.

Just imagine what it would be like to really feel her under him, against him, as he reached his peak. Unfortunately, he'd never get the opportunity. His imagination was all he had. Hank comforted himself with the thought that even though she would never belong to him, there was a part of her he would carry with him always.

Hank cleaned himself up and rolled over onto his side, exhausted but satisfied,

"Goodnight, sweetheart," he murmured, and quickly fell asleep.

Chapter Nineteen

Cherry understood the need for Bletchley to be constantly in operation. The enemy didn't halt the war to sleep so neither could the British, but the midnight to 8 a.m. shift was a rather dreary affair. She never got a good sleep in preparation, and toiling the whole stretch in darkness made the hours wear on. At least today she had come to work with hope in her heart.

Her plan was underway. She'd left a message for Hank at his squadron building requesting his presence at the Ponsonby's that Sunday afternoon. She knew he had the time off, it was the day they'd planned to visit her family. She'd said she needed to speak with him on a matter of grave importance. There was no intent to be overly dramatic. Cherry considered their future happiness to be a matter of grave importance, and she feared that if she simply stated she wanted an opportunity to convince him he'd made an error he would decline her invitation. She'd found that few men, if any, enjoyed being contradicted.

She genuinely believed that Hank did love her and had intended to propose. He'd only jilted her out of concern over her happiness. A misguided belief that he was robbing her of something.

Despite her privileged upbringing, Cherry had never been particularly enamoured of luxury. If she had been, she'd have paired off with one of the chaps that had been repeatedly and well-meaningly thrust at her during the past several years. She was a healthy girl, not too hideous to look at, with a good pedigree and flawless education. She'd been told by more than one matron that she would be a credit to any house. While none of the fellows had particularly caught Cherry's fancy, there had been a few that she'd believed, with a little encouragement, could have been charmed into offering for her. Her mother had even told Cherry she'd received a few queries in that direction. As Cherry had told Hank, she could have lived in a grand house on some country estate. But a life without love was, to her, a fate worse than poverty.

And so she would defy her refined breeding, her etiquette lessons, all the rules about good girl behavior that had been driven into her during her formative years in a grand scheme to win back the love of her life. It was enough to inspire a yellow-backed novel.

Cherry hadn't seen Gilda at all today. Or rather, yesterday. The other woman had been on the day shift. But the recently cleaned teacup at Gilda's workspace told Cherry that she'd been there. Of course she had. Gilda would soldier on, like everyone else who had lost someone to this terrible war. Cherry liked to think that if Hank really were killed, the next day would find her at work, beavering away as usual.

Just as she should be getting on with her work now.

Benötige 200 Gläser.

"Hmmm. Need two hundred binoculars," Cherry murmured to herself, jotting down the translation on her form.

I wish there were some way for me to retransmit the message and substitute "Käser" for Gläser, she thought. *Wouldn't Goering be surprised when two hundred cheesemakers showed up at his Stützpunkt?*

For all she knew, British Intelligence already had MI5 feeding the Germans just that kind of misinformation. But as Bertie was constantly reminding Cherry, her job was translations, not espionage, so she'd better keep at it.

"[Wind] northwest [force] 5, [atmospheric pressure] 15 millibars rising, good visibility."

Cherry finished scribbling the translation and moved on to the next one on the pile. She was translating messages that had been received earlier in the day. The Engima settings used by the various German military branches were changed each day at midnight, and it could take hours for the cryptographers to break the day's code. Once that happened the messages that had been received utilizing the new code were sent to be decrypted, and then on to the Cottage for translation.

Every once in a while the cryptographers were unable to break a particular code. This would send BP into a tumult, but it rarely happened with the Luftwaffe codes. Generally the Kriegsmarine, the German Navy, was the Enigma that gave Hut 4 fits.

As Cherry's eyes scanned the paper on the desk, her mind involuntarily drifted back to thoughts of Hank. She'd never been a particularly patient person, especially when she was waiting for something this important.

She wasn't sure how she'd get through the next thirty-six hours. It was closing in on 4 a.m., and she wondered idly what Hank was doing right now. Sleeping, hopefully. Like all sensible people.

She took a determined breath and refocused her energies on the slip of paper before her. The message had been received at 1543, or quarter to four that afternoon. She began, as always, by studying the five letter patterns and spotting any easily identifiable German words.

"Let's see what we've got," she muttered. "Ich freue mich zu teilen... I am happy to share... Oh no." Her pencil began to tremble and her breathing quickened. "Neuigkeiten über den Graduierung... news of the graduation of... *Dear Lord.*" She whispered a prayer, but it did no good. Her worst fears were confirmed when she saw that the final words of the message read "meines Neffen."

She shot out of her chair, clutching the message. It was four o'clock in the morning. Bertie wouldn't be in for another four hours. Cherry needed to get this message into someone's hands now.

"I'm off to Hut 3, back in a mo," she called behind her as she dashed out the door, the slip in her hand.

She ran all the way to Hut 3 in the absolute darkness of the blackout, tripping several times and nearly missing the low building in the gloom. She rapped sharply on the door, wondering who she would find in charge and whether they would believe her about the importance of the seemingly innocuous message.

The door cracked open and she slipped in, glancing around at the tables of silent workers casting long shadows in the dim light of the overhead bulbs. Her sudden appearance and frantic manner drew some strange looks, but Cherry had no time for pleasantries.

"Who's the ranking, then?" she asked the woman who had let her in.

The woman nodded towards a man at the far end of the Hut with his back to them. *Hugh.* Cherry groaned inwardly. Undaunted, she gathered herself and marched to the rear of the Hut.

"Yes, Duck?" Hugh asked, without turning.

"How did you know it was me?" she asked, briefly distracted.

"Despite your petite yet shapely stature, you have the distinctive clomp of a water buffalo," he replied.

So much for Miss Vacani's training, Cherry thought wryly, and then remembered why she was there. "I need you to get word to Air Ministry of an impending attack."

Hugh turned to her, his face somber. "Something in that message?" he asked, looking down at her hand. She handed him the paper, but her brows knitted as he read it and the ever-present smirk returned.

"Bit of an overreaction to some German using the cyphers for family dos. What makes you think this message signals an impending attack?"

Cherry took a deep breath and tried to determine how much detail it would take to convince Hugh the message indicated what she said it did.

One of the many layers of secrecy utilized at BP was compartmentalization. Most workers had no idea what went on in other buildings, or what happened with the information once they'd processed it. This helped ensure that if any one cog in the machine spilled the beans, they would not be able to provide a complete picture of how the whole machine worked. But it made situations like her current one much more problematic. Every minute she wasted explaining to Hugh the significance of the messages was one less moment the RAF had to prepare for the impending attack.

And yet it must be done.

Cherry bustled Hugh over to a relatively quiet corner and walked him quickly through the trail of messages she'd found and how they matched up with messages that had preceded Operation Paula. As she spoke, she was relieved to see the skepticism leave his face.

"And now the final message has come, is that about it?" he asked, indicating the paper in his hand.

"Hugh, this is real." She looked into his eyes, willing the good man, the man who had offered her his shoulder to cry on, to really hear what she was saying. "The attack is coming. We have to ring the RAF and find someone who will listen to us."

He may be difficult, she thought, *but he's not stupid.* He believed her.

"Aye," he nodded grimly. "Even if they have to wake up Air Chief Marshal Dowding himself."

Hugh got on the direct line to the Air Ministry and requested that the highest ranking member be brought to the phone. Cherry perched on a wooden stool and waited as Hugh's silence lengthened. An icy chill passed through her as she realized it was possible that whoever was on the other end of the phone might have no idea of the nephew message's significance and might not be made to understand.

After what seemed like an eternity, Hugh began speaking, slowly and clearly, to the person on the other end of the line. They must have been a high ranking individual indeed, because Hugh was providing the specifics of the relations' celebrations messages.

The work done at BP was so secret that most members of the British Armed Forces weren't even aware that the German transmissions could be decrypted. There was an entire team at Bletchley called "The Watch" dedicated to altering the intelligence gathered from the decoded transmissions to make it look as though it had been obtained from another source. The most commonly used "source" was that a spy had retrieved a piece of paper from a dustbin in German headquarters. It must have appeared to some that the Germans were quite careless with their confidential paperwork. But luckily, whoever had come to the phone was someone Hugh felt comfortable telling about the messages themselves.

Cherry had a sense of déjà vu from the night she'd passed along her suspicions regarding the destination of the *Prince Heinrich,* but this was exponentially worse. It was true that the German warship had been viewed as a great prize, but the information she was trying to pass along now could save the lives of possibly dozens of RAF pilots, including the man she loved.

Cherry was convinced a large scale attack was coming, probably today, which left her petrified for Hank's safety. She had never felt so helpless in all her life as she sat there listening to Hugh walk some scrambled egg at the Air Ministry through her logic. She wanted to find a phone, to make a frantic call to Hank's squadron and warn them all. To tell Hank not to fly, to do anything rather than put himself up in that plane today. But of course, that was impossible.

Like everyone at Station X, Cherry had signed the Official Secrets Act. And even if she hadn't signed it, it still would have barred her from telling anyone what she knew. A phone call like that would have been treason. She was aware that there were individuals much more important than her who carried larger secrets and had more reason than her to break their silence, but none of them had. They knew that the real secret they protected, the fact that the German transmissions were being intercepted and decrypted, was one of Britain's most valuable weapons in the war against Germany. Cherry would not be the one to break the silence, not even to save Hank's life.

She told herself that even if she were willing to risk treason, there was no chance that anyone would believe her. Even to those who had some inkling of what went on at BP, the information it provided sounded like fortune-telling. If Cherry rang up Hank and insisted she had proof of a massive raid coming today he would probably just think she'd gone mad. And with all the emotional ups and downs she'd experienced in the last few days, she was beginning to feel as though that was an accurate description of her mental state. Even if he believed her about the large scale assault, would that information make it more likely he'd stay out of a plane, or more likely he'd get in one? Knowing Hank, probably the latter.

Cherry glanced up as Hugh put down the receiver.

"Well?" she asked.

"I dunno. He followed the logic of the messages, but they apparently have no reason to expect a large-scale attack today. The Luftwaffe have been quite predictable in their pattern of attacks, focusing mainly on the aerodromes and aeroplane factories, and there haven't been any deviations that would signal a change in strategy. We can only hope that someone higher up than him puts more confidence in your hunches."

"Thanks for making the call," Cherry said glumly, sliding off the stool and heading towards the door.

"Duck," he called softly after her. "I am sorry about your chap. He seemed a decent sort."

"He is," she replied with a sad smile and headed back towards the Cottage.

Chapter Twenty

Hank looked up from the chessboard in the Dispersal hut and took in the group of men around him, reading, lounging, playing cards. His squadron.

The room was unusually crowded this morning. For some reason the higher ups had deemed that all twelve squadron pilots would be on ready alert today, rather than the usual six. RAF leadership must know something he didn't. Thus far all had been quiet.

Glancing out the window Hank saw that while there was some light cloud cover, the skies over England were a brilliant blue and relatively clear. Arguably good weather for Hun attacks. His flight was first on alert, but fortunately it was the type of alert that allowed them to play games and read magazines rather than just sit in their cockpits.

After Dickie's death Hank had attempted to isolate himself, not feeling up to the joking and frivolity that was a normal part of pilot downtime. His squadronmates wouldn't hear of it. They'd all experienced loss and knew that wallowing in misery wasn't a productive way to deal with tragedy. They'd even gone so far as to challenge Hank to games of chess, which was saying something. Fighter pilots were a competitive group and generally avoided contests that left them no hope of winning.

"Now I know your heart's not in this game," Johnnie joked, as he plucked Hank's bishop from the board.

His heart. No, Hank's heart definitely wasn't in this game. Didn't seem to be in his chest either. He'd lost it somewhere between ditching in Southwold and getting back to Chicksands that endless night. He felt as though he'd been moving on Gyropilot for the past week, just going through the motions. Existing, but not living. It didn't help that he was exhausted and overworked just like the rest of the pilots. One day bled into the next. The next sortie, the next alert watch, the next dogfight.

The RAF had been under constant barrage for the past two months, and the Luftwaffe showed no signs of letting up. If anything, the attacks had intensified. Targets were almost always airfields or factories striving to churn out planes faster than the Huns could destroy them. The last few weeks had been especially rough. Briefing papers provided to the air crews every few days listed casualties on both sides. According to the intelligence dope, the RAF had lost over one hundred pilots in the past two weeks, in addition to the one hundred and twenty wounded. Not to mention three hundred planes destroyed, but of course pilots were harder to replace.

Hank knew that level of attrition could not be maintained. At only twenty-three he was one of the oldest pilots in the squadron, and only three others, including the squadron commander, had more combat experience. Not that that particular commodity was hard to come by these days. With such high numbers of casualties, the remaining pilots were being put to a terrific strain to cover all the sorties, and everyone was running on fumes.

Despite everything that had happened, despite the death, and the loss, and the exhaustion, Hank still knew that this was where he was meant to be. This was what he was meant to be doing. Exhausted as he was, he'd never felt so useful, or more alive.

He was due an entire two days' leave, starting tomorrow. The break should have been a welcome reprieve but the empty hours stretched in front of him, mocking him with the reminder that he had no one to spend them with.

"Did you see this, Yankee? There's a message for you."

Hank glanced up to see Fergus, a wiry dark-haired sergeant, waving a slip of paper in his face. He was still adjusting to his big "secret" being so openly bandied about. After Dickie's departure, Hank had been quite heartened to discover that his entire squadron was aware of his citizenship. It had apparently been an open secret, but because he never spoke about it they kept their mouths shut as well. Once it had been established that there was no danger of anyone turning him in, Hank was more than proud to claim his status as an American. He'd even heard that he wasn't the only Yankee in the RAF. There were apparently several others in different squadrons who had likewise risked their citizenship to fight for the Brits.

Hank reached out to take the paper, but Fergus jerked it out of his grasp and made a show of sharing its contents with the assembled pilots.

"It seems a Miss Cherry Spence needs to see you on a matter of grave importance." He looked up with a knowing smile. "A matter of grave importance, eh? What could that possibly be? A knobstick wedding perhaps? Sounds like you got your 'cherry' all right."

The room went silent. Fergus' smile faded as he sensed he'd made some terrible mistake. The man was new to the squadron and not aware of Hank's history with Cherry or their recent split. But several of the other pilots knew and glanced over at Hank to see how he would react.

"You want I should pummel him for you, mate?" Johnnie asked across the table after Hank's continued silence.

Hank stood up suddenly and pushed his chair back from the table. Nobody else moved. It was like a scene from a Western. Hank walked slowly towards the Scotsman with his fists at his sides.

"Easy, big fella," Fergus said, backpedaling with his hands in the air. "I meant no harm." He stopped when his back hit the wall of the hut and flinched as Hank reached out and snatched the paper from his upraised hand.

Hank was not a violent man. Far from it. He'd always been big, as long as he could remember. But if he'd taken the bait every time he'd been teased growing up he wouldn't have made it past grammar school. If the bullies hadn't tanned his hide, his father would've. That didn't mean he was above using his size to intimidate the sergeant a bit to quell any future mention of his ex-sweetheart.

Cherry.

He could barely allow himself to think her name.

Once the other pilots saw there would be no bloodshed they returned to their activities. Fergus took the opportunity to flee to the other side of the room. Hank stared down at the note, his chess game forgotten. In the bold scrawl of the corporal who answered the phone at Dispersal, the note read:

Miss Cherry Spence invites you to her lodgings the afternoon of Sunday, 8 Sept, to discuss a "matter of grave importance."

Grave importance? What could that mean? Hank was painfully aware that it couldn't possibly be the reason Fergus had so lewdly intimated, although Hank's lower body hardened mutinously in response to just the thought of making a baby with Cherry. It was a fantasy he'd had frequently, a warm place he'd gone in his mind during many a long cockpit alert and lonely night in his bunk.

He couldn't imagine what Cherry might want to discuss. He'd assumed she would initially be upset with him but eventually come to the conclusion that he'd been right to bow out. Now that her father had come into his title she was probably being set up with all sorts of fancy folks.

Sunday, September 8th. That was tomorrow. She knew he had leave.

Hank was torn. On the one hand, Cherry wasn't the kind of person to exaggerate so maybe he should take her at her word that he was needed. He couldn't imagine what the problem might be, but if she said it was important, it likely was. On the other hand, he was trying to do the right thing, but he was weak. He wasn't entirely sure that he could be in her presence without begging her, on his knees most likely, to take him back. It had required every bit of willpower he had to walk away from her the first time. He didn't think he'd be able to do it again.

The phone rang in the next room and everyone in Dispersal paused expectantly, waiting to see if they'd be sent up. The orderly ran to the door and yelled "Green flight take off! Patrol Wittering at 25,000 feet."

Hank's flight had been designated Green flight for today, so he, Johnny, and Poolie, the other pilots in his flight, slung on their Mae Wests, grabbed their helmets, and shot out the door. Pete, good man, already had his prop spinning by the time Hank vaulted up into the cockpit. He clipped himself into his parachute harness and buckled his helmet.

A quick salute to Pete and he was off. Once in the air, Johnnie and Poolie formed up on his wings and they pointed south and headed up towards the designated altitude. Control came over the R.T. and clocked a bandit off to port, heading back towards the Channel.

Hank still hadn't decided what to do about Cherry's summons, but at least he had something else to think about for a while.

"Bugger was almost to the Netherlands before we got 'em," Poolie was saying excitedly, as the pilots of Green flight entered the Dispersal hut a while later.

"We?" Johnnie raised an eyebrow.

"Right. Johnnie and Hank got em, that's half a Jerry for each," Poolie amended.

Hank tugged off his lifejacket and slapped his helmet and gloves down on the table. It hadn't been much of a battle, chasing a lone bomber back across the Channel. Clear skies and nothing more than a single Dornier. Looked like it was going to be a quiet day after all.

It was after four o'clock when the phone rang again. There was a long pause, and then the orderly skidded excitedly into the main room.

"Squadron to your aircraft, all flights, patrol base at angels ten! There's a one hundred plus raid plotted, coming across further down the coast. It may turn and head our way."

One hundred plus. That meant over one hundred aircraft. *Guess the RAF knew something after all,* Hank thought, grabbing his helmet and gloves. The fact that his squadron had been ordered to patrol their own aerodrome meant that either Control wasn't certain of the

318

Luftwaffe's target, or they expected the aerodromes themselves to be the targets.

He took off with the rest of his squadron and formed up over the aerodrome. Almost immediately his squadron commander's voice came over the R.T.

"Control reports the one hundred plus has become two hundred plus."

Hank whistled through his teeth. *Two hundred enemy aircraft.* He wondered if other squadrons had been scrambled as well.

"Squadron, patrol Maidstone at angels twenty."

Hank wheeled his Spitfire around in accordance with his squadron leader's directions, taking care to keep his place in the large formation. Maidstone was slightly inland, but still close to the narrowest Channel crossing from France. It was logical that the German force would make land near there.

Hank had never seen a formation of two hundred planes, at least not all together. He wondered if this was some sort of large scale attack on one location, or more likely the Luftwaffe was intent on taking out all the RAF airfields simultaneously.

Not if he and his fellow pilots had anything to say about it.

As Hank's squadron approached Maidstone, a shadow appeared on the horizon. It was similar to the "swarm of gnats" he'd seen during his first aerial engagement but much denser and larger in size. He looked out of his cockpit and was shocked to realize that the German formation stretched as far as he could see in both directions. It must have been twenty miles wide.

"Cor blimey! There's the whole German Air Force, bar Goering!" Poolie's voice came over the R.T. and was almost immediately cut off by the commander.

"Cut the nattering, chaps! Keep the radio open!"

The massive formation grew larger, filling the whole of his windscreen, and Hank nearly came out of his cockpit as the enormity of the force hit him. He'd never seen so many planes in the air at one time. This wasn't two hundred planes. Damned if it wasn't a thousand planes. Then he glanced off his right and left wingtips, at the other eleven Spitfires facing this tremendous threat.

Once again, the thought that popped into his mind was *"Where do we start?"*

If the huge formation followed the pattern of previous raids, it would break into pieces and scatter to bomb multiple targets. But to Hank's surprise, the formation stayed largely together and advanced relentlessly towards Maidstone.

That doesn't make any sense. There aren't any high value military targets in all of Kent that would warrant an attack of this size. Unless…

Hank's Spitfire was facing the coast and oncoming waves of enemy planes. But immediately astern, past his tail, was London. There were five aerodromes surrounding the city that would make juicy targets for the oncoming Huns.

"Prepare to engage." The commander's calm voice came over the R.T. Hank checked his position in formation, armed the firing ring of his trigger, and prepared for battle.

The bombers droned on towards the city and the cloud of fighters dove down toward his squadron.

"Break by flights, attack at will."

Hank saw his commander's Spit plunge forward toward the closest bomber in the Luftwaffe formation that now filled hundreds of miles of sky around him. The two planes on the commander's wingtips followed suit.

Hank's agile mind took in the mess of targets before him and selected a bomber that had fallen slightly out of formation.

"On me, Green Flight," he transmitted, and dove for the bomber. He trusted that Johnnie and Poolie were just off his wings, as they were supposed to be, and his trust was rewarded when the bullets from his eight machine guns were joined by the fire from sixteen more. He saw smoke start to pour from one of the Dornier's engines, but didn't have time to confirm its fate.

There were enemy planes everywhere he looked. There were *planes* everywhere he looked. Diving, swooping, filling his windscreen. Hank tried to get a good line on another bomber, but swarms of 109s had descended from above and were striking out at any RAF fighter that got close. The front of the bomber formation had moved past his squadron, heading, as he'd feared, towards London. It was likely they'd break formation over the city and send a portion of their numbers to each of the aerodromes. With a group that large, they could do severe damage to the airfields and possibly cripple the RAF's defenses of the capital city.

Anti-aircraft artillery had opened up along the banks of the Thames. He could hear the *Whoomp! Whoomp!* over the buzz of his engine. White puff balls appeared below him as the "ack ack" shells burst, but they didn't shoot high enough to touch the German formation.

Hank felt some relief when he realized that there were definitely more RAF planes in the air than just his squadron. Several other squadrons of Spitfires and a number of the older model Hurricanes had been scrambled as well. But from the quick glimpses he could manage it appeared as though the Brits were outnumbered by a factor of ten with just fighter planes alone, not counting the bombers. That was not good. Those bombers were going to level the airfields.

Hank hauled back sharply on his spade grip and turned his Spit around, just missing another flight of Spitfires.

"Oy!" he heard over the R.T. It sounded like Trotter, leader of Red Flight.

"Red leader, let's get in front of this mess and see if we can hit some bombers before they drop their loads."

"Righty-o. You've got lead, Green flight."

Hank pulled the lever for emergency power and felt the familiar exhilaration as the thrust drove him back into his seat. He shot past dozens of dogfights, the pilots all gripped in graceful battles for their lives as they swooped about an attempt to gain the upper hand.

Hank's R.T. was abuzz with transmissions. He was lucky Trotter had heard him over the din. The voices all blended together into a bewildering cacophony until Hank was forced to tune them out, concentrating instead on staying out of the path of wayward Messerschmitts. His fighter could fly circles around the relatively slow, lumbering bombers, but the sheer number of planes in the air made it a feat of piloting simply to catch up to the front of the large formation without slamming into another kite, friend or foe.

There were several 109s that crossed in front of him and provided him with what would normally have been favorable targets, but he only had thirteen seconds of ammunition.

"Save your bullets for the bombers, if you can," he said into his R.T., hoping the other pilots could hear him. His wasn't the first voice to give that instruction. Several squadron leaders had already provided reminders over the air. It was standard practice for the RAF to avoid the fighters as much as possible and target the bombers.

Hank could see the front of the formation as it headed up the Thames Estuary. He expected it to break up soon and wanted to try and hit it before the bombers split in different directions. Tugging back on his spade grip, he pulled his Spitfire up into a climb in order to gain some altitude. A quick glance to the sides told him that his two wingmen were still with him. He hoped Red Flight was back there as well but he couldn't spare a glance in his rear vision mirror for fear he'd run right into another plane.

Once he'd gotten several thousand feet of loft under him, Hank flipped the fighter, inverting it before plunging back in the direction he'd come. His plane accelerated and the familiar grey tunnel began to close in. Applying the tried and true techniques of tensing and leaning forward, he managed to keep his senses while his plane accelerated down towards the oncoming Dorniers below.

His plan was to attack the bomber formation head-on, firing at them hard when they got close and pulling up at the last second to avoid a collision. Because the Spitfires and bombers would be going in opposite directions, their aggregate speed of closing would be around 550 mph. It sounded suicidal, but it was actually one of the most effective methods for engaging large bomber formations. It served to destroy some of the bombers and split the large formations so that the bombers were forced to separate and could be shot down more easily.

Hank looked out at the bombers as they grew large in his windscreen, waiting for them to fill the crosshairs of his targeting sight. His thumb floated over his trigger button and his breathing slowed.

And then something completely unexpected happened.

The Dorniers dropped their bombs.

All of them.

On London.

Hank was so startled he nearly took his hand off the yoke. *The whole formation of bombers just opened up on the city.* The deadly barrage cascaded down towards the city below like leaves falling from a tree. Everywhere the bombs struck, pillars of fire shot into the air. They fell on dockyards, warehouses, factories.

Apartments. People. Children.

Hank's flight was nearly on top of the bomber formation. The minute the lead Dornier's wings filled his gunsight he plugged everything he had into the ship and pulled starboard at the last moment, cutting close enough to see the startled face of the pilot as he blew by.

He couldn't believe what had just happened. A few stray bombs had been dropped on London in previous raids, but those were widely viewed as anomalies and likely the result of navigational error. This was a full scale assault on the most populous city in England.

He didn't have much time to reflect on the horror of the situation. Johnnie's Spit came shooting past on his right side, pursued by a 109. The light blue underside of the Hun plane flashed past Hank's windscreen. Hank yanked his grip to starboard and hit the firing button as the 109 drifted across his gunsight. He didn't know if the 109 went down but it did veer off its pursuit of Johnnie's plane.

Hank noticed that some of the rounds he'd shot in that last barrage were tracer rounds, leaving their glowing red trails in the sky. It meant he was almost out of ammo. He grimaced at his windscreen, which was awash with targets. Normally he ran out of fuel before he ran out of ammunition, having to chase his target all over the skies trying to get a good shot. Now there were targets everywhere and he had maybe twenty-five rounds left.

He turned toward the closest bomber, some of which were already angling to head back across the Channel. He managed to get close enough to be guaranteed his shots would count and jammed his thumb down on the trigger until the guns stopped firing.

Short of crashing his plane into one of the bombers, there was nothing more he could do. The thought frustrated him to no end. Dozens of bombers were still coming in low, dropping seeds of flaming death on the capital city. Spitfires and Hurricanes were making a good showing, but there were just too many 109s to prevent the bombers from completing their deadly mission.

Angrily, he wheeled his plane back towards Chicksands, thumping his spade grip with his fist.

Hank wasn't the first one on the ground. A few others had also run out of ammo and headed back, and several Spits looked as though they wouldn't be airworthy any time soon.

As his craft taxied to a stop, the fuel truck roared up and several men jumped into action to get him rearmed and refueled. Pete started his thorough walk around, checking every flap and panel for damage. Two armorers were already up on one wing reloading the eight Browning machine guns. They were meticulous. As many times as Hank had fired his guns, he'd never had the ammo jam or experienced any other weapons malfunction. There were also a rigger and a fitter who would inspect the aircraft for damage and effect repairs, as well as restock oxygen, replace the battery, and so on. The men who took care of his Spit had the same pride in it that he did. The ground crew had managed to trim down the entire process of refueling and rearming a Spitfire to about twenty-six minutes.

Hank studied the comparatively peaceful skies above Shefford. One would never guess that an unprecedented bombing attack was currently taking place just sixty miles away. It still galled Hank that he'd had to let so many Huns complete their deadly mission unmolested. He had no idea what the thinking had been behind the monstrous attack on London. Hitler must be crazy if he thought the Brits wouldn't retaliate. Hank tried to remind himself that the city had bomb shelters for just this type of thing, and hopefully the air raid sirens had given people enough time to seek shelter. He briefly offered a prayer of thanks that at least Cherry was safely out here in the country.

He pulled his bandana out of his pocket and wiped his sweaty brow. *I've got to get back there*, he thought. He pulled his watch out of his pocket.

Twenty-three minutes to go.

By the time Hank and the other five members of his squadron with airworthy craft managed to get back to London the 109s had long since departed, leaving their bombers unescorted. While this made the bombers easier targets, the sheer number of them meant that it was hard to produce any visible results. Hank figured there must have been at least twenty RAF squadrons in the air, but they couldn't shoot the Dorniers down fast enough to prevent the bombs from falling on the city.

When he'd run out of ammo for the second time, Hank reluctantly headed back towards Chicksands, taking in the burning city below. The skies were red with the flaming inferno that had engulfed whole swaths of the docklands. Huge clouds of black smoke billowed up into the skies. Miles of warehouses burned, as well as ships in the docks and the estuary. He'd never seen anything like it. There must have been hundreds of tons of artillery dropped on the city. Even from his elevation, he could see sprays of water from firefighters attempting to douse the flames. They had their work cut out for them tonight. He'd wager they had a more dangerous job than he did today.

Then again, he had no idea how many of his squadronmates would be joining him on the ground. The Huns had leveled the docks, and Hank knew they'd taken their toll on the RAF as well. It would be anxious times until the rest of his squadron was accounted for. He'd wanted to get rearmed and head to London for a third time, but he could see that the German bomber formation was already heading back across the Channel. They'd be gone by the time he got airborne. It was time to get to ground and find out what fate had befallen his fellow pilots.

When Hank finally managed to bring his Spit down he saw that three planes had beaten him back, with one kite looking more like a kitchen sieve than a high tech aircraft. He wandered over and was hardly surprised to find it belonged to Novi, the Polish pilot.

"They say I no take it back up," the Pole lamented. Hank grinned.

"It looks like you were lucky to get it down," he said.

"Bloddy Germans," Novi muttered, shaking his head. "You want drink?" he asked.

Hank considered the invitation. His hair was stuck to his forehead with sweat, his clothes plastered to his body after a series of nerve-wracking sorties in the late summer weather. What he should do was shower and fall into bed.

But a drink suddenly seemed much more appealing.

"Sure."

The two headed into the Officer's Mess and Novi scrounged up a bottle of whiskey from somewhere along with two teacups.

"I pour," he said, depositing a healthy slug in each cup. "To killing Germans," the Pole declared, raising his cup.

Hank lifted his cup by the delicate handle, and gave his comrade a bemused look.

"You hate them, don't you?" he asked, after taking a swallow. Novi poured another shot into each of the cups.

"You hate them too, if they kill your mother, give your sister to soldiers for brothel."

Hank considered this. He knew that the Germans had invaded Poland and that some Polish pilots like Novi had managed to escape, but he hadn't really considered what it would be like to know that you had to leave everyone behind, at the mercy of your enemy, to continue the fight.

The men drank in silence for a moment, and then Novi frowned.

"Why you sad? Today, you live. Shoot many Germans."

Maybe it was the two shots of whiskey, or his companion's frankness, but something made Hank answer honestly.

"I miss my friend," he said simply. "And my girl."

"You friend is dead, nothing can do," Novi replied. "Why you not with girl?"

"I think she's better off without me."

"You make problem where is no problem." Novi shook his head. "You love her?"

"Yes," Hank replied.

"She love you?"

"I think so."

"Then be together. Is good to have life, when so much death."

Hank wished it were that simple. He still thought Cherry would be better off with someone of her own station, but after surviving today's barrage he'd decided one thing for sure. He would go and see her tomorrow. If he could face the entire Luftwaffe, twice, he could face one rather petite woman. Even if it cost him his heart.

Chapter Twenty-One

Cherry didn't know whether Hank was alive or dead.

Her hunch about the attack yesterday had been spot on. She'd have given anything to have been wrong. The Luftwaffe had stormed across the Channel with almost three hundred bombers and more than six hundred fighters in the largest aerial attack in history. The first wave had appeared around four o'clock in the afternoon, and just as the last bombers were turning back towards the Channel, another wave had come at eight in the evening. Because the sun had already set, there were no defensive fighters to meet the German bombers as they rained their terrible cargo down on London. Word at BP was that things could have been worse, but the RAF casualties were understandably high for a single day and Cherry had no way of knowing whether Hank was among the missing.

The bombing had continued until almost four in the morning, an ungodly hour which had found Cherry at her desk with her translations. As she'd sat in the silence of the Cottage early this morning, her fertile imagination conjuring up what three hundred tons of bombs might sound like falling on a city, she would have traded any chance she had at happiness with Hank, just to be assured he was all right.

And now the moment of truth was upon her.

She'd dressed especially nicely, in a soft chiffon dress dyed a deep coral. There was shirring at the shoulders and waist, giving her the appearance of someone with a shape. It was a bit old fashioned perhaps, but with even clothing being rationed one had to make do with previous seasons' frocks. Besides, it was what she wore underneath that would likely be the more significant fashion choice this afternoon.

Cherry tried sitting in one of the Ponsonby's brocade chairs, but the tapping of her small foot on the parquet floor echoed through the oppressive emptiness of the drawing room and threatened to drive her mad. She tried standing, but found herself wandering aimlessly from one of the front rooms to the next, never wanting to be away from the windows that lent her a view of the circle drive.

What sort of imbicile would issue an invitation for an important rendezvous without providing a specific time? she chastised herself. When she'd made the call, she'd felt it was better to leave the timing open-ended in case Hank had some difficulty making his way down from Chicksands. But the unfortunate result was that she could very well spend the next few hours alternately pacing and fidgeting in acute anxiety, unsure as to whether he was delayed in securing transportation, or floating in the Channel with the wreckage of his Spitfire.

Cherry didn't know how much more of this she could bear.

It was fortunate that no member of the household was there to see her fussing and fretting. The Ponsonbys had thoughtfully left Katie, the housemaid, to see to anything Cherry might want. And Cherry had thoughtfully given Katie the day off to see the chap at the butcher's for whom the girl carried a rather large torch. Cherry fully expected the maid to take advantage of every stolen moment provided to her, and would be surprised to see her return before late that evening.

It was queer, Cherry could almost hear the old home settling around her. She couldn't remember the last time she'd been alone in a large house. Growing up, there had always been family in and out or members of the household staff. The closest she'd come was arriving at the Ponsonby's after a late shift at BP, creeping through the side door at midnight and silently padding to her room. But this was the middle of the day, and because she was truly alone here she was free to do anything she pleased.

And she planned to use that freedom to secure a proposal from Hank.

If only he would come.

She stopped her pacing for a moment and spared a glance down at her dress, wanting to ensure everything was in order. To her dismay, she spied a small spot of brown liquid on her skirt, about the size of a halfpenny. *Must've fallen from one of the two cups of tea you drank to calm your nerves*, she thought. She fled to the kitchen to try and dab up the spill, after casting a last fleeting glance out the front window to assure herself there was no one in the drive.

On the one hand, it seemed ridiculous to be worried about something as trivial as a spot of tea on her skirt when there was every chance Hank had been wounded or even killed in yesterday's massive battle. Her stomach lurched at the possibility, and she didn't allow her mind to dwell on such a terrible thought. On the other hand, if he had managed to make it through, she truly believed this was her one chance to win him back and it was too important to overlook even the smallest flaw.

"After all the effort that went into you acquiring a social polish," she muttered to herself, "you can't manage through two cups of tea without soiling your—"

Whap! Whap!

Cherry had become so engrossed in blotting the stain that the knock on the door took her completely by surprise. She dropped the tea towel and bolted for the front door, skidding dangerously on her leather soles as she reached the foyer. Her heart slammed in her chest as she twisted the large knob with both hands and yanked the massive wooden door back to reveal her guest.

And there he was.

Hank.

"Thank God," she breathed.

He stood on the doorstep, looking handsome as ever, and also a bit bewildered at her startled appearance. She'd intended to be the picture of composure as she gracefully opened the door, instead she had the look of someone who'd just completed the Olympic hurdles.

"Are you all right?" he asked, looking understandably concerned. After all, she had left that mysteriously dramatic phone invitation and here she was, eyes wide and gulping air like a fish out of water.

"Yes, of course," she murmured, regulating her breathing. "Won't you come in?"

Her hands were shaking and she nervously smoothed her skirt as she backed into the house to allow him entry. She tried to remain calm, but inside she was doing somersaults just to have him there, apparently in fine fettle.

"Thank you," he replied, stepping up into the entryway.

She had quite forgotten how big he was. Her whole body melted at the sight of him, solid and strong, and she realized that until that very moment she'd secretly harbored the unspoken fear that she would never see him again. It was all she could do not to throw herself into his arms and beg him never to leave her again.

"You look really pretty," he said softly. His blue eyes were gentle, looking down at her. A warmth spread through her body as his deep, mellow voice reverberated in her like a tuning fork.

"Thank you, so do you," she replied. Then considered the ludicrousness of that statement, and quickly amended, "Fit, I mean. Natty. Quite spruce." *So much for composure.*

And he did look wonderful. His navy blue RAF uniform coat accentuated his broad shoulders and tapered down to his narrow waist. The sunlight streaming through the open window made his golden hair gleam, and his full bottom lip left her itching to reach out and touch it. To feel its softness against hers. If her plan worked, she would experience that and more soon enough. Her heart was beating so loudly at the thought she felt he must surely have heard it.

Once inside he looked around, seemingly taken by the house itself. He stepped slowly into the foyer and peeked into the rooms beyond, marveling at the high ceilings and tasteful furnishings.

"Would you like to see the rest of the house?" she asked.

"Sure," he replied with an easy shrug of his big frame.

She led him first into the drawing room where several wingback chairs flanked a large ornate fireplace with a dark wood mantle. It was a comfortable room, and Cherry often enjoyed curling up here with a good book. Hank seemed interested in every aspect of the room, from the carvings on the fireplace to the silk draperies. The house was quite nice, Cherry reflected, with its large, airy rooms and ornate wood trim. She didn't often take notice of it, but she supposed if one were unused to the splendor of English country houses it would be a rather impressive showing.

She then took him through the library, dining room, and kitchen. He seemed equally taken with all of the rooms, and made a thorough study of each as they passed through.

Cherry wasn't quite sure what to say. She didn't want to intrude on what appeared to be his genuine interest in the old manor house, but as the hostess she felt she should be offering some sort of witty chatter. Nothing

342

particularly witty occurred to her, so she maintained a respectful silence until they came around to the stairs leading to the second storey.

"Would you like to see the upstairs?" she asked lightly, motioning towards the staircase.

"Yes, I would," he replied, seeming genuine.

As she led him up the wooden staircase, Cherry considered the remarkable turn of events that had brought her to this point, alone in someone else's house, leading a man up to her bedroom. Hank's country upbringing had apparently left him blissfully unaware of how inappropriate this was. Either that or he was so distracted by the house itself he wasn't thinking clearly. Regardless, she refused to question her luck, as her plan was going smoothly.

She obviously wasn't going to invade the Ponsonbys' privacy by showing him the rooms used by her hosts, so instead they poked their heads into a few guest rooms, made a quick sweep of the W.C., and then stopped at the doorway of the room Cherry occupied. She entered ahead of him and stood in the center of the room, keeping a careful distance from the bed.

"And this is my room."

The room was painted a cheery robin's egg blue, with warm golden draperies and a white and gold bedspread. The furnishings included an armoire, a chest of drawers, and a dressing table. They were done in dark wood, but dainty enough to fit well into a woman's boudoir.

Here Hank paused, suddenly unsure of himself. Even he could sense this was unusual, if not entirely taboo. But then, appearing to come to a decision, he stepped over the threshold and followed her in.

He seemed somehow enormous and even more masculine than usual within the confines of her bedchamber. Although he did nothing more overt than stand with his hands at his sides, several paces into the room, his mere presence in the space felt shockingly intimate. Cherry had never before invited a man into her bedroom. At least, not one to whom she was unrelated.

"Shall I put on some music?" she asked, mincing briskly over to her gramophone.

Hank nodded, looking a bit bemused.

Cherry had given a lot of thought to what would be the ideal music to accompany her scheme, and had finally settled on the Ink

344

Spots. It was the most provocative record she owned. Most of her collection was classical, and while there may have been a few Tchaikovsky preludes considered saucy in their time, it was not really proper music for modern seduction. She probably could have borrowed something more appropriate from Gilda, but didn't want to bother her friend over this ridiculous exercise while the woman was still in mourning.

Cherry switched the machine on and set the needle down, wisely electing to skip the first track on the album, "It's All Over but the Crying." With her background music in place, she took a deep breath and decided if she were really going through with this hare-brained scheme of hers, she'd better get on with it.

"I suppose you would like to know why I summoned you here," she said finally.

Hank just looked at her intently and waited for her to continue.

"I'm afraid you dismissed me so quickly the other night I didn't have a chance to plead my case," she explained. She'd elected to start there. If he would just listen to reason, she might not have to resort to the other part of her plan.

He looked down at the floor and shook his head.

"You grew up in a house like this?" he asked, finally looking back up at her.

She hesitated a moment, and then nodded. "Yes," she said.

"Yours was larger than this, wasn't it? More grand?"

"Yes," she admitted.

"And there were people to clean it for you, and cook for you, and take care of your things?"

She took a step towards him, willing him to look into her eyes, to trust her.

"Hank, you must believe me when I tell you I don't care about any of those things."

"Not everybody had a life like yours, Cherry. Not everyone would be able to give all this up so easily."

"You think any of this matters to me?" She motioned absently around the room. "Do you know how many girls I know with huge, empty houses and huge, empty lives? What good is a mansion if it's not a home? I'd live in a potting shed if I had a man who loved me to share it with."

She could see that he wanted to believe her, but somehow he still wasn't able to accept the truth of her words.

For the first time she noticed he was holding a small paper wrapped bundle.

"Is that for me?" she asked.

He looked down at the package, a bit surprised, as though he'd forgotten he was holding it.

"It's a notebook of Dickie's," he explained. "He'd written some nice things about Gilda. I thought… I don't know, I thought maybe she'd want to have it."

A sadness washed over Cherry as she remembered what it had felt like to share the sad truth of Dickie's death with Gilda. It was kind of Hank to have saved the book for his chum's sweetheart.

"Thank you, I will see that it gets to her. I'm sure she will find it a comfort."

"And what about you, Cherry?" he asked softly, placing the package on her nightstand. "Would a notebook of poems be enough for you to remember me by?"

He still didn't understand. Didn't think he was enough.

"I want to be with you, Hank," she said simply. "For however long we have. I don't know what's going to happen to any of us, or how this is going to end. But I do know that I want to spend whatever time I have left with you. I want to be with you, in every way possible."

She glanced meaningfully over at the bed and her face reddened. Apparently she was bold enough to conceive the plan, but too British to actually say the words. It took Hank a moment to realize the significance of her look, and then he flushed as well. At least she thought he did.

"I'm not a smart man, Cherry. There aren't a lot of things I know for sure. But I know I love you." Her mouth fell open at his words. She'd ached to hear those words, to know that he felt the same way about her that she felt about him.

"Love you enough to know that you deserve better than me," he added firmly.

"How can you say that? You think I'm entitled to make up my own mind about who to dance with but not who to marry?"

"You're an Honorable. And I'm, well, I'm a dishonorable." He smiled but there was no humor in it. "I'm a man with no country, Cherry. I have nothing to offer you."

She shook her head in disbelief. "You can't possibly believe the words you're saying. You have no country, as you put it, because you risked your citizenship, and your life, to come and save my country."

He didn't look convinced. He glanced quickly at the bed, and then back at her.

"Don't you understand that if we do this, you'll be thoroughly—"

She cut him off, unable to bear hearing his lips form the word.

"Don't you dare say I'd be ruined. I was ruined when I thought you were dead." Her eyes blazed and her voice broke. "I love you, Hank Clarkson. More than fancy houses and servants to fill them. More than any man I've ever known. You broke my heart when you left, but I won't let you do it again."

Her heart was racing as she stepped gingerly out of her shoes. She watched Hank's eyes as she slowly unzipped her dress. They never left hers, even when she pulled the dress down her shoulders and let it pool at her feet. She next removed the black satin slip, her fingers trembling as she drew the straps down her arms and let it, too, fall to the floor. She glanced down and noticed that his hands clenched and unclenched at his sides, but nothing else moved.

She stood before him wearing only her brassiere, knickers, garter belt, and stockings. They were all black, but for her stockings. She'd felt that to bring off her plan she must somehow paint herself as a woman of experience rather than the fumbling virgin she truly was. She'd thought that her usual peach or pale blue smacked of purity and innocence, and that wasn't what was needed now.

Hank finally allowed his eyes to wander down over her almost naked form, and it warmed her as it went until her whole body felt flushed with the heat of his gaze. She stood there for a moment, waiting for him to speak, and when he didn't Cherry decided she might as well go ahead with the rest of her plan before she lost her nerve.

Gingerly placing one foot on the stool of her dressing table next to her, she unclipped the stocking from her garter belt. Then she raised up on her toe and slowly rolled the stocking down her leg until it was free. There was no deliberate attempt to be seductive, in truth she had little knowledge of how to entice a man. It was simply a method she'd developed to better protect against ladders.

350

Hank's breathing was suddenly audible above the Ink Spots softly crooning "If I Didn't Care." Neither one of them spoke as she lifted her other foot and repeated the routine, removing her second stocking and setting her bare foot down on the floor with its mate. She unhooked the side of her garter belt and let it drop down next to her stockings.

Cherry stood there in her bra and knickers and pondered what to do next. She had reached the end of her plan. By this point she'd expected that Hank would either have ravished her on the bed or have fled the room in disgust, horrified at her lewdness. But he'd done neither. He simply looked at her, his face a mix of sadness and something she didn't recognize.

She had no idea what to say so she slowly crossed the room until she stood right in front of him, the toes of her bare feet touching his black leather shoes. She put her hands flat on his chest and could feel his heartbeat racing beneath her palms.

She looked up into his eyes. At this proximity he was unable to hide the heat of his desire.

"So, are you going to turn me away again?" she asked, giving up any pretense of dignity, and waited breathlessly to see whether her mad gamble had paid off.

Chapter Twenty-Two

Hank looked down at Cherry in his arms and made a low sound in the back of his throat. A primal, desperate sound.

He'd known it was a mistake to go to her. But the truth was that the week without her had been excruciating and he would have given almost anything just to see her face. It was all over the moment she opened the door. He could not leave her again.

He'd wanted to be a better man. He'd tried so hard, but in the end he was swept away by his overwhelming desire for her, just as Cherry must have known he would be. He wanted her, more than anything he'd ever wanted in his life. Wanted to worship her body, to love her as well as he was able. To be with her for whatever time he had left on this world.

"Sweet Charity," he whispered, before swallowing her whole.

His arms crushed her against him, his mouth moved on hers forcefully, urgently, as though she were providing the very oxygen he needed to survive. He kissed her with every desperate urge built up over countless lonely nights, nights filled with fantasies that began in a moment such as this.

He was delirious with the fierce longing to feel her warm skin against his body. Her little hands went up inside his coat, running their whisper soft touch over his chest and shoulders. Without pulling his mouth away from hers, he frantically tugged at the buckle of his belted coat, his urgency making the process take twice as long as normal. He shrugged out of his coat and pulled off his suspenders, in a comically rough imitation of the sensuous striptease she'd performed for him.

Her fingers plucked at the buttons of his shirt, and once he'd freed himself of his trousers he simply ripped the two sides of the garment apart, sending several buttons skittering across the floor of her room.

She pulled away from him to giggle.

"My goodness, I thought I was keen."

He looked down at her smiling face, her brown eyes sparkled up at him with laughter. And love.

She loved him.

It was incredible to contemplate. And there would be plenty of time to contemplate later, but right now he just wanted to feel her against him.

He stood before her in only his boxer shorts, his erection making them jut out from his waist in a way that seemed to fascinate Cherry. He couldn't keep his hands off her body. The contrast of the black lingerie with her milky white skin was incredibly erotic. He was burning to see what was concealed under the few garments that remained.

Tucking a thumb under each bra strap, he eased them gently down her arms, marveling at the velvety softness of her skin. Bringing his face back down to hers, he captured her mouth for another eager kiss as his fumbling fingers attempted to unclasp her bra. He couldn't seem to get his clumsy digits to do the job.

"Here, allow me," she offered politely with an impish grin, and the bra snapped open.

"I suppose you should be glad I'm not an expert at brassiere removal," he joked. In truth, even at his age he'd only had the opportunity a handful of times. And none of those girls had come close to possessing the

355

spectacular breasts Cherry had. As her bra fell to the floor, he looked down, mesmerized.

They were full and round, like ripe fruit, each capped with a perfect rosebud that he ached to take in his mouth. He knew he was staring, but he'd never seen such lovely breasts outside of a magazine. She did indeed look just like the *Esquire* pinup. His fantasies had been right on the mark.

Hank sank down to his knees so that the pink tips were at eye level, and looked up at Cherry with undisguised heat in his eyes as he took one in his mouth. Cherry made the most wonderful sound, a soft "Oh!" that was both innocent and sensual. As his tongue teased the hardening bud she grabbed fistfuls of his hair and held his face against her. He gave a low chuckle, never letting the nipple out of his mouth.

His hands skimmed over her back, unable to get his fill of her warm skin. It felt like the outside of a summer peach. He wanted to touch every inch of her. It was as though he'd been given permission to indulge in all those fantasies he'd concocted in the dark of his bunk, the lonely isolation of his cockpit. He didn't know where to start.

Hank pulled his head reluctantly away from her nipple and left a trail of kisses across her silky stomach. She made a soft sound of protest, but when he continued his exploration down the front of her satin panties she quieted. He squeezed her hips in his strong hands, delighting in the supple roundness of her womanly shape, and brought his mouth down to the warmth between her legs. Cherry gasped and whispered his name. He kissed her there, licking and teasing her gently through the thin, silky fabric. Her fingers twined in his hair and she let out a soft moan that made his groin tighten.

Her earthy, feminine scent through the satin was almost enough to finish him off. He was going to have to be careful if he wanted to last long enough to make it good for her. He was desperate to make it good for her. Hank wasn't a virgin, but neither was he very experienced in the art of a woman's sexual pleasure. He was determined to do what he could to please Cherry.

She seemed to be thoroughly enjoying what he was doing with his mouth. Her head fell back, her eyes closed, and her hands were still clutching his head as if to center herself.

She shifted her weight, swaying a bit, and he tore himself away from her panties in order to catch her before she plumb tipped over. He put an arm behind her knees and wrapped the other around her back and scooped her right off her feet.

Cherry squealed at the sudden gesture and looked at him dazedly.

"There's no champagne or candlelight, but there's a bed, and I'll be damned if I don't make you as comfortable as possible," he muttered, gently depositing her on the mattress.

Not wanting to be separated from her softness for a second longer than necessary, he came down on top of her, his lips finding hers as he propped his bulk up on his elbows and knees. He teased a nipple with his thumb and she whimpered into his mouth. His lips left a trail of kisses across the smooth skin of her stomach as he eased his body down between her thighs. When he reached her waist he hooked a finger under each side of the waistband and drew her panties slowly down her hips.

Here Hank paused, looking up at her beautiful face. He had never been so shocked in his life as he was when she'd unzipped her dress and removed her clothing. Of everything he thought she might do at that moment, undressing would have been the least likely. He was so stunned it had taken a moment for his brain to process the fact that it was happening at all. But he'd adjusted quickly and was now an enthusiastic participant in what she'd initiated, as long as he knew she was still willing.

He was relieved to see that her expression was the picture of bliss, eyes closed, cheeks flushed, mouth open in wordless ecstasy. She gave no sign that she wanted him to stop, so he eased the scanty bit of black satin down her legs and took in the heavenly sight of her naked body. She was dimpled and soft and round, and oh so feminine. The stuff dreams were made of. He was desperate to bury himself in her plump folds.

His erection was making him uncomfortable in his shorts, so he vaulted off the bed and yanked at the buttons. His sudden movement made Cherry look up to see why he'd pulled away. The boxers fell to the floor and his manhood sprang free. She seemed fascinated by the sight of it.

"Do you want to touch it?" he asked. She nodded.

Hank stepped close to the bed and as she ran a finger delicately along its length, he groaned and propped his hands against the wall behind her head. Her touch was almost his undoing.

"It's hard and soft," she said in fascination. "And as beautiful as the rest of you."

And then, incredibly, she leaned forward and kissed it. Hank glanced down at the sight of her sweet pink lips against his shaft and felt a familiar tightening in his loins. Justifiably afraid of releasing his seed right into her lovely face, he swiftly pulled away from her.

She looked up in surprise, and he explained "I want to kiss you some more." Mollified, she lay back on the bed with an enticing smile and held out her arms.

"Not there," he said, moving back to his position between her legs. She observed him, curious. Despite her earlier seduction, Hank suspected she was a girl of limited experience and he wanted to gently ease her into lovemaking. At least as long as he could hold out.

He began lazily tracing random patterns on the inside of her thighs, making his way ever closer to the warmth at the apex of her legs. When he finally reached it and fingered the soft tuft he found there she gasped. He slowly eased one digit into her warmth, marveling at the fact it was already wet with her own dew. She wanted him as much as he wanted her. Taking care to be slow and gentle, he slid his finger further into her passage, and then back out again. She shifted slightly, but did not seem to object to the incursion.

Hank meant what he'd said about wanting to kiss her. Taking one last look up at her charmingly flushed cheeks, he leaned forward and buried his face in the mound of dark curls, inhaling deeply as her sweet scent drenched his senses. He parted her folds and found the bud that he knew would bring her pleasure. He flicked it experimentally with his tongue, and Cherry whimpered and clutched at the bedspread beneath her hands. Encouraged, he began slowly tracing circles around the nubbin of flesh and she raised her hips and moaned wantonly. He could feel his own excitement building as he pleasured her, and his grip tightened on her soft thighs.

Cherry was making very encouraging noises, panting and whispering his name in that sexy accent of hers. Hank loved that he

361

was the one responsible for bringing her pleasure, but when her fingers tightened on his hair, pulling him back up to her face, and that breathy voice begged "Now Hank, please," he was more than happy to oblige.

With the utmost care, he grasped his shaft and placed it at her opening. He knew if any part of sex would be unpleasant for her, this was it. He would do everything he could not to hurt her.

He gritted his teeth as he inched himself forward into her narrow channel. Beads of sweat formed on his brow as he strove to maintain control. She was so tight, so damn tight.

Cherry looked up at him with concern.

"Hank?" she asked.

The idea that he might be causing her pain or distress was the only thing that could have stopped him. With a Herculean effort he pulled away from her, easing himself back out, but she grabbed him by the shoulders and hugged him tightly against her, her little nails digging into his back.

He was going to stop. They'd only just begun, and he was pulling away from her. In the past twenty minutes Cherry had experienced more sexual pleasure than in all the previous moments of her lifetime combined. From Hank's searing gaze making her whole body flush, to the intense sensation caused by his scandalous kisses between her legs. All the things she'd longed for him to do, all the places she'd longed for him to touch her, it was all coming true. And now, at the ultimate moment, he was pulling away from her.

She wouldn't let him. She knew the strength in her body was laughable compared to his, but she was desperate that he continue. She wanted him to fill the empty, aching space inside her. To join with her as no man ever had. To make her complete. To consummate their love.

"No!" she said. "I want this. I want you, Hank. Please."

He looked down at her, his earnest blue eyes searching her face.

"God help me, I want you."

His voice was a strangled cry and his lips came down hard on hers, swallowing any sound she might have made as he edged his length back into her passage. She should have expected it would be as generously proportioned as the rest of him. She could tell he was doing his best to be careful not to hurt her, but she still felt as though she were going to explode. As though there were no way for him to possibly fit all that girth into her body.

It felt nothing like the lazy, sensuous kisses he'd left in her most private place, kisses that made her feel like melted chocolate was being poured all down her body. And still she wanted it, wanted him. She knew this was lovemaking, and she wanted Hank to be her first and only, even if it tore her in two. And it was beginning to feel as though it just might.

He let out a shuddering breath as she felt his hips bump hers.

"Is that all of it?" she asked politely. He looked down at her in surprise and then barked a laugh.

"Yes, that's all of it," he replied, taking a deep breath. Then as gently has he'd entered her, he pulled back out, leaving the space empty once more. "Again?" he asked in a strained voice, as though holding a great weight on his back.

She looked up at him and nodded. "Kiss me," she said, placing a hand on his cheek.

He dropped down onto his elbows and captured her mouth as he entered her again.

It was easier this time, her body growing accustomed to the fullness. By the third and fourth stroke it felt almost pleasant. Hank shuddered against her as he continued his slow and deliberate movement, and reached down with one hand to find that magic spot between her legs. Cherry's thighs dropped open, feeling herself relax as he gently stroked her secret place.

A pressure built inside of her, bubbling up from where Hank touched her. It quickly became a full-blown storm, making even the effects of his previous kisses seem like mild flutters in comparison. She briefly reflected on the only advice she'd gotten on lovemaking from her mother, namely, "It will hurt, but it will get better."

Yes indeed.

She gasped as the storm overtook her, spreading a flush up her face until even her scalp felt on fire. Hank's jaw clenched and he made a guttural sound as he drove hard into her, attempting to fuse their two bodies together. She cried out and the storm clouds exploded, unleashing a torrent of pleasure that spread through her body in waves. Hank gave a triumphant shout as every muscle in his body tensed under her hands.

And then it was over. The waves of pleasure gradually receded, like the tide going out, leaving her to bask in the glow of contentment, cradled in the arms of the man she loved. Hank collapsed on top of her in an exhausted heap before rolling to the side and propping himself up on one big arm. He left the other draped across her stomach, as though he couldn't bear to completely relinquish her.

Once he'd caught his breath, he gave her a heart-melting smile and gently asked "Are you all right?"

She nodded, unable to find the words to describe what had just happened.

"Has my lovemaking robbed you of your power of speech?" he teased, gently running a finger across her stomach.

She shook her head.

"I hope not. I'm dying to hear that accent again."

"I'm glad you came," she said simply.

Cherry could scarcely believe her plan had worked. Looking over at him, the hard planes of his body outlined in the soft glow of the afternoon sun, it seemed he must be a figment of her imagination. Conjured out of daydreams and desperate longing. Only his warm hand resting on her stomach allowed her to accept he was really there in her bed.

He chuckled. "I don't know that I could have held out much longer," he replied. "Apparently I'm much too selfish to really give you up."

"Then ask me to marry you," she said.

She had bet everything on the fact that Hank really did love her, and wanted to be with her. There was always the chance that he'd used her upbringing as an excuse to get out of the relationship, but she'd felt it was worth the gamble. Despite his earlier words, she knew him to be an honorable man who would do right by her if they slept together. She didn't have the heart to tell him if she were the kind of girl who bothered with appearances she'd have been ruined the moment he'd stepped into the house.

"Why me?" he asked. "Why were you willing to go through with this just to be with me?"

"Because I love you." He looked uncertain, so she took his big hand in hers. "You said you loved me too, and part of love is trust. I need you to trust me that I know what will make me happy. Nothing makes me happier than being with you."

He studied her face and seemed to come to a decision.

"You should probably know that I've been engaged before." His began absently massaging the back of her hand with his thumb.

She looked over at him in mild surprise, but his eyes were focused on their joined hands.

"A girl from back home. Irene. I suppose it doesn't matter now, but it seemed like something I should mention."

Cherry didn't care a whit about the fact that he'd had a previous fiancée, but Hank seemed to be struggling with it so she waited to see if he would continue.

"She broke it off, before we'd even set a date."

"I can't imagine any woman in her right mind leaving you," she said finally.

"It wasn't entirely her fault. She…" Hank laughed darkly and shook his head.

"You can talk to me," Cherry said gently. "If you want to."

Hank looked up at her finally. "She didn't grow up with us, she went to a school in a different county. Her family moved to town when she was eighteen. We hit it off and started seeing each other. There was another boy, a kid I'd known in school, who liked her. She didn't pay him any mind until I took it upon myself to propose marriage. Then he told her..." Hank looked back down at their hands, and gripped hers tightly.

"He told her I couldn't even read and all our kids would be retarded."

A flush spread across Hank's face as he admitted what was likely one of his most shameful moments, but it was nothing compared to the hot fire that spread through Cherry as she considered the hurt that a comment like that would have caused Hank, her brilliant Hank, who could coax magic out of engines and fly circles around the enemy.

"She was an idiot," she said, stating the obvious.

He laughed at her certainty, but quickly quieted. "You don't share her concerns about our children having this curse?"

A warm glow spread through Cherry at the sound of his words, "our children." But his question deserved an honest response. "If any of our children are lucky enough to be born with a mind like yours, I suppose we will

369

tell them they may be anything up to and including a decorated war hero."

Hank looked at her for a moment, and then brought her hand to his mouth and kissed it. "In the whole world I never imagined I'd find a girl like you. I guess it makes sense I'd have to travel across the ocean to do it.

"I do want to marry you Cherry, but I can't promise you a life together any more than I could the night I walked away. Every day I go up is a day I might not come back down. But I made the biggest mistake of my life that day and I'm not about to repeat it, so I guess you're stuck with me now."

"I know that things are more casual in America, but is that all I can expect by way of a proposal?" she asked, grinning up at him.

"I will happily get down on one knee and participate in whatever ritual you Brits find acceptable, but I'd like to speak to your father first."

Hank looked at her intently. There was no sign of any doubt or reluctance on his part. Rather his eyes shone with love and his smile was tender.

"All right, but you'd better kiss me now, while we can. Katie'll be home soon and the last thing a new engagement needs is a scandal."

Chapter Twenty-Three

Exactly three weeks later, during his next forty-eight hour leave, Hank found himself once again driving Cherry down a country lane, this time in a much nicer automobile. The squadron commander had lent Hank his sedan for the occasion, and the plush leather felt luxurious beneath the arm draped around a nestling Cherry. They were finally making the oft-discussed trip to visit her parents.

Dickie's advice, while well-meant, had sown the seeds of anxiety in Hank's mind that Cherry's parents might cast her out if she deigned to marry a commoner. Especially one as common as Hank. Cherry assured him that her parents would find no fault with him and joked that they would be happy that someone was finally willing to take her off their hands. But Hank was dead set on ensuring that his marriage to Cherry wouldn't do any harm to her relationship with her kin. He leaned over to breathe in the floral scent of her hair, enjoying the feeling of her warmth huddled up against him. She was wearing red today. It brought out her pink cheeks and scarlet lips.

Hank had managed to be the consummate gentleman in the intervening days since he'd shared Cherry's bed. Not that his every waking moment hadn't been filled with thoughts of feeling her softness against him, of burying himself in her warmth. But he'd already taken one liberty with her virtue, and he intended to keep his hands to himself as much as possible until they were lawfully wed. Even if it killed him.

He'd been enjoying the drive through beautiful rolling countryside when an enormous building rose up before him as the car crested a hill. It was the single largest structure Hank had ever seen, with a three-story rotunda in the center and wings extending from both sides, either of which would have dwarfed the stone mansion where Cherry currently resided. The edifice was pleasantly situated at the end of a tree-lined lane.

"That's your house?" he asked, finally managing to close his gaping mouth. It seemed almost ludicrous to call such a magnificent structure a "house."

"My grandfather's house," she corrected him. "And now my father's house because of his title. It's beautiful and historic, but if you ask me he'd be happy to unload it in favor of a nice townhouse in the city. I'll be curious to see if mum and dad decide to keep it."

Hank looked down at Cherry, perplexed by her detached response. While he couldn't imagine growing up or living in a palace like this, he was equally unable to imagine wanting to get rid of it.

"It's very expensive to maintain," she explained. "And while the household does employ a few people from the village there are certainly better uses for it than a private residence. There's been talk of it being converted to a hospital or convalescent home for wounded soldiers. I can't think of anything my grandfather would have preferred."

Hank could certainly appreciate that idea, having seen firsthand the ravages of battle.

"I wanted to mention, you look particularly dashing in your uniform. Especially with the new DFC ribbon." Cherry looked up at him, her eyes sparkling.

Apparently one of the scrambled eggs at Fighter Command thought Hank deserved an award for lasting as long as he had, and he'd been presented with the Distinguished Flying Cross. He brushed it off as luck, but Cherry would have none of it and after listening to her speak of his bravery and skill one would have thought he'd fended off the entire Luftwaffe single-handed.

As the car approached the circle drive in front of the stately edifice, Hank could see that several people were gathered outside. He pulled the car around in front of them and a young man in a black suit stepped briskly forward and opened Cherry's door.

"Welcome back, miss," Hank heard him say as Cherry nodded at him pleasantly.

"Good to see you, Jimmy."

A handsome older couple approached the car and the woman immediately enveloped Cherry in an affectionate hug.

"Darling, how are you?"

"Hello, mum," Cherry replied, pulling back and glancing over at Hank who stepped forward to greet the couple.

"And you must be Flight Officer Clarkson. We are delighted to have you as a guest at our home."

Cherry's mother looked nothing like her daughter, except for the sparkling smile. She was tall and statuesque, and reminded Hank a bit of Gilda. She held out her hand and, unsure of what to do, Hank shook it and returned it to her. He was relieved when she smiled warmly and gave no indication that he'd done anything wrong.

"Please ma'am, call me Hank."

"Yes, of course. And you must call me Ellen, and this is George." She motioned to the man at her side.

"How do you do, son?"

Cherry's father stuck out a hand, which Hank grasped in a firm handshake. George was shorter and slighter in stature than Hank, but bore a head full of dark hair only just fading to grey and moved with a distinctive energy of a younger man.

"Please, come in," Ellen put an arm around Cherry's waist and led her up the front steps. "Let's get you settled."

Hank looked back at the car, and saw that his and Cherry's bags were being retrieved by several of the young men who had been present to greet them. He shrugged and turned to follow Cherry and her parents into the palatial residence.

If Hank thought the outside of the structure was impressive, it didn't compare to the inside. It looked like nothing he'd ever seen. The closest he could reckon was Tara, the grand mansion from Gone with the Wind, but even that seemed a little gaudy and overly festooned compared to the graceful elegance of the manor in which he now stood.

There was wood everywhere. Beautiful dark mahogany and cherry paneling and carving that trailed all the way up to the vaulted cathedral ceiling above. The walls were hung with colorful woven tapestries and classic portraits, and the intricately designed Persian rug on the floor stretched the length of a swimming pool. He made a conscious effort to keep his mouth from dropping open, but he couldn't keep his eyes off the sumptuous setting. He'd never seen a place like this in a movie, much less in person. And the girl he wanted to marry lived here. At least, her family did.

Hank glanced over at Cherry, who was talking animatedly to her mother and seemed oblivious to her surroundings. He didn't hear the entire conversation, but caught snatches of something about "the spring" and "orchids would be lovely."

"Can I interest you in a drink while the ladies catch up?" George motioned for Hank to follow him into a room just off the entrance hall.

"Yes, sir. Thank you." Not that Hank normally drank in the afternoon, but this was his future father-in-law and he would have said yes to just about anything to avoid offending the man.

He followed George through a high arched doorway into another opulent room. This one had a huge fireplace at one end and more books than Hank had seen outside of a library. Shoot, maybe even inside a library.

"Is scotch all right?" George asked over his shoulder, heading for an ornate wooden bar.

"Whatever you're drinking is fine with me, sir. I was raised on moonshine."

George chuckled and lifted a decanter of brown liquid.

"My wife left something out when she introduced you, didn't she?" George finished pouring and turned to Hank with an unreadable expression.

"Sir?" He stood up a little straighter.

Cherry had assured Hank that her parents were aware of his citizenship and it hadn't made the slightest difference to them, but he now wondered if the man's cryptic comment was in reference to him being an American.

"Your name should have been followed by DFC, if I'm not mistaken."

Hank tried to disguise his immense sigh of relief. "Oh, yes sir."

"Well done." George held out a leaded crystal glass containing two fingers of amber liquid. Hank took it and waited for his host to take a sip before likewise imbibing.

It was very good scotch. It went down like velvet compared to the stinging burn of his dad's homebrew, but Hank could barely taste it. He was interested in getting to know Cherry's parents, but he wouldn't be able to relax and enjoy himself until he knew how they felt about him marrying their daughter.

"I wanted to fight in the Great War, you know," George mused, casually propping an arm up on the bookcase. "But of course my position as only son prevented me from doing anything but the Home Guard." He looked over at Hank. "I admire you for what you've done. I know some of the sacrifices you made to come here. I'd like to personally thank you for your service to this country."

Hank didn't think he'd get a better opening than that.

"Sir, I'd like your permission to marry your daughter."

George studied him for a minute in silence, so Hank continued.

"I will never be a rich man, but Cherry will want for nothing if it is in my power to give it to her. And she will never have a reason to question my love."

Hank felt this was his strongest suit. Looking around him, he knew he'd never be able to provide Cherry with the lavish lifestyle she grew up with, but if she said his love was enough for her, then the least he could do was give her the trust she deserved.

George looked down into his scotch, and finally spoke.

"I have a nephew, my sister's boy. They live nearby and he's been like a son to me and a brother to Cherry. The patent would not have allowed Cherry to inherit the title or property. And she's never been of a particularly aristocratic turn of mind. I may be unusual among the men of my set, but all I've ever wanted was for Cherry to find someone who would love her for who she was, and not who her father was."

George crossed the room to a large wooden desk and opened a drawer, pulling out a small box.

"If you're interested in passing on a family heirloom, I thought you might propose to her with this." He slid the box across the desk towards Hank.

Hank approached the desk and picked it up. Upon closer inspection, the box itself looked as though it must have been valuable. The black lacquer exterior was embellished with brightly painted birds and exotic flowers that looked vaguely Asian in origin. He carefully lifted the lid.

Inside was a ring. A delicately beautiful ring of white gold, and in its center the largest diamond Hank had ever seen. It was surrounded by a halo of tiny diamonds, and on either side, more diamonds set into delicate scrollwork made to look like flowers. It was stunning, and beyond even the wildest dreams of someone in his position.

Hank was shocked. He hadn't really expected to get Lord Fairfield's blessing, he would have been content with grudging acceptance. But apparently George not only approved of the match, but had prepared for their meeting in advance.

"I know it must seem presumptuous to expect a man to propose with someone else's ring," George continued. "But this should be on the finger of a young bride, not locked away in a vault somewhere. It's been in the family for several generations and I would be pleased for you to place it on my daughter's finger."

Hank looked down at the ring. It sparkled in the light from the fire. He knew that in a lifetime of flying, he would never be able to afford to give Cherry a ring like this. He also knew that there were two ways to interpret this gesture.

George was looking at him expectantly, waiting to see how he would react. This could be George's way of reminding Hank he'd never be able to afford what Cherry deserved. Or it could be simply what George had said, a lovely family treasure and a way of showing Hank that he approved of the match.

Hank closed the box and slipped it into the pocket of his tunic.

He lifted his glass, the facets of the intricately etched design mirroring the brilliance of the diamonds.

"To Cherry," he said.

George smiled genuinely and clinked his glass against Hank's.

"Welcome to the family, son," he replied.

"My, he is tall, isn't he?" Ellen remarked casually, as she directed one of the upstairs maids in unpacking Cherry's clothes. Cherry sat on the bed, picking at the floral embroidery on the counterpane.

"Mmmm hmmm," Cherry responded with a contented smile. "And handsome. And brave."

Ellen looked fondly at her only child, overjoyed that Cherry had finally found a man with whom she could share her future. After several unsuccessful Seasons in society, Ellen had begun to fear that finding a suitable husband would be an uphill battle for Cherry. Her intelligence and self-reliance would unfortunately make married life a misery with anyone who viewed her as simply an heir bearer. And that wasn't the sort of match Ellen wanted for her daughter. But with the war ramping up, the number of eligible men in the country was rapidly dwindling, leaving fewer possible beaux with every passing week.

It now appeared that Cherry had finally met someone who could make her happy.

Ellen would never presume to decide for Cherry something as important as whom her daughter should marry, but she knew that one's life partner determined so much of one's happiness. She needed to know that her daughter hadn't simply been swept up in the tide of patriotism and fervor that led many a bride into a hasty marriage to the first dashing military man they encountered.

"Darling, I would never question your choice of husband, but as your mother I feel it is my duty to ensure that you've thought this through. You know that your father and I have nothing but admiration for how Hank has chosen to spend his life, and it must all seem terribly romantic, but are you sure this is what you want?"

"What do you mean?" Cherry seemed genuinely puzzled. "Does it bother you that he's an American?"

"Not in the least," Ellen answered honestly. "I meant the fact that he's an RAF pilot. They're not known for their career longevity."

"Believe me, I'm already well acquainted with that particular aspect of his job." Cherry's knowing tone led Ellen to eye her daughter suspiciously. There was clearly something Cherry had failed to mention.

"He seems to bring it up every time we discuss marriage," Cherry explained, possibly in response to her mother's look. "One would think he was trying to talk me out of it."

"At least he's honest," Ellen pointed out. "But it hasn't been enough to scare you off?"

"I would be scared, of all of it," Cherry admitted. "If it were anyone but Hank."

Her mother smiled. "I remember thinking the same thing on my wedding day, as I walked down the aisle towards your father. That's when I knew he was the right man for me."

"I love him," Cherry said simply. "I feel more myself around him than with any other man I've ever met."

"Then let the planning commence," Ellen replied with a smile.

"You know, he hasn't actually asked me yet. He wanted to speak with Father first."

"I shouldn't have any worry on that account," Ellen remarked, her eyes sparkling. "Although no man will ever be truly worthy of his daughter, I happen to know he is inclined to approve the match."

Chapter Twenty-Four

Just after eleven, there was a scratching at Hank's bedroom door. He had only been in his room for half an hour and was just sliding between the luxurious silk sheets. He considered a number of things it could have been, from the old house settling to mice in the walls, but ultimately decided he should at least check to see if someone was there. With all of the formalities he'd witnessed that evening it wouldn't have surprised him if it had been a butler or maid asking if they could turn down his sheets.

He swung his legs over the side of the bed and crossed the carpet towards the heavy wooden door. When he pulled it open, he was astonished to find Cherry standing there.

She glanced surreptitiously to either side and whispered "May I come in?"

He grinned at her, ostensibly sneaking around her own house, and stepped back to allow her entry. Once safely inside she turned to face him.

Hank inhaled sharply when he saw that she was wearing *that* nightgown. The one from the horrible night where he'd made the worst mistake of his life and walked away from her. He hadn't had the time or the light that evening to fully appreciate the way she looked in it. But now he let his eyes roam over her every curve, admiring the way her pale skin glowed beneath the gauzy aqua fabric. In the soft light of his lamp he could see that it was quite sheer, leaving the supple outlines of her full breasts visible, and even the darker pink circles and peaks of her nipples.

He'd had a hard time keeping his hands to himself during the long yet pleasant evening spent in the company of her parents. After the meeting with George, which had thankfully removed the stone in the pit of his stomach upon learning that his marriage to Cherry had her family's blessing, he'd washed up and prepared for dinner.

George and Ellen had invited several friends who lived nearby to join the foursome for the meal. Hank should have viewed this as the compliment it was, but the desire to be alone with Cherry had driven all other thoughts from his mind. In preparation for

387

dinner, Cherry had changed into a sleek dress of teal brocade that hugged her curves and left Hank's fingers itching to touch her. Over pre-dinner cocktails he had managed to drift near enough to run his hand lightly along her hip, but that brief touch had only left him desperate for more.

Dinner itself had been pleasant yet somewhat interminable, as Hank had been seated in a place of honor next to the hostess, but across the wide table from his soon-to-be fiancée. He could only cast hungry glances in Cherry's direction, hoping the heat in his eyes conveyed the desire he felt to be alone with her. After dinner the gentlemen, including Hank, had retired to the library for another glass of the marvelous scotch, while the ladies had done who knows what. George and his friends had been warm and complimentary and Hank had received many slaps on the back and congratulations both on his conquest of Cherry's heart, and his surviving the Battle of Britain thus far.

Much to Hank's dismay, once the sexes rejoined he was only able to give Cherry a brief peck on the cheek before glumly watching as she ascended the stairs to bed. She'd been accompanied by her mother, and halfway up she'd turned to Hank and winked. He hadn't been sure at the time what it could mean, but if he'd known it foreshadowed a late night rendezvous in his room he would have bounded up the stairs with more spring in his step when he retired shortly thereafter.

None of that mattered now. He'd been half aroused all evening just watching Cherry talk and laugh with her parents and their friends, every now and then sneaking him a knowing smile that made his insides tighten. And here she was, in his bedroom, practically naked.

He studied her face, searching for a sign that her nocturnal visit was prompted by anything other than simply a desire to be alone with him. All he sensed was a trace of self-consciousness.

"I know it must seem a trifle odd to sneak into your room like this, but we hadn't really gotten a chance to talk alone since we arrived and I wanted to…" Looking at him seemed to cause her to lose her train of thought.

Hank had realized too late that it probably would have been a good idea to pack a set of pajamas. He'd gotten out of the habit of wearing them at the aerodrome, and like most of the boys he slept in an undershirt and shorts so that's what he'd packed for the trip. And that was how he stood before her.

"Yes?" Hank prompted, feeling his lip twitch.

"See to your comfort," Cherry replied finally. And then blushed down to her toes. Hank's grin widened. "I mean, make sure you were... settling in all right," she finally choked out.

"Very considerate," he murmured.

"Yes, thank you. I, ah..." She stared straight ahead at his chest, and actually reached out with one tentative finger and touched it. Almost immediately her hand dropped and she muttered "Yes, well, there you are."

"And where is that?" he teased, edging slowly towards her until he could feel the heat from her body through the thin fabric of his clothes.

"In your bedroom," she whispered, looking up at him.

He took another step forward and felt the softness of her breasts bump his ribcage as he looked down into her lovely eyes.

"Actually, I couldn't bear the thought of you being just down the hall and dropping off to sleep without feeling your lips on mine," she breathed.

It was exactly the words Hank wanted to hear, but even he could hardly keep the surprise from his face that she'd said them out loud.

"Yes, it's true," she admitted. "You should know that you've fallen in love with a shamelessly wanton woman who–"

While Hank was curious about how she would have ended the sentence, watching her pink lips moving was simply too tempting and he brought his mouth down on hers, wrapping one arm around her waist as her hands slid up his chest. The taste of her released a torrent of desire he'd kept under strict control since he'd picked her up that morning.

Like every kiss they'd ever shared, it did not remain gentle for long. She opened her mouth for him, inviting his tongue to plunder her sweetness as she tilted her head back and melted into his body. His hand slid down to cup her rounded bottom and hold her more tightly against him. He groaned as the silky material of her nightgown slid beneath his fingers.

You're in her parents' house, Hank thought to himself. *You haven't even properly asked for her hand in marriage. You've already taken her virtue, she should be able to rely upon you for some measure of self-control.*

But all he wanted to do was slide the slinky garment down her shoulders and rake her smooth skin with his tongue.

His body tingled as he felt her softness all along his length, from her ample breasts to the warmth between her legs, which was pressed up against his hardening erection. The delicate floral scent of her hair tickled his nose, and the more subtle feminine perfume of her desire left him straining against his control like a hound on a leash.

Hank made himself tear his mouth away from hers and separate their bodies with a gentle hand on each of her shoulders.

"Cherry, if you want me to stop, I need you to tell me to stop." His voice was ragged, as though the words were being wrenched from him.

"Oh Hank, I know it's not proper, but I don't think I can wait."

Her cheeks were flushed and lips swollen with kissing, her eyes wide and luminous in the glow of the lamp. Her darkened nipples

392

tented the gauzy fabric where they peaked and her breasts rose and fell with her quickened breathing.

Thank God she doesn't need me to stop, he thought wryly, as he pulled her against him once more and reclaimed her mouth. He drew her back with him until his knees hit the bed, and then sat heavily on the soft mattress, his lips never parting from hers.

Although the gossamer gown did little to hide her luscious body, Hank wanted nothing to come between his hands and her skin. He tucked a large finger under each of the delicate straps and drew them gently down her arms, exposing her creamy breasts to his gaze and touch. They were inches from his face, and he couldn't help but take one pink tip in his mouth.

"Oh, Hank, yes," she whispered, her hands burying themselves in his hair, holding his face against her body. As though he had any intention of pulling away. His tongue traced circles around the hardened berry, until Cherry moaned and he took it tenderly between his teeth, tugging gently before moving to the other side. As he suckled her, his hands eased the silky gown down over her rounded hips and left it in a pool at her feet.

His hands explored the smooth satin of her knickers, and he pulled back to study the one garment still covering her nakedness. They were identical to the black pair she'd worn in her bedroom, but these were powder blue.

"I think I caught a glimpse of these at the dance," he remarked, tucking a finger playfully under each side of the waistband.

"Likely so," she replied. "I believe I was also wearing a similar pair when we met. And no stockings," she added, with a naughty smile.

"Really? I can't believe I didn't notice." *I was too busy trying not to peek down your blouse*, he thought.

And now he didn't have to peek, he was free to look and taste his fill. He slid the knickers down her shapely legs and they joined the nightgown on the carpet. His hands ran up her calves and thighs until they reached the source of her warmth, where he gently separated the curls to reach the place he knew she liked to be touched. He stroked her and teased her until her little hands clenched in his hair and she gasped his name.

"Hank."

He looked up at her and she bent down and left a gentle kiss on his lips.

"I want to touch you," she said, a becoming flush pinking her cheeks.

"Where?" he asked hoarsely.

"Everywhere," she replied. "I don't know where to start."

"How about here?" he asked, pulling his shirt up and over his head and bringing her hands down to his chest. She knelt between his legs, running her fingers over the hard planes of his body. He closed his eyes as her feather light touch skimmed over his chest and shoulders, and down his arms. She leaned forward and kissed him softly just under his throat.

"Hank?" she whispered.

"Yes?"

"I want to touch you the way you touch me."

He opened his eyes and found her looking earnestly up at him. He was having a difficult time focusing on her words, focusing on anything except her naked body between his thighs. But she seemed so serious he forced himself to concentrate on what she might mean.

He must have looked confused because she cast a significant glance down at his erection, which had almost worked its way through the opening in his shorts.

The way you touch me.

She wanted to touch him there.

Hank jumped up and quickly unbuttoned his boxers, yanking them down his legs and dropping back down on the bed. His manhood stood at attention before her and he watched Cherry study it for a moment. She grasped it tentatively in her small hand and at his sharp intake of breath she looked up.

"Show me how to touch you."

Cherry had spent a disproportionate amount of time the past two weeks thinking about the afternoon she'd spent in bed with Hank. The feelings at the time had been almost beyond her understanding, but the overarching memory had been how much pleasure he had brought her with his touch. She knew she was still lacking in experience, but she wanted to learn how to bring Hank the same kind of pleasure he'd brought her. Giggled whispers in various powder rooms had concluded that all men enjoyed sex, whether the woman actively initiated anything or not. But Cherry knew there must be things she could do to be a better partner. And she was a willing student. She just needed Hank to teach her. She'd decided she would simply ask him and do what he said.

He paused only a moment and then wrapped a big hand around her smaller one, gently easing her hand up and down his shaft in a slow, regular rhythm. The motion of her hand seemed to heighten his arousal, and if possible his member became more rigid and full in her grasp. He leaned back, propping himself up on his strong shoulders, eyes shut and head back. A low, guttural noise emerged from his throat and Cherry smiled as she continued her motion.

He was clearly enjoying the sensation, and she wondered what would happen if she used her other hand as well. Deciding to satisfy her curiosity, she continued rubbing along his shaft and brought her other hand up to touch the swollen flesh that hung beneath his manhood. Cherry was fascinated by it. She'd never had an opportunity to study the male anatomy up close. She cradled it delicately in her hand, somehow sensing it must be incredibly sensitive. It felt like two small eggs in a velvet pouch. She massaged it gently, running a thumb around the twin bulges where they joined his groin beneath.

Hank made a sound that was somewhere between a cough and a shout, and sat up abruptly, capturing both of her hands in his.

"Did I hurt you?" she asked, concerned. He laughed.

"Not at all, sweetheart. But I don't want you to finish me off before I have a chance to be inside of you."

"Oh," she said, blushing and relieved.

He gathered her up in his arms and pulled her back onto the bed. She loved the way his naked body felt beneath hers, strong and solid and male. Her softness seemed to fit perfectly against the hard contours of his frame. His erection pressed against her leg and Cherry ached for him to fill the emptiness inside her. She looked down into his handsome face, not quite sure how to proceed.

"Would you like to try something?" he asked.

"Of course," Cherry responded enthusiastically. She was willing to try almost anything that involved her body pressed up against Hank's.

"Can you sit up? I want to look at you."

It took her a moment to understand he wanted her to sit astride him, and she reddened remembering how she'd had this exact fantasy back on the picnic blanket that sunny afternoon. She placed her hands on his chest, enjoying the crisp curling hair under her palms, and pushed herself into a sitting position.

It was incredible, her body was completely bared to this man, her breasts exposed, nipples tightening at the sudden rush of cold air, and yet she was not embarrassed. The heat in his eyes as he studied her made her feel desirable. Powerful, even.

"You are so beautiful," he whispered.

Cherry smiled down at him. She knew she was not beautiful, but his words and his expression made her believe he found her so. And that was a precious gift.

He placed his strong hands on her hips and lifted her up, lowering her to cover him with such exquisite care that a sweat broke out on his brow. As he entered her there was an intense sense of fullness that was completely lacking the painful stings of the previous encounter. He still seemed very large, but she had become so stimulated by their earlier lovemaking she was slick and ready for him and he slid in quite smoothly. When her bottom settled back down on him she wiggled slightly, adjusting to the feeling of having him inside of her, and Hank let out a groan and tightened his hands on her hips.

"Let's take this slowly," he said, his voice thick.

He moved her hips back and forth in a rhythm that spread a pleasurable glow up her spine, originating where their bodies joined. In this position she was able to rub against Hank and stimulate the magic place he had found between her legs, even without him using his fingers.

A familiar flush spread over Cherry as her breath quickened and muscles began to twitch in her core. Hank's hands on her hips were strong and he pulled her faster now.

"Sweet Lord, Cherry, you feel so good," his voice roughly tender.

Cherry loved the way it felt to ride him, his body all hard muscle beneath her thighs. During their prior interlude, she had reveled in the weight of Hank on top of her, gloriously strong and masculine, but the lovemaking had felt like something that had happened to her. This way felt more like something they were doing together.

400

She was enjoying the fluid motion of her hips on him, feeling him buried deep inside of her. But as the sensations neared a fever pitch she hungered to feel the powerful in-and-out thrusting of his body against hers. The way he'd driven into her as he neared his climax. She wanted to feel the strength of his need for her as she came apart.

Cherry toppled down towards his chest, propping herself up with a hand on either side of his head. Hank gave a satisfied growl to find her breasts within reach, and took the closest nipple in his mouth. Cherry squealed in delight as his teeth nipped at the sensitive bud. Keeping her hips in his hands, he bent his knees and thrust upwards with his muscular thighs, driving himself into her with the force she craved.

"Yes, Hank, oh yes!"

She buried her face in his shoulder as he entered her again and again, his hoarse groans echoing in her ear as his release overtook him. There was no pain this time, only the gripping satisfaction of Hank surging into her. Her whimpers became a cry as she felt her body shimmer and then explode in a shower of light like a Catherine wheel.

Hank wrapped an arm around her shoulders and claimed her mouth for a deep kiss, swallowing the last of her sounds. She felt his body tremble beneath her with the last throes of his climax. He eased his hips back down to the mattress, and she pushed her body up so she could see his face.

"Cherry, I—" he began.

A board creaked in the hall just outside the bedroom.

They both heard it and froze. Hank looked up at Cherry in alarm, and she just shook her head, unsure of what the sound could mean. They lay comically still for several moments, waiting for the sound to be repeated or some explanation to present itself. Then Cherry collapsed on Hank's chest with an unladylike giggle.

"That was probably the ghost of a distant ancestor of yours, wondering what a commoner was doing in his bedroom," Hank joked.

"Or someone overheard us and thought one of us was in pain. I'm fairly certain some of the noises I made could have also indicated distress. I'll have to remember to be more quiet in future."

"Dammit, I don't want you to have to be quiet. I want us to be in a place where I can hear every sweet sound that comes out of your mouth. In fact…" Hank trailed off as he gently rolled Cherry off him and down onto the bed. He reached into the drawer of the nightstand and pulled out a small box. It was a box Cherry knew well.

Without bothering to cover his nudity, he knelt next to the bed and gently opened the box, holding it out to her.

"Miss Honorable Charity Spence, would you make me the happiest pilot in the RAF and agree to be my wife?"

The ring sparkled in the glow of the lamp. It was her Grandmama's ring. Cherry had always admired it, but never dreamed it would be offered to her along with a marriage proposal from a man like Hank. A fearless, selfless man who loved her for who she was, and had chosen her knowing nothing about her family or pedigree. A man who made her feel beautiful and cherished.

A stunningly handsome man who knelt beside her without a stitch on.

Another woman's attentions would have focused on the lovely ring, but Cherry found she could not look away from Hank's glistening form. She was so distracted she failed to answer his question.

"How could a girl say no to a ring like that?" he asked softly. His words made her look back up at his face.

"I would have said yes to a band of twine," she said.

"It bodes well that you appreciate the simple things," he joked.

"It's you I care about, not the jewelry. I love you, Hank Clarkson."

He reached out with a shaking hand and slid the ring onto her finger.

"Wait, if you come down to breakfast wearing the ring, how will you explain when I gave it to you?" he asked.

"Let them wonder," she replied with a smile, wrapping a hand around his neck and pulling him close for a kiss. "I'd thought, perhaps, a spring wedding. But I don't think I can wait that long for you."

"I've waited my whole life for you," he said, and the love she saw in his eyes made her breath catch. As she bent down for another kiss, she knew he wouldn't need to read to see what was in her heart.

Epilogue

Present Day

"Gramps flew in the Battle of Britain?"

Cherry looked fondly at her eldest great-grandson. She knew she wasn't supposed to play favorites, but Kent was the spitting image of Hank, aside from the dark hair he'd gotten from his mother's side. He was sitting on her ruffled floral couch, studying the contents of a dusty shoebox she'd found in the back of the closet.

She'd stumbled on the box while searching for mementos of her time in England during the war. Apparently, BP had become a tourist attraction of all things, and they wanted her to come and give a speech on the work she'd done there.

Old habits were hard to break, so before she would agree to do the talk she'd contacted the boffins at British Intelligence to ask for an exception to the Official Secrets Act to ensure her talk wouldn't be an act of treason. A very young sounding man had told her, "Of course you may, you're not likely to say anything that would be of any interest." She'd thought that was bloody rude, but asked them to send it in writing.

Kent held up a star shaped medal attached to a ribbon with a gold bar reading "Battle of Britain."

"Oh, yes. I believe he shot down nine planes altogether."

Kent stared at her in amazement. "Nine planes?"

"He was very skilled. And very lucky. Although I daresay I much preferred it when he got a training assignment and was no longer shooting at anyone."

Kent reached gingerly into the box and pulled out several other items. "This is a Silver Star. A Distinguished Flying Cross. No, two DFCs. There must be eight or nine air medals in here. GG, what's this one?"

Kent called Cherry GG at her insistence. "Great-grandmother" sounded like someone unfathomably old. She looked down at Kent's hand, which held a small gold pin shaped like a caterpillar with red eyes.

"He received that from the Irving Company. It was sent to anyone whose life was saved with one of their parachutes. They called it the 'Caterpillar Club' because the parachutes were made of silk."

Kent looked down at the faded ribbons and tarnished awards and shook his head.

"I had no idea. How come he never talked about it?"

Cherry shrugged. "He'd lost so many friends, it was hard for him to talk about it. After the war he wanted to look ahead to our future together. To happier times, building a family and a life here."

She had been so proud of Hank's accomplishments, as had her parents. And to her intense relief, so had Hank's family. He'd received a hero's welcome when he finally brought his bride back to Kansas after the war, and Cherry still remembered how Hank's father had been choked up when he'd laid eyes on his son for the first time in years. Hank had extended a hand for a shake, and the older man had pulled him in close for a hug. Judging by Hank's startled reaction, Cherry could sense that the elder Mr. Clarkson was not known for showing affection. But it appeared that whatever had come between the men before the war had been healed through time and distance.

"You both were pretty good at keeping secrets," Kent observed. "I didn't even know you'd worked at Bletchley Park until mom mentioned it when I said I was driving down to visit. Then I had to look up Bletchley Park."

"That's because we were all good at keeping secrets. It's how we won the war."

"Was it hard for you not to be able to tell Gramps what you'd done? The contributions you'd made? Mom said you helped predict the Blitz."

"He knew all the important things. He knew I loved him. And I'm sure, with your job, you keep secrets from your girl. Work was work, but my life was Hank. The most important part of my job was keeping him and his fellows safe, and that demanded secrecy. And I did tell him, eventually."

But not until the 1970s when that scoundrel Winterbotham's book came out, Cherry thought to herself. Of the hundreds of people who had come through Bletchley, it wasn't until 1974 that anyone had spoken of what was done there. That year, Captain Winterbotham wrote a book about the codebreaking at Bletchley that gave all the secrets away. Every other man and woman had kept the secret, just as they'd sworn to do. And for years after the war, the codebreaking had remained an important tool for the Allies in other conflicts against other enemies.

But once the secrets were out in print there didn't seem to be much use in staying silent, so Cherry had told Hank everything. At least, everything she could remember. By then it had been over thirty years. If she had any regrets, it was that she would have liked to have told her father about her work. He would have been very interested in what really went on a BP. But, of course, he'd passed away by then.

"What did Gramps say when you told him?" Kent asked. Cherry laughed, remembering.

"He was so proud, he went out and bought every copy of that Winterbotham book he could get his hands on. He gave one to everyone we knew and told them 'This is what my wife did during the war!' I always felt he might have suspected I was more than just a secretary."

"Speaking of secrets," she continued. "When were you going to tell me you'd gotten engaged? I didn't even know you were dating anyone until your mother emailed me."

Cherry did quite well with email, but couldn't seem to master text messaging. At ninety-eight, those little buttons on the phone just seemed so small.

Kent looked sheepish for a moment, but then a broad smile spread across his face.

"It happened kind of fast, but I'm positive she's the right girl. She reminds me a little of you, actually."

"Really?" Cherry was intrigued. "Is she a stubborn old biddy?"

"No," Kent laughed. "She's brave. And smart. And loves kids."

"Well then, I'd like to wish you both a lifetime of happiness. And offer you this."

Cherry went to her antique secretary desk and opened a drawer, carefully removing a small black lacquer box. She handed it to Kent and sat back down as he opened it.

"If your Ellie is a modern girl, she probably wants to choose her own ring," Cherry remarked. "But your mother mentioned she has a record player and likes old music so I thought she might fancy this."

Kent stared at the ring for a moment, watching it catch the afternoon light.

"It might interest your sweetheart to know the ring was made using diamonds from my great grandmother's tiara. She was the daughter of a Duke. It's quite old, but I hear the vintage look is popular these days."

He snapped the box shut and looked up at his great-grandmother.

"It's an incredible gesture, but this is your ring. I can't take it from you."

"I would have worn it forever because your grandfather put it on my finger." Cherry felt a rush of warmth flood through her at the memory. "But with my arthritis the doctors threatened to cut it off. I couldn't bear to let anything like that happen to it. It should be on the finger of a young bride."

Kent looked back down at the box, wavering.

"As the eldest great-grandson you would have gotten it anyway," she said gently. He grasped the box in his palm and she knew she'd convinced him.

"Do you miss him?" he asked gently.

He was a dear boy, Cherry could tell he wanted to ask more about Hank, but also wanted to spare her feelings.

"Every day," she replied. "But we had a wonderful life together. And as he always told me, he had a lot of friends up there waiting for him."

411

Cherry found it ironic that after all of Hank's concerns about leaving her a young widow, they'd had seventy happy years together. Much longer than many of her younger friends.

The rest of the afternoon's visit flew by as Kent peppered her with questions about her work at BP. Cherry was certain he would have rather heard tales of air battles, but even after seventy years as a pilot's wife she was a poor substitute for her husband in that regard. So he settled for tales of codebreaking and seemed quite interested. Even with the odd letter or holiday card, Gilda, Hugh, and Bertie had been ghosts for so long it was nice to spend an afternoon with them again.

Cherry was sad to see him go, but he promised to call and let her know how his fiancée liked the ring.

As she cleaned up the dishes from their afternoon tea, she passed a wall of family photos and spent a moment looking at each one. She and Hank had been blessed with four children, eleven grandchildren, and seventeen great-grandchildren, with another one due that fall. Generations of family who existed because of Hank's love for her.

"And you said you had nothing to offer me, Hank Clarkson," she gently chided.

She passed other photos, pictures of Hank in front of the Cessna 120 he flew to work every day. Despite his anxiety on the subject, his reading difficulties hadn't kept Cessna from hiring him as a test pilot immediately upon his return from the war. His valuable insights had helped make future models of aircraft safer and more efficient. He'd flown almost every day, until cataracts had finally taken enough of his vision to prevent it.

Cherry had been so proud of her husband's work, and he'd been equally supportive of her career. She'd loved staying home to raise the children, but once they were all in school she'd managed to get a job as the first female professor in the Language Department at the University of Kansas. She and Hank had taken several trips to Europe over the years, and she had been overjoyed to see that the vibrant, welcoming Germany she'd known growing up had been restored after the horrors of the war.

She sat down on the couch and began carefully replacing the medals and ribbons in the shoebox. She'd offered them to Kent, but with all the moving around he did he was justifiably concerned that they would get lost. He'd gently offered to take them when he settled down, but it was still early in his career and Cherry thought it was likely he'd receive them well before that.

As she placed the little gold caterpillar back into the box her hand brushed something at the very bottom. She hadn't noticed it earlier, it was cardboard and had blended in with the box. She reached in and pulled out a very old, very tattered pub coaster.

The name of the pub was undecipherable, and the handwritten number was so faded it could no longer be read.

But just like Hank, she knew the number, and everything that had followed, by heart.

Author's Note

While writing this book, every effort was made to ensure authenticity, from the style of clothing and design of uniforms, to RAF strategy and period cologne. I borrowed liberally from the records of the real experiences of RAF pilots and Bletchley girls with the sole intention of accurately reflecting their lives, sacrifices, and dedication. Some liberties were taken regarding plot points, but the most unbelievable moments are almost certainly taken from real life. I cannot overstate the debt owed to those who fought, in any capacity, to ward off an evil that threatened all of humanity.

This book would not have been possible without the following reference sources, and if you are interested in further reading I encourage you to start here:

Tally Ho! Yankee in a Spitfire, Arthur G. Donahue
Spitfire Pilot, David Crook, DFC
Spitfires, Thunderbolts, and Warm Beer, Philip Caine
It's a Piece of Cake, C.H. Ward-Jackson
The Debs of Bletchley Park, Michael Smith
The Secret Lives of Codebreakers, Sinclair McKay
The Bletchley Girls, Tessa Dunlop
The Road to Station X, Sarah Baring

Amanda Page has been interested in romance novels since she started sneaking them from her mother's bookshelf in junior high. Her favorites were always those that featured brave men in uniform.

Amanda was so captivated by these tales of military chivalry that she went to work for the Air Force right out of college and ended up as Director of Youth Programs at Langley Air Force Base where her fascination with fighter jets really took off. Surrounded by the speed and power of these lethal machines, she set about to create stories reflecting the lives of the men who flew them. The result was her "Flyboys" series.

Amanda lives with her two children and active duty Air Force husband, wherever he happens to be stationed.

Made in the USA
Middletown, DE
26 December 2021